# THE SECRETS
# THEY LEFT
# BEHIND

# THE SECRETS THEY LEFT BEHIND

## A MYSTERY

## Lissa Marie Redmond

CROOKED
LANE

NEW YORK

Published in the United States by Crooked Lane Books, an imprint of The Quick Brown Fox & Company LLC.

Crooked Lane Books and its logo are trademarks of The Quick Brown Fox & Company LLC.

Library of Congress Catalog-in-Publication data available upon request.

ISBN (hardcover): 978-1-64385-299-7
ISBN (trade paperback): 978-1-63910-300-3
ISBN (ebook): 978-1-64385-320-8

Cover design by Melanie Sun

Printed in the United States.

www.crookedlanebooks.com

Crooked Lane Books
34 West 27th St., 10th Floor
New York, NY 10001

First Edition: April 2020
Trade Paperback Edition: February 2023

10 9 8 7 6 5 4 3 2 1

For my sister, Lorri

# Prologue

**Wednesday, December 28ᵗʰ, 2016**

**Christmas Break**

Skyler slammed the front door behind them as they rushed in against the biting winter wind. The three girls kicked their boots off in unison, scattering snow around the hallway. It immediately began to melt and sink into the carpet, leaving dark splotches in the plush pile. The house was dark but warm and silent as the girls stripped off their winter coats and hats. Their escape complete, they stood in the hallway soaking the remaining melting snow into their socks, holding their outerwear, looking at each other. Olivia was the first one to speak. "This is bad."

The hallway led directly into the formal living room, with its couch no one ever sat on and its chairs that had to be dusted. Skyler threw her coat on the far end of the show-couch and her two friends followed suit, piling theirs on top.

Olivia pulled her cell phone from her purse and checked it. No new messages. She needed to think. The grandfather clock in the corner bonged loudly. They didn't have much time before her parents came home.

Skyler went over to the pristine, less-than-state-of-the-art entertainment center that never got used and clicked on the television. Her wild blonde hair was matted to her head from her knit hat that now lay limply on the pile. She hated that hat, but it was freezing out and there was no way around not wearing one if you wanted to keep your ears. Remote in hand, she stared at the flat screen and flicked through the channels. With the other hand, she spun the daisy wheel on the old-fashioned iPod Nano tucked into the docking station, looking for a song. The noise of the TV mixed with the music of the stereo in an assault on the ears. But Skyler was looking for white noise, something to focus on without focusing.

Neither Olivia nor Emma said anything. You could still see the wet stain running up the side of Skyler's tight jeans where Joe had splashed beer on her. She was seething, and if she'd had the proper target right then, she'd have smashed something.

Emma sat down in an overstuffed floral armchair, cradled her head in her hands, and asked, "Now what?"

"Look, I'll take care of it, okay?" Skyler snapped. She was frantically texting something, eyes locked on her cell screen. Emma fell silent, staring at Skyler's stocking feet, falling into a position of defeat.

Olivia's cell had only one bar left. "I'm calling Kayla. She's not answering any of my texts. She doesn't even know what's going on." She dumped the cell into her purse and jumped up, going into the kitchen to use the house phone.

Skyler turned from the entertainment center, eyes rimmed with red. She watched Emma's blank expression, getting more agitated by the minute. She wanted to scream at her. She wanted to kill Joe. She wanted to go home. But things had to get fixed, and she was the only one of them who knew what to do. For once she had to be the responsible one.

Olivia came back into the living room. "What'd you tell her?" Skyler demanded.

"Nothing. I just wanted her to know why we left. She said Joe carried on for a while and then she went home. She was just walking in when I called. She asked what happened, and I told her I didn't want to get into it again."

"Again?"

"You know what I mean." Olivia tried to hold on to the fact that they would all be back in school once winter break was over, except maybe Skyler. Olivia could do without this whole mess. She'd thought she missed this town when she went away for freshman year. Now she wished she'd never come back. Nothing ever changed. And now she knew there was a whole big world out there. She could walk away from Kelly's Falls and never come back. But that had been her plan all along, right?

The sound of a car pulling into the driveway made all three of them swing their heads toward the front picture window. There was a tense silence as the car idled in the driveway. The headlights were mirrored in Emma's eyes. Olivia swallowed hard and said, "Someone's here."

## Monday, February 20th, 2017

If I had known the best thing that was going to happen to me that day was a black eye, I would have called in sick.

At the ripe old age of twenty-three, I'd been working as a patrol officer in the City of Buffalo Police Department for about two and a half years. While all my friends were out partying, doing entry-level kiss-ass work, or getting their master's degree, I'd been standing in snowbanks writing tickets and arresting drunk drivers. I know how that sounds, like I'm ungrateful, but I really did love the job. Every day was something different and I was never bored. You just had to learn to take the bad with the good. That day just happened to be bad.

I was working the day shift, which was thought to be cake duty since most of the residents of South Buffalo were mainly middle-class Irish who worked in one of the few remaining factories or for the city. Most of the violence was domestic and beer inspired. It was considered an easy tour in a slow district.

I was riding with Patrick Malloy. And he hated riding with anyone other than his steady partner. Not that he wasn't nice to me—he was as nice as he had to be—but it's not the same as being with a real partner. I had left my real partner behind when they reassigned me to a special detail over the summer. I was trying to figure out a way of getting back to my old district as soon as possible.

At one o'clock we got a disturbance call from Delaney's on Seneca Street. A lot of plant guys eat their lunches in the bars down that stretch. As we rolled up on the scene, two guys were locked in a death grip, struggling in a snowbank.

Some of their buddies were trying to break it up, but these two guys were really going at it. Pat grabbed one of them by the back of his neck and swung him around to the ground in one single fluid motion. Pat's no small man and pretty strong, considering the size of his beer gut.

I came up from behind and grabbed the other guy, pushing him against our patrol car. He took one look at me, at my five feet six inches and one hundred twenty pounds of pure police intimidation, and punched me right in the eye.

My head swung back, but I didn't let go. Pat saw it, took one step toward us while still holding the other guy by the collar, and slammed my guy onto the cruiser. He was cooperative after that.

"Are you okay?" one of the combatant's friends asked me as I grabbed a hunk of snow from a drift and pressed it to my face.

"They're both garbage men," another one offered, brushing snow off the front of his coveralls. "We have to get back on the truck."

"He just assaulted a police officer," I told him, opening our cruiser door to deposit our fighters inside.

"But he didn't know you were a cop," the guy pleaded with me.

His handcuffed friend piped up, "I didn't know it was a cop grabbing me. I would never hit a cop. I never would've hit a girl."

Of course he'd never hit a girl. Or a cop. Just the girl-cop who showed up to his fight.

I ducked his head in the door and closed it. My eye was throbbing.

Pat tried to talk to me all the way down to central booking and while we were doing the paperwork for the prisoners, but I didn't feel like chitchatting. I was feeling pretty foolish for letting myself get hit.

On the way back to the station house, Pat looked over at my face and told me, "You did good today. You got out of the car, you weren't afraid, and you didn't let go after taking a hard shot."

*That's what cops are supposed to do,* I wanted to say, touching my swollen eye with my fingertips. *That's my job.*

I knew he was trying to be nice. I knew he was old-school and set in his ways. Not only was he old enough to be my father; he was actually friends with my father. He wasn't a monster or a bully or trying to shame me. He was just a guy I worked with.

It still stung worse than my eye.

Parking the patrol car, we trudged through the drifts in the unplowed police lot to the side door of the station house. Coppers coming and going had worn a slushy path through the dirty snow.

As soon as we walked in, Tony Miciwitz, the desk officer, looked up. "What happened to you?"

"I got hit by some drunk over at Delaney's." I walked over to his desk, which had all our blank reports and forms on it. "You should see the other guy."

He laughed. "Good for you, kid." I sat down and started writing out our arrest report in the hopes of ending any further discussion of my eye. By the time I entered it into the computer, it would be time to go home.

"By the way, some guy from the FBI called you. I left a note on your locker," Tony told me as our captain came out of his office with a coffee in hand.

"What's the FBI want with you?" The captain leaned in his doorway and blew the steam off the top of his coffee mug. "Why didn't he call your cell?"

I shrugged. "Maybe they want to talk about one of my reports. Have a question about something. And why would he have my cell number? I'm not a snitch." I hunched over my report, trying to cut the conversation off.

The details of the Terry Roberts serial murder case weren't public knowledge. My participation in the detail was being kept quiet until after a judge decided whether Roberts was sane enough to stand trial. The court had imposed a gag order on all parties. In the court papers and affidavits, I was officially known as "The Undercover Officer to Be Referred to as Officer Jane Doe." As far as everyone in the police department knew, I had been out with a bad case of appendicitis. That was the official story. When I came back after six weeks undercover, they transferred me to the South District. Nobody I worked with knew what had happened. Or what I had done.

Or what had happened to me.

My ancient wooden chair creaked uneasily underneath me. Our station house was only a year old, but all the new chairs and tables that had come with it had mysteriously disappeared. Cops are notorious station house thieves.

"Maybe he heard what happened at the bar and wants to investigate reverse police brutality?" the captain suggested, still hugging the doorway.

"I thought she was going to need a trip to the hospital after the shot she took," Pat laughed. I just sat there, smiling and nodding like a good sport. Because that's what the guys expected you to be: a good sport.

My captain let me out a little early because of my eye, which was nice of him, because we were a little shorthanded that day. I guess he didn't want me going to calls with a big juicy shiner. I changed my clothes and drove over to the FBI building.

Bill Walters hadn't always been at the Buffalo branch. He'd moved all over the state and then all over the country before landing here as the special agent in charge. Bill had been born and raised in Buffalo, just making it back when the Roberts case broke. His background was in psychology, but he wasn't one of the famed FBI profilers who were all the rage. He liked to be involved in cases, get his hands dirty, be in charge of them. That was how our paths had crossed. I had been working at Delta District when he saw me dropping off a witness downtown. He ran down the hall of the homicide wing and said, "I need to see your boss."

I should have shot him then.

After jumping through the many hoops that comprised entering the federal building downtown, including having an escort, I found Bill sitting quietly at his desk when the lesser agent dropped me at his office. I had been picturing him as I walked down the hall, sitting there, waiting with a far-off look in his eye, staring at his computer. And sure enough, that was how I found him. His pinstriped gray power suit was perfectly pressed and accented with just the right red tie. He was in his late fifties, fit for his age, and tan. He always looked rested and serene, like he'd just gotten back from some exotic location. He was most calm when he was in control of a situation.

I hung back in the doorway. "Hey, Bill. I got your message. You wanted to see me?"

"You changed your cell phone number."

"All things considered, I thought it was a good idea."

He smiled. "Come in. Have a seat." He motioned to the comfortable leather chair in front of his highly polished wood desk. His desk was almost empty except for a computer monitor and keyboard, an in-box neatly stacked with color-coded files, and the multiline Bureau phone stationed next to him. He had his cell phone facedown next to his right hand—in case he had to snatch it up quickly for some FBI emergency, I guess.

The rest of the space was completed by two chairs, a printer/copier in the corner, and a white dry-erase board that covered most of the wall to the left of him. Even his garbage can was empty. He wasn't one to clutter himself up. It was part of his whole serenity thing. I hadn't seen him for almost four months, since I'd testified in the grand jury, and nothing had changed.

"What's up?"

"How have you been?" Zeroing in on my eye, he added, "Looks like you've had some trouble."

I smirked and said, "I totally pummeled the guy's fist with my face. It was brutal."

"Smartass." He had taken a kind of fatherly affection toward me, which shouldn't have been a stretch, because his own kids were older than I was.

He leaned back in his chair, same wistful smile on his face. "You know me, Shea. I'm not one to beat around the bush, so I'm going to get right to the point here. I've got an interesting case on my hands, and I thought maybe you could help with it."

"I didn't know you had an active case in the city again." A chill ran up my spine. They had lots of cases in the city, but Bill was interested only in the worst ones.

"I don't. This is something special. I've never seen anything quite like it. Not in twenty-five years on the job. I must admit, I'm stumped, and you know how I hate to be stumped."

"I don't understand. If it's not in the city, how can I help you? It's not my jurisdiction. The Bureau can't just step in and take over a local investigation."

"You know the Buffalo branch covers counties all the way to the Pennsylvania border."

I could feel my forehead creasing in concern the more he talked. "What does this have to do with me?"

"It's a town called Kelly's Falls." He went on as if I hadn't even spoken. "It's right on the state border with Pennsylvania. Three young girls, all college freshmen, just disappeared. No clues. No traces. They went to one girl's house after a party and vanished. Their purses were left, their jackets, their cell phones. The TV was on. There was no sign of a struggle; they were just gone."

"I think I read about this in the paper. It happened during Christmas break, before New Year's."

"That's the case."

"Where do I come in?" I asked again, eyeing the stack of folders on his desk.

"Well, I figured after the job you did with the Roberts case, this would be right up your alley. I thought we could plant you in and see what we come up with."

The Roberts case. My own personal albatross. Over the course of eight months last year, three high school students had been murdered, one after another.

"That was different," I protested. "You knew Roberts was the killer; you just couldn't prove it. Something like this is out of my league. Don't you have anyone in the Bureau to do it?"

"I'm a man who utilizes my assets. What I have before me is a twenty-three-year old police officer with almost three years on the force who looks like she's eighteen. I could stick you in any school in the country and you would blend in." He leaned forward, palms down on the desk for the clincher. "On the other hand, your youthful looks are a liability on the streets. Who wants to be partners with someone who looks like she should be at cheerleader practice? I've been there; I know. I'm offering you a chance to do some good here."

"What about manpower shortages? We're averaging a shooting a day right now. Do you think my department supervisors are just going to let you take me off on some—"

He waved his hand, dismissing the words right out of my mouth. "I already have permission from your commissioner to grant you a leave of absence. The local county district attorney is on board, although he won't know your identity. The Bureau will pick up your regular salary, plus expenses."

I sank back into my chair. I wish I could say I was stunned, but I was intimately familiar with Bill's style. "You've got it all figured out, haven't you?"

He smiled again and ran his hand through his salt-and-pepper hair. "I think my clearance rate proves I know how to close cases. And I know how it is to be where you are." He added gently, "I see you being wasted as a police officer. Are you really happy writing tickets and pushing papers?"

"I didn't get this from pushing papers," I said angrily, touching my eye.

"I'm sorry. I didn't mean it like that. I'll tell you what, look over these reports I've got for you on the case. I have a feeling you'll be interested in this without my having to convince you." With that he pulled a large manila folder out of his desk and tossed it to me. I glanced down at it, leafed through the paperwork, and looked up.

"Couldn't you have just emailed these to me?"

He shrugged. "Call me old-fashioned. I want you to really look at these reports, not scroll through them on your iPhone."

The folder was thick, but not thick enough. "Where's the complete file on this?"

"You don't get any of that. I want you to go in practically blind. No preconceived notions. I want to see what you can come up with on your own. Most of this you could get on the Internet."

"No backup. No surveillance. You're throwing me in without a net. Again."

"I wouldn't ask you to do this if I didn't think you'd be safe. But there's always an inherent risk when you're trying to track a killer."

"I thought you said they were missing."

"No bodies. It's been ruled a kidnapping due to the insistence of the parents and the circumstances of the disappearance. Is it a kidnapping? Human trafficking? A triple homicide? Who knows at this point? The county attorney approached the FBI for assistance because the local authorities and state police have come up with absolutely zero. I don't think these girls up and ran away. Once you read the file, I'm convinced you'll agree with me."

I folded all the papers back in place and got up, trying to seem noncommittal. "Okay, I'll take a look at these."

As I was walking to the door, Bill said, "When this is all over, we'll see about you coming to work for the Bureau. We'd love to have you."

I wanted to say *No thanks.* I wanted to say *Go screw yourself.* I wanted to throw his old-fashioned paper files back at him and storm out of his office in righteous indignation, but instead I reached for the doorknob and muttered, "We'll see."

"Take care of the eye, Shea O'Connor."

I walked out.

I managed to keep my composure as I strode across the steel-gray carpets that lined the pictureless, sterile walls. I gave the security guard my visitor's pass and walked back through the metal detector to the side door. As soon as I made it across the parking lot and into the sanctity of my car, I burst into tears.

Bill knew what buttons to push on people, and he had hit every one of mine. I knew I looked like a kid. I knew no one wanted me as their backup. Every cop has the moment where they're tested and you either pass or fail under the eyes of your peers. I'd had my moment and I'd passed, I'd survived, but no one knew about it. The judge had issued a gag order on all parties so as not to taint the jury pool because of the depraved and extreme nature of the crimes. Until Terry Roberts's sanity hearings were over, no one would know what I'd done to catch that sadist fuck, or that it was even me who'd done the catching. If the court decided Roberts was fit to stand trial, they'd go forward with the evidence and the people's case would be open to discovery for all the world to see.

Until the gag order was lifted, I had to struggle every day with my own reflection in the mirror. Along with the emotional and the physical scars, the case had left me drained and isolated.

I drove home knowing that Bill had won, but not knowing whether I should be grateful. It was only a five-minute drive from Bill's office over to my apartment in Allentown. Closing my eyes and practicing the breathing technique my roommate had taught me, I got myself together after I parked my car behind our building.

I lived on Elmwood Avenue, considered to be the trendy, artsy Buffalo neighborhood. People were snapping up the old Victorians and had reinvented the area as The Elmwood Village. Our landlord had renovated an old shoe store that had stood vacant for almost a decade into two oversized apartments.

The downstairs tenant/landlord was shoveling his walkway. "Hey, Shea," he called as I sifted through my keys. "I did yours, too."

"Thanks, Marcus. You always come through for us."

"I'm out here anyway. Just keep me safe, girl."

I laughed. "Will do."

My roommate, Karen, was already home when I walked in, lounging on our couch, watching the news with the remote in her hand. "Who dotted your eye?" She clicked the remote, turning off CNN. "Boy, you look like crap."

"Thanks," I groaned, and threw my things over the armchair. My scarf slid off my coat and pooled on the floor. I just left it. "I got decked at work."

"Pretty." She moved her feet so I could sit down next to her. "What's that?"

She was eyeing up the case file I still had in my hand. I put it down on our coffee table. "Bill Walters called me today. He left a message for me at the station house, and of course I ran right over to see him."

"What did he want?" She propped herself up on one of our throw pillows. "To gloat over the raise he got for the case you solved?"

"No, nothing like that. He wants me to work for him on a new case. He wants me to go undercover again."

I had told Karen about the Roberts case. If I hadn't talked to someone other than the shrink they assigned me, I would have gone crazy. "Can you do that?" she asked. "Will the department let you after what happened last time?"

I waved away some of her secondhand smoke. "The department practically gave me to them. They could care less."

Karen reached over to the bowl of candy on the coffee table and popped a chocolate into her mouth. "You know what I say?"

I rolled my eyes. "No. What?"

"To hell with them." She sat straight up and gave me a hard poke in the chest with one of her bony little fingers. "If it weren't for you, Terry Roberts would still be killing students and drinking their blood. You almost got killed. And what did it get you? A one-way ticket back to patrol in South Buffalo. You're just another beat cop to them, nothing special. If Bill Walters wants you to work for him, do it. At least he knows and appreciates what you did."

Karen was a force of nature when she got going. She worked as a nurse at the Erie County Medical Center in the trauma unit and had pretty much seen it all. She looked like a bimbo: long hair extensions, colored blue contacts, fake boobs. The only thing left on her that was real was her mouth. She talked like a truck-driving psychiatrist. We had met in college when we were both students at the University at Buffalo. I had dormed for one semester before deciding it was a waste of money, and she had been my roommate. Now she was my rock. She always gave it to me straight, no matter what.

"You're right. I know you're right. All I want is someone to know what happened. For my coworkers to know that I'm not useless."

"And then what? If they can't see it now, who cares?"

"I do. I know I shouldn't care, but I do. I went above and beyond, and the only person who knows it is you."

"Well, I hope it all comes out soon. I'm getting really tired of you moping around feeling sorry for yourself. You're obsessed, and it's getting boring."

"Thanks."

She tucked an arm behind her head. "What you really need is a man. What about Ben? He's nice and he's got a job."

"He's a bouncer and he lives in his mother's basement."

"No one said you had to marry him."

"Thanks anyways, best friend." I got up, grabbing the file with me.

I wanted to go over it undisturbed, so I twisted up the staircase to my loft bedroom and flopped onto my king-sized bed. Our cat, Boyd, lay curled up next to the heat register, purring like a revving semi, nose tucked under his tail.

I opened the file and fanned everything out across my bed.

Kelly's Falls was a small town on the Pennsylvania border. It had one small factory that made office supplies, which employed a few of the general population. There was also a lot of old money in the town. Once there had been oil in those hills. Nothing major, a couple rigs around the turn of the century, but enough to make a few families very wealthy.

Once those dried up, a new source of income had come to a lucky few—natural gas. There were huge deposits of it that stretched across the Pennsylvania border. Since Governor Cuomo had banned fracking in New York a lot of people were making a ton of money crossing the border into Pennsylvania to do business there. Over half the town's population drove twenty miles every day to work in the fracking industry, bringing their paychecks back over the state line at the end of the week. Which was a little nuts, considering New York State's high taxes.

With those things going for it, Kelly's Falls was a middle-class town, no different than any other upstate burg. The only thing of note to have happened in the last twenty-five years was the girls' disappearance.

Over a month and a half after they were last seen, there were still no leads. As far as I could tell from what Bill had given me, local law enforcement had reached out to the state and Feds right away. The families had organized search parties, set up a reward fund, and scoured the woods that surrounded the town over and over again. They'd held press conferences and begged for information about the girls' whereabouts. The national media had been all over the story the first month; then a tot had gone missing from her bedroom and the mother's boyfriend was arrested, changing their focus. Leads had come and gone. Nothing had panned out.

The girls were just gone.

Bill had been right. It was interesting. Interesting enough for me to want to look into it. Three girls. Threes. The irony was not lost on me. Terry Roberts had murdered three girls. I rolled over on my bed and watched the sun set over the gingerbread rooftops. As the sky changed from gold to red to orange, I turned over the situation in my head. If it were my friends, my family, my neighbors, wouldn't I want the authorities to do whatever was necessary?

That might help me sleep at night, but that wasn't why I was going to say yes.

I was a glutton for punishment.

The next morning, against my better judgment, I held a raw steak over my purple eye and made a phone call to Bill Walters. Just like that, I was a transfer student at Harris Community College in Kelly's Falls, New York.

**Saturday, March 18<sup>th</sup>**

The morning after St. Patrick's Day, with my eye as good as new, I found myself being driven by Bill Walters to my new identity. I would be posing as an eighteen-year-old college freshman, just like the missing girls.

Registered at Harris Community College under the name Shea Anderson, I would be staying with the town police chief's friend, who ran a boardinghouse. We were going on the premise that I was the chief's niece from the city whose parents had just been killed in an auto accident. The town police chief would be the only person who knew who I really was. The boardinghouse was next door to his own house. I would be staying there under the pretext that he was an unmarried man who lived in a one-bedroom home and had no experience with raising teenagers.

I wasn't crazy about that cover story, but Bill insisted that people would ask fewer questions about a girl who had just lost both parents.

"Aren't we stretching this a little far?" I asked when he laid it all out for me. "And thank you for giving me the whitest white-girl name ever."

"Kelly's Fall's isn't exactly diverse. Things aren't so liberal in small towns," he assured me. "We had your records sent. You start school on Monday."

"What records did you send?"

He glanced over from the driver's seat with a raised eyebrow. "Why, yours, of course. From North Side High School. You're still on record there as a former student. I have you transferring from the Erie Community College West Campus. I have a friend in admissions there; he set it all up."

"You amaze me sometimes."

I had to admit, I was nervous and excited. I didn't want Bill to see, to let him know how I was feeling. That my stomach was in knots. Because I was feeling useful and this was important. Those girls needed to be found. It was a ton of pressure, but I thrived on that. Truth be told, I had spent the last few weeks looking forward to this day, to jumping in again undercover and seeing this through.

"You gave your family the cover story?" He wanted to hear me say it again. For the third time.

"I'm taking a leave of absence to rethink my job. An extended road trip with some money I saved. Call them when I can, from wherever I am." Rethinking my job had become my actual job lately, so it wasn't much of a stretch.

"And you went over the FBI guidelines for undercover operations again?"

I let out an exasperated breath. "About a million times. And we went over it with your legal counsel, and I remember it from when I started the Roberts case."

"Remember, everything has to be double-checked with me."

"Except what I encounter in the field. Then I have to use my discretion. I got it. I know."

He nodded, satisfied with my reply. "Cell phone reception can be spotty in Kelly's Falls. The Wi-Fi can be as bad. Try to keep me updated daily. Hourly, if it comes to that."

"I'll follow you on Instagram," I told him.

"Funny. We have all your social media accounts set up. Don't go on Facebook; they use facial recognition software—you know, how they tag you in pictures? Don't follow anyone you know from Buffalo. Don't follow anything that can connect you back to Buffalo. We'll be monitoring them."

My poor follower-less accounts. I was starting out as a loser. "I'll try to keep the selfies to a minimum."

As Bill drove, I watched the scenery unfold, from the iron grays of the city to the dirty browns of a Western New York spring. The farther we got from the city and then the suburbs, the muddier and more barren the landscape looked. The hills rolled by out the window, dotted with farms. Farms with sagging snow fences and red grain silos. Farms that had cows. Cows that didn't even turn their heads as we drove by; they just kept chewing at the ground, or staring off at each other, mouths working, working, working. I was on another planet. It was an alien landscape to me.

"I hope I can pass. I actually feel like I'm starting a new school for the first time," I said, running my fingers through my choppy, unnaturally straightened brown hair.

"You'll fit in. You look like a million bucks, kid. And look on the bright side. It's March eighteenth now; only a few more weeks and you get to go on spring break."

"Only if you foot the bill," I countered.

"Imagine that line in my expense report." Bill chuckled and glanced around. "Looks like we're here."

The town was bigger than I expected. Bill pointed out various landmarks to me as we rolled over a bridge onto a wide street lined with brand-new old-fashioned lampposts. I saw a pizza place, a McDonald's, even a large shopping plaza with a Target and a grocery store. He took a left, past a car dealership/body shop, and then another right. I was getting the full tour. We passed the high school and the athletic field across from it where the Kelly's Falls football team played in the fall and the baseball team played in the spring.

Circling back toward the bridge, Bill drove through the Main Street area. "The townies refer to this as downtown," Bill told me, slowly cruising past cutesy boutiques, a coffee shop full of people, and a very fancy bank building, probably built in the 1920s, restored to its art deco glory.

"Kelly's Falls even has a country club," Bill announced, as if that would make me giddy with joy.

"It's a nice town," I admitted, peering into a bridal shop with a gorgeous white beaded dress in the window. "Nicer than I expected."

"What did you expect?"

I shrugged. "Something from *Deliverance*."

He turned the car around in a deli parking lot and went back the way we came. "I'd take you to the crime scene, but we don't want you connected to us in any way. You're on your own. This place has been crawling with cops, reporters, troopers, Feds, you name it, since the girls disappeared. So these people are suspicious of everyone. Got it?"

"Nothing like sticking an undercover operative in to spy on them, right?"

"Welcome to post-nine/eleven America."

"It feels dirty, somehow." I crossed my arms against my chest. "I still don't like it, lying to these people."

Bill laughed. "You sure fit the role. You're as crabby and opinionated as my own kid."

I suppressed the overwhelming urge to stick my tongue out at him.

We rolled off Main Street and down a side road lined with pretty, well-kept houses. I watched as he pulled into the driveway of a three-story, white Victorian with an impressive wraparound porch that sat at the corner of a crossroads.

On one corner stood Theresa Parker's Boardinghouse, announced by its hand-painted sign hanging from a post on the lawn. On the other side of the street, directly across, was the police station. It was a square, squat one-story structure with glass block windows and a massive double door right in the center, dividing the building perfectly in two.

On the other side of the crossroads stood the volunteer fire station, with its red-brick facade, complete with an old-fashioned fire bell out front. It was the kind that looked like a big metal hoop. The firefighters would bang on it with a hammer before sirens were invented to wake the town. The only reason I knew that was because my uncle had been chief of a volunteer fire company when I was a kid, out in the suburbs, and I used to climb on the "bell" when they had family parties at the fire hall.

I wondered if they had banged the bell the night the girls went missing.

"This is some town," I said, reaching for the door handle.

"It's one of those quiet towns the tabloid TV shows love, where nothing ever happens, except when the city folks come down for hunting season and shoot each other, drunk in the woods." He swung his door open. "Take my word for it, small towns have the worst secrets, the most skeletons. Let's see if you can dig up a few."

He helped me extract my four overstuffed suitcases and shuffle them to the front porch. I looked up. Standing in the doorway was a gray-haired woman in her seventies. She reminded me of those ladies you see in the adult-diaper ads, all smiles and apple pie.

"Welcome! Welcome, Miss Anderson. I'm Theresa Parker," she called, pushing forward to grab a bag. "Your Uncle Roy has told me so much about you. I'm so sorry to hear about your parents, dear. Tragic—that's what it is." She swung one of my bags up onto the porch with surprising ease. "But you look hungry, so you go on upstairs and get settled, and I'll make you something to eat."

She grabbed another bag, swung it up, and then stuck her head inside the doorway. "Henry!" she called. "Come down here and carry Miss Anderson's bags." She gave me a pat on the arm and disappeared down the hallway.

"One last thing," Bill said quietly, coming up next to me. "I want you to remember you are not a cop here. You're just here to get us some leads. Whoever we're dealing with is dangerous. No unnecessary risks. You're to consult with me on everything, got it?"

"Go home, Bill. I'll call you in the morning."

"Good-bye. You just be careful." He glanced toward the stairs for a moment, turned, and left.

I stood there on the porch for a second, not knowing what to do, as Bill's car pulled out of the driveway. Then a man appeared at the top of the stairs in an old flannel shirt and overalls. He looked like he was in his early sixties, painfully thin, with wild, white hair. Marching down the steps, he scooped up three of my bags at once. "I have bad knees," he said gruffly. His left front tooth was chipped clean in half, giving him a slight lisp. "You'll have to carry the big one."

"That's all right." Grabbing the handle, I bumped my suitcase up the stairs and followed him down the second-floor hallway.

"I'm Henry Jones." He pushed open the last door on the corridor with his hip and set my bags inside. "I stay down the hall."

"I'm Shea Anderson." *Anderson, not O'Connor*, I reminded myself. "I'm Chief Bishop's niece."

"Yeah, we all heard you were coming. I'm real sorry about your mom and dad. I think you'll like it here. You've got the nicest room in the place. Key is on the bed. Just give me a holler if you need anything."

I set my big bag down. "Thank you."

He brushed past me, and I watched him slide inside his own room three doors down. Shutting the door behind me, I sized up the place. It wasn't as bad as I'd thought it was going to be. It was actually quite cozy and comforting in a way.

It was really two rooms. As you walked in, there was a bed, all made up with an old-fashioned comforter and ruffled pillows. Next to that was a nightstand with a pretty white-and-pink lamp on it. A small archway led to a sitting room of sorts with a bay window that overlooked the police station across the street. An old armchair faced an even older TV. The rooms smelled like the lavender sachets my grandmother used to put in all her drawers. Thankfully, I had my own bathroom. Henry was nice, but I didn't want to share a shower with him.

I checked out the bathroom and then went back to the bedroom to unpack. I started to put my shirts in the antique dresser across from the bed. Its mirror was oval shaped, and I could still smell the glass cleaner.

"Honey? Are you hungry? I've made some sandwiches." Mrs. Parker was in the doorway, smiling like some painting of a country aunt come to life.

"I guess I am. It was a long ride."

I threw my last shirt in the drawer, closed it, and followed her back downstairs to the kitchen. I sat down with her at the huge white table, big enough to serve breakfast to all her guests, complete with a blue vase in the center filled with perfect pink carnations. She had it all set up with sandwiches, pastries, and a big glass pitcher filled with milk. In my entire life I'd never poured myself milk from a pitcher. It always came from white plastic jugs.

"I don't want you to feel like I'm trying to mother you, but we do have rules around here, and I might as well get this out of the way now. They apply to you and to everyone else that stays here, too. And I also don't want you to think I'm babysitting for your uncle. Even though you're only a freshman in college, you're eighteen and an adult, so I'll treat you like one."

"I appreciate that, Mrs. Parker. Believe me, I won't be any trouble."

"Good," she said, and tucked a piece of white hair that had come loose from the bun on top of her head behind her ear. "Now, about those rules. Here they are: No loud music, ever. There are too many people who live here to be blasting music all around. No pets, unless you want to keep a goldfish; that would be all right. Henry has two named Romeo and Juliet. No parties at all. And the last one . . ." She paused for a second, trying to figure out how to put it to me. "While I know how things have changed with young people these days, I'm afraid I'll have to ask you not to bring home any overnight male visitors. It just wouldn't be appropriate, you being in my care in your uncle's stead. He trusts me to look after you. I hope you'd be above that sort of thing anyway. You seem like such a nice girl."

I had to suppress a laugh at how serious this woman was trying to be. "Don't worry, Mrs. Parker. I just want to finish out this semester of college. I'm already looking at schools upstate for next year. I'm not looking for a boyfriend."

Theresa Parker sighed, poured a glass of milk, and said with a smile, "That's exactly when you find one."

There was a knock on the back door just then, and a strawberry-blonde woman stuck her head in. "Is your new guest here yet?"

"Sarah Rose, come in. She's right here," Mrs. Parker told her. She came inside with a little girl, about seven, who had the same red hair as her mother. The color I had tried to achieve for two years with my hairdresser and could never quite get. A natural golden red that practically sparkled.

"I'm Sarah Rose Gifford. I live two doors down." She put her hand out to me, and I shook it.

"Shea Anderson. Nice to meet you. And what's your name?" I asked the little girl, bending down so we were nose to nose. She hid behind her mom, who herself was not all that big. Sarah Rose was barely five feet tall, and I doubt she even broke a hundred pounds.

Sarah Rose's delicate red hair was cut in a cute bob that matched her daughter's. "This is my baby girl." Sarah gently pushed her forward toward me.

She twisted the end of her little denim dress and said, "My name is Emily Rose."

"But we just call her Emily," Sarah Rose corrected. "Too many Roses in our family. What happens when you get too many roses?"

"Thorns," Emily replied in a whisper, and I laughed.

"Emily is a pretty name," I told her. She went back to trying to hide behind her mom.

"We stopped by to give you your pan back and to say hello. Jake said to say thank you, he loved the pie."

Mrs. Parker took the pan from her and put it down on the kitchen counter. "It was nothing; I love to bake. Once Mr. Parker passed away, I didn't have much reason to, until I started taking in boarders."

26

"You keep cooking like that, and I'll be your next boarder." Sarah Rose smiled. "We're just stopping in. I wish we could stay longer and chat, but I have to go pick up the baby and make Jake's dinner. It was nice to meet you."

"Nice meeting you too, and you, Emily," I said, waving to her.

Sarah Rose smiled and ducked out the back door. Emily waved to us and followed her. Mrs. Parker picked up the pie plate and put it into the cupboard. "Sarah Rose is a lovely girl."

I took a sip of my milk, and noted a touch of tightness in her throat when she said it. "Is something wrong?"

"You never really know what goes on between two people." Mrs. Parker wiped her hands on her skirt. "I had hoped for better for her." She left it at that, and I didn't pry. I went upstairs to get my things organized. I liked Mrs. Parker. I was a little more optimistic about my role in Kelly's Falls. I told myself to think of it as a working vacation. I'd been hoping that the girls would suddenly return and I could go home after a couple of days.

Somehow, though, I knew it wasn't going to be quite that easy for me.

## Sunday, March 19th

I didn't get to meet my new Uncle Roy until the next morning around breakfast time. I spent the night getting settled in and making some notes before going to bed. At eight o'clock that morning, I got a knock on the door. It was him, Kelly's Falls' trusted chief of police. "Shea? I'm Roy Bishop," he said quietly. "May I come in?"

I stepped aside. "It's nice to meet you."

He had a baseball hat clenched in his hands as he stepped through my doorway. Younger than I expected, he had the typical brown-and-tan police uniform on, complete with a shiny black Glock on his hip and handcuffs. I had found out the night before that besides being the youngest police chief at thirty-eight, he was also the town's most eligible bachelor. I had to admit, he was a very good-looking man, in a cowboy sort of way, with perfectly combed light-brown hair and startlingly blue eyes. He was on the short side, for my taste, but had an athletic build, like he worked out every day. I could see his easy smile and polite ways making him the talk of the town's women's league. "I'm sorry I didn't get a chance to come over last night, but I was busy working."

"That's all right. I sat around and got to know Theresa and Henry. I met Marlene and little Peter as well. We're all going to be one big happy family."

He laughed at that one, and then took a long look at me. "You're really a cop?"

And there it was, right out of the gate. I nodded. "I really am. I carry a gun, and they gave me a badge, and once in a while I get to drive the police car with the lights on."

"I didn't mean to be rude. It's just that you look so—young."

"It's okay, I get that all the time. But then again, so do you, I bet." I threw that in to try to level the playing field a little. He wasn't exactly an old-timer himself, even if he was the chief.

"Is there anything special I should know about your family?" I asked, running my hand through my flattened hair, trying to smooth it out a little. It tended to frizz up as the day went on. That was the Irish in me.

He seemed to think on that for a moment, like he wasn't sure how much he had to reveal. "I came here as a patrol officer about ten years ago from Utica, so no one here knows too much about my family life. I told everyone you were from Buffalo, but I suppose you should be aware of the Utica connection."

"I lived there as a small child, but we moved when I was very young, so I barely remember it. My parents were Jim and Katie Anderson," I said, trying to remember all my lies.

He nodded. "Jim and Katie."

"Just recently died in a car accident. Katie was your older sister. I have no other family."

"Yep, that's about it."

"So," I said, sitting down on my bed. I was still in my T-shirt and shorts. "Do you really have a sister named Katie?"

"I do, alive and well in California with instructions not to call, text, email, FaceTime, or write. Your FBI friends even made up a fake *Buffalo News* with her obituary in it."

"Those were real. They submitted a fake death certificate to the paper. Just a precaution."

"You people really go all out."

"Don't call them my people. I work for the Buffalo Police Department. I'm on loan."

"I'm sorry." He shook his head with a laugh. "I really can't picture you as a cop. Especially not a cop in Buffalo."

Wow. That was funny to him? I'd seen more action in three years in Buffalo than he'd see in Kelly's Falls in his whole career.

"Why do you think they brought me here?" I shot back, trying to control my temper. I dug my nails into the palm of my hand. Stupid, misogynistic, sexist hick. I could make first-impression labels, too.

With that, he clapped his hands together, realizing he had just insulted the shit out of me. "Why don't you get dressed and meet me at the police station after breakfast?"

I mustered up my best fake smile. "Sure."

"We'll talk more in my office later."

"Okay, Chief. I'll see you there." He left without another word. I took a few deep breaths to exhale my anger. I wasn't used to him and he wasn't used to me, but we'd have to work together. I knew things between us would smooth out. He'd see that I wasn't useless and I'd realize that he wasn't a dick. At least, that's what I hoped for.

I took a shower and changed into a pair of jeans and a sweat shirt. It was a cold day despite all the sunshine. By the time I made it downstairs, everyone was already eating. Young Peter Martin, not even ten, loudly slurped the milk from his cereal bowl. His mom, a thirty-something divorcée with a high-pitched voice, told everyone about the continuing troubles she was having with her boss down at the convenience store.

I ate my breakfast, carefully listening to everyone's conversation for some talk of the missing girls, but it didn't come up. I scraped my egg residue in the garbage, put my plate in the sink, and informed everyone I was going over to the police station. "Make sure you tell that uncle of yours I said hello," Marlene told me.

"Will do," I said with a cheerful fake smile, making my exit.

Outside, the snow was melting and you could feel spring starting to slowly creep up. Purple crocuses had broken through the thin frost that crusted the front flower beds. I crossed the street to the police station and walked in.

"Hello," I said to the officer hunched over an ancient computer on top of an even older desk. "I'm looking for Chief Bishop."

"Hello there. You must be his niece. He's right in there; that's his office," the cop at the desk said eagerly, as if he didn't get to see too many people. The station itself wasn't much. It was probably built in the fifties and hadn't had a lot of updating. The main office had a few empty desks and a couple of random computers sitting on a long table against the back wall. Above the table, wooden shelves stacked on top of each other were overstuffed with paperwork. A brand-new copy machine sat in the corner, looking out of place in the vintage office. Missing posters were plastered everywhere. It was the perfect police station for a town where nothing much ever happened, except when it did, and then it was much too small.

I gave the cop a pleasant nod, walked over to Chief Bishop's door, and knocked.

"Come on in." He was sitting behind his desk in his little office. On the walls were framed newspaper clippings, various awards, and a picture of him holding up a huge fish he must have caught somewhere. An old-fashioned coat rack was propped in the corner, weighed down by police jackets for every occasion and season. I noticed he had a cot with an old army blanket against the back wall, which I thought odd, because he lived practically next door. I sat down in one of the two chairs he had set up in front of his desk.

"So here we are," I said, smiling, but now he wasn't smiling back. Not even out of politeness.

"Look, I didn't want to say anything at Mrs. Parker's house, but I'll say it now. I don't want you here. I don't approve of you spying on my friends and neighbors, and I don't see what you could possibly find out that we don't already know. I also don't like being forced into some crazy charade about you being my niece. My cooperation in this matter is being given under protest."

Here we go, I thought. Game on.

"We're only doing this to help those girls," I told him, trying to tame my tone.

"You people don't give a shit about those girls. You just want to clear this case. You don't care if they're dead or alive. The Feds just want to wrap this all up in a neat little package labeled clues, suspect, arrest, conviction."

"I'm not a Fed," I pointed out. "I care about finding those girls. I didn't have to come here."

"Why do I get the feeling you are not as selfless as you pretend to be?" he asked bluntly.

"Whatever the reasons, the fact remains that I'm here, and you'll have to get used to it and work with me on this. You know as well as I do that three college-age girls do not just up and disappear together without so much as taking their cell phones. Someone knows something."

We sat facing each other for a moment. It was over before it started, I thought, as he drank me in with his eyes. I knew that look. Then the chief sighed, stood, and said, "Well, now that that's over with, I'll show you around the town and let you in on some things."

I paused for a second to see if there was a caveat to that sentence. When none came out, I said, "Thank you, Chief. I just want to help."

"Please," he said, smiling a little, almost in defeat. "Call me Uncle Roy."

I laughed, relieved that all the cards were on the table and he was going to try to work with me instead of fight against me. "Very funny."

"What do you want to see first?"

I shrugged. "Everything and anything connected to this case would be nice."

"The Bureau did a fantastic timeline for us of the events of the night—on paper, digitally, and video. With the help of the state police and county sheriff's office, we did over a hundred and forty interviews in the first week alone. Forty-seven people were at that party over the course of the night. The Feds pieced together pictures, videos, texts, live streams. I'm old. I never realized how documented people's lives are now." He opened a desk drawer and pulled out a flash drive. Holding it up, he told me, "It's all on here. Including the connection chart. Take this."

He was right about that. The first thing I'd done that morning was check my texts, and now my assumed-identity Instagram and Twitter feeds. Before I'd left for Kelly's Falls, I'd had to tell my friends and family back home that I'd violated the police social media policy and had to deactivate my accounts or face suspension. But even virtually friendless, I still spent almost an hour every morning on social media. I was just as connected as an imposter as I had been in real life.

"I'll go over this tonight," I told him, picking the thumb drive off the desk where he had dropped it and putting it into my purse. "This will be a huge help."

He slapped his palms down on his desk. "Right this way for the grand tour." Crossing the room, he opened the office door for me. I walked back out into the front with him right behind me.

"Jack, we're going for a little ride. I'm going to show my niece around our lovely town."

The chief's office must really have been soundproof, because things had gotten a little heated in there for a second, but his officer had no clue.

"You two have fun, boss," he replied happily. He acted like it was a great treat to be left on his own at the station house.

"I'm taking my chief's vehicle. If anyone needs me, call me on the horn."

"You got it. 'Bye now," he called after us as we walked out the back door.

I hopped into the chief's new giant white Chevy Tahoe. *Chief of Police* was emblazoned across both sides, complete with the Kelly's Falls official town seal of an oil rig against the yellow rays of the rising sun. I guess fracking didn't have a cool emblem to put on their police patches yet.

He pulled out of the parking lot and headed down the road to Main Street. "Kelly's Falls has a pretty simple layout," he explained, waving to a white-haired man in front of Kilkenny's Dry Cleaning. "Hey, Mr. Kilkenny!"

Mr. Kilkenny waved back and straightened the sandwich board in front of his shop.

"Main Street is the center of town, with three major side streets. You are now currently residing on Oakbridge. Going south, toward the school, we have Carlisle and then Bainbridge.

That pretty much makes up the heart of downtown, so to speak. But right now, we're headed north," he said, swinging around in the parking lot of the supermarket.

"Where to?" I asked.

"To the residential section off Oakbridge, on the other side of Main where Olivia and Emma lived. Skyler lived down on one of the rural roads in the trailer park."

I sat there taking in all the scenery and all the landmarks he pointed out. "This is really small-town America, huh?"

"You may think we're a bunch of hicks, but at least we can walk the streets at night." He paused for a second, then added, "Or at least we could until we lost those girls."

"You think they're dead, don't you?"

The chief adjusted his hat and sighed. "You know, I hope and pray, we all hope and pray, but in my heart I know they're dead. I'm not naïve enough to think after twelve weeks they're going to show up at the Los Angeles City Mission, trying to call home."

We pulled into a neighborhood of large, pastel-colored country houses. Almost all had big wraparound porches and spacious lawns. Even in the muddy March springtime, they seemed warm and inviting. The chief stopped in front of one of the biggest homes on the street.

"We can only stay a second. I know Mr. and Mrs. Stansfield are down at the location center at the church. They go there every day to coordinate the search effort. Emma Lansing's house is right there." He pointed to a similar house about five doors down.

I craned my neck around, trying to take in as much as I could without getting out of the vehicle. "This is the scene of the crime?"

"Yes. Emma's car was parked right here when the Stansfields came home. Everything was fine. The girls were just gone."

"No physical evidence? Nothing?"

"We accounted for every fingerprint in the house. Luminol tests came up negative for blood. We believe they got into a vehicle that pulled in the driveway, but it was slushy that night. No usable tire-track marks or even shoe prints."

A brown sedan drove by, slowly, the driver watching us. "We better go."

Chief Bishop backed out of the driveway and headed down the street. On the way, we passed an older white pickup truck driven by a guy with dark hair. The driver nearly broke his neck swiveling around to eyeball us. "That was close," Roy commented, glancing back in the rearview mirror. "That's Olivia's older brother, Nick."

"A narrow escape, huh?"

"Yeah, but I would have said I was just checking on the house. Nick is a great kid. He goes to school up at RIT in Rochester. He took the rest of the semester off to be with his folks through all this." The chief turned down another road and added faintly, "A real good kid."

"I wanted to ask you about Skyler's boyfriend, Joe Styles."

"That punk." The chief rolled his eyes. "He works nights at Fitzgerald's machine shop in town. Goes to Harris Community College under the adult education program to get his GED. He's been a thorn in my side since the day I took this job."

"Really?"

"He and Skyler got in a lot of trouble together." He swung the truck around to Main Street. "She lives over in the Rainbow View Trailer Park, just over Hoyt Bridge on the south side of town. Down the road, west of that, is St. Mary's Cemetery. That was where Joe decided to make some skeleton art. That kid is really something—into drugs, always picking fights. His old man, Frank, died in Attica. He got stabbed to death by another prisoner."

"Can we go by Skyler's place?"

"Sure. Hopefully Brandy Santana is sober today."

We crossed over Hoyt Bridge and came upon the Rainbow View Trailer Park. It was a big, depressing mess. I watched row upon row of squat little box trailers pass by, some decorated with plastic pink flamingos on the lawn. The place was dirty, run-down, and shabby-looking. A bunch of kids played in the swampy grass, throwing mud at each other, while a mangy hound chained to a stake in the ground howled in someone's yard.

"A hurricane should pay this place a visit and do the town a favor."

"Our town is unique that way; we got rich and we got poor, and there ain't too many in between."

He rolled up on a particularly horrible dwelling at the bottom of a dead-end street. Sitting out front on some small steps was a woman in her late forties. Her hair was dirty and limp and hung in her face as she smoked a cigarette. Two little dark-haired boys played trucks on the muddy lawn in front of her. When she saw the vehicle pull in, she waved, and the chief waved back.

"Hi, Chief. What brings you out to see me today?" She didn't get up.

"Hello, Brandy." The chief hopped out and motioned for me to follow. "I just stopped by to see how you were doing."

She stared at him for a second, then looked over at me. "Who the hell is that?"

"This is my niece, Shea. She's come to live with me. This is Brandy Santana."

I gave her a smile. "Hi."

Brandy, who was still sitting, took a long drag of her smoke. "That was real smart. You can't find my girl, but you'll bring another one into this shithole town. Real fucking smart, Roy."

"You been drinking again?"

"Yeah." She had smoked her cigarette all the way down to the filter. She stubbed it out and flicked it across the yard.

The chief hitched his thumbs in his gun belt. She glared at him with red-rimmed, bloodshot eyes. "Too drunk to look after your boys?" he asked.

"Nope. Just one beer after the baby went down for his nap." She fished a pack of smokes out of her coat pocket and lit another one with a disposable lighter that fell out with it. "So what? You gonna arrest me?"

"No, I'm not going to arrest you." He sighed. "I was just checking up on you. Come on, Shea, let's go."

"Yeah, go home," she called as we got back into his truck. "Have fun with your niece. If you're not looking for my daughter, get the fuck out of here." The boys never looked up once from their trucks the entire time we were there, not even when we started to pull away.

"Pleasant lady," I remarked. "I see she's taking it pretty hard."

"Brandy has always been a drunk. She likes to frequent the bars around town. I've arrested her twice for DWI since I've been here. The father of her boys isn't around much."

"Not the same guy as Skyler's dad?"

The truck got stuck for a moment in the ruts that passed for a road, and he threw it into reverse and forward again to rock it out. "No. Skyler's dad took off years ago. Brandy hooked up with a guy named Will Garrette. He likes to make kids but not take care of them." The truck finally found some traction and shot forward, away from Skyler's trailer.

"Where to now?" I twisted in my seat to watch Brandy Santana stare off into space while her boys played in the mud.

"The cemetery."

The chief turned us around and got us out of that hellhole of a trailer park. After a minute or two, he turned down the road to take us to the cemetery. "It used to be a real beautiful place, until the kids started to have their parties here," he said as he turned onto a gravel road. He didn't risk pulling off into the mud, so he parked the truck in the middle of the road, and together we walked down to the entrance.

A huge padlock secured the rusty wrought-iron gate. The chief picked out a key from the many that hung on his huge key ring.

"They used to keep it open all the time, so you could drive in, but ever since Joe Styles went crazy in there, they keep it buttoned up tight. It's only open to the public one weekend a month until we get it back into shape, or if there's a funeral."

Twisting the key in the lock, it popped open. The chief let it and the thick chain wrapped around the two halves of the gate fall to the ground. He cinched the key ring back to his belt and pushed the gate open enough for us to get inside. The wrought iron squeaked loudly, startling a bird from its perch on top. It flew away with a screech.

As soon as I walked in, I could see what the chief meant. Spray paint covered some of the old tombstones, and a lot of them had been toppled over and cracked into pieces.

"What kind of a twisted sicko would do all this?" I asked in amazement, turning in a circle to get the full view.

"Little Joey Styles," he replied. "Watch yourself. Be careful." He grabbed my hand and helped me over a fallen tombstone. A lot of the damage was still evident, but you could also see brand-new stones mixed in. Families had had to entirely replace their loved ones' headstones. They stuck out: black shiny granite blocks next to their weathered, defaced neighbors.

"The town is trying to help restore and maintain this place, but the money just isn't in the budget, and all of our local volunteers are focused on finding the girls right now."

He led me through the cemetery to the mausoleums tucked far into the back corner. I noticed trash and beer bottles littering the ground in front of well-kept graves topped with wilting flowers. A few had American flags stuck in front of them. I felt sorry for the families who had to visit their loved ones there. The place was a mess.

We stopped in front of a large tomb. The name *SCHULTZ* was written across the top in the pitted concrete. Its door was new, though, and locked, with an iron gate in front. Crisscrossing the door was bright-yellow crime scene tape. Posted in red letters was a plastic sign that read: *Crime Scene. Do Not Enter. All Trespassers Will Be Prosecuted.*

He walked over to the gate. "It was here that Joe Styles, who was high on crystal meth at the time, brought Skyler Santana one night about four and a half months ago. He broke open the door and proceeded to build a sort of mosaic with the bones. Skyler agreed to testify against him."

"That's really sick."

"We had to dismiss the case when Skyler disappeared. Lack of evidence, so he walked."

"Is he the same age as the missing girls?"

"He's twenty and only made it to the tenth grade and dropped out. You'll see him milling about the Harris campus. He's taking adult GED classes, but mostly he hangs around in the student union, selling weed and pills, so rumor has it. Campus security is always having problems with him."

I looked around. "Let's get out of here. I've seen enough."

He motioned over at the tomb. "We've had to keep this one sealed up because it's still a crime scene. Just in case we ever get enough evidence to go after Styles again."

Even though it was daytime, the whole place had a dark and gloomy feel to it. "Yeah, well, this place is giving me the creeps, so let's go back."

We picked our way through the uneven lines of tombstones and jumped in his truck. I was glad to leave the crumbling, desecrated cemetery behind us.

We rode back into town, stopping to have lunch at Maronetta's Cafe on Main Street. I sat across from the chief and watched as the waitress flirted and filled his coffee mug every two minutes. I was willing to bet his Tinder account was full of Super Likes.

There was a short silence between us, as if we were both thinking about what we'd just seen. I sat back and sipped my coffee. That was one thing I had to have: coffee. I drank it every day, all day long. And I took it black. Another one of the many bad habits I'd picked up as a police officer: coffee addiction.

Finally, I said in a low voice, "I'm going to start with Joe; it's too coincidental. She goes missing, the case gets dropped."

"His alibi is airtight. We have multiple videos and cell phone pictures that were posted on social media that show him passed out. We confiscated just about every kid's phone who attended that party. Watch the videos. We've got close to five hundred pictures of that night, but nothing incriminating on Joe."

"But he's a start. I just have to introduce myself to him."

"I don't think you'll have a problem meeting him. You're going to attract a lot of attention to yourself being the new girl on campus. Joe tries to be quite the ladies' man, I hear."

"Some girls just love those bad-boy types."

"Do you?" he asked pointedly, but I think he was trying to be funny. I was having a hard time getting a read on my new uncle. Sometimes he seemed good with me being there, other times not so much.

"No," I replied. "I like mine clean-cut, all-American looking. And preferably not potential murderers."

Just then, the chubby blonde waitress set our food down in front of us. "Here you are, Roy. I hope you enjoy it."

"Thank you, Jennifer." He patted her hand, and she walked over to the counter with a radiant smile.

I shook my head and smirked at him. "My uncle's a player."

"You better watch it," he told me, smirking back, "or we just might end up becoming friends after all."

The little bell over the door of the café jingled, and the guy who had driven past us in the pickup by the Stansfield house walked in. He strode over to our booth, hands clenched together in front of him. "I've been looking for you all over the place since you passed me. I was wondering if you were coming by with news for my parents."

"No, Nick, nothing like that." The chief motioned to me. "I was showing my niece the town, and I thought I'd check on your house. I was just making sure everything was all right."

"Oh." He let out a breath. "I was just wondering."

"But where are my manners? Nick Stansfield, this is my niece, Shea Anderson. She's come to live with me here. This is Nick."

I reached out and shook Nick's hand. "Hi, it's nice to meet you." It was warm and callused, but not rough.

Roy gestured to our booth. "Sit down. Have a sandwich with us."

"Okay. Just for a minute." He slid into the seat next to me, his arm brushing mine as he settled in.

I studied Nick Stansfield with what I hoped were discreet sideways glances. His eyebrows were knitted together in concern over deep-brown eyes. He was tall, with the build of a life-long athlete that carried to the way he held himself. His thick, dark hair was cut short, gelled up just a little in the front. A rough five-o'clock shadow shaded his face, as if he hadn't had time to shave in a couple of days. He had on a pair of faded Levi's and a heavy unbuttoned flannel shirt with a black tee peeking out from underneath. I knew from reading Bill's files that he was the older of the two Stansfield children. His mother had almost died giving birth to him, hence the adoption of Olivia from South Korea.

"So," he began after he ordered a cup of coffee, "how do you like Kelly's Falls?"

"It's not as big as Buffalo, but then, Buffalo is not exactly a booming metropolis anymore either."

He gave me a forced smile. "Compared to here, it is. And they really did some cool things at Canalside, near the hockey arena. Up at school, we go to Buffalo all the time when we get bored."

I was becoming more and more aware of how nice he smelled, like Irish soap and fresh laundry.

"Where do you go to school?" I asked, playing dumb.

"Up at RIT in Rochester. But the bars there suck, so we drive over to Buffalo. Did you ever go to McMulligan's or the Boxing Room?"

"No, I'm only eighteen. I can't get into those bars, but I know them, you know?" I felt like an idiot. I'd been going to those bars since I really was eighteen.

He sat back a little, as if to get a better look. "You're only eighteen? Wow, I thought you were my age. I turned twenty-one four months ago." His knee grazed my leg lightly. The waitress came over and set his coffee cup in front of him. He took it black, like me, picking up the mug and blowing across the top lightly before taking a sip. "That's hot," he said, and put it back down on the table.

"Yep, she's going to be taking classes at good old Harris Community College on Monday. She's a freshman," the chief chimed in. Good old Harris CC.

"A freshman, just like my sister. She went to Penn State—goes to Penn State," he said softly, and tried sipping his coffee again. He suddenly stood up and put two dollars on the table. "I've really got to go. My parents should be home soon. It was nice meeting you, Shea." He touched my arm as he got up. "'Bye, Chief. If you hear anything, please let me know."

"Will do. 'Bye now, son. Tell your mother hello for me," he called after him.

"He seems like a nice guy," I commented, taking a bite out of my sandwich.

"He won't go back to school. He says he's staying here until we find his sister."

"I believe that. You can tell he's devastated."

"They were very close. His whole family is just torn apart. I don't know that they'll ever be able to put the pieces back, no matter how this turns out."

We paid the bill, and Roy dropped me off at the boarding-house with the promise he'd bring over everything he had on Joe Styles for me. I went up to my room to go over the files I had hidden in my closet and take some notes.

Flipping through the printouts I had scattered across my pale-green bedspread, I pushed all other thoughts to the back of my mind. My job in Kelley's Falls was to help find the girls, whose faces stared up at me from the pictures Bill had given me. Olivia Stansfield's senior portrait was on top of the stack. Picking up her photo, I felt a knot in my gut. *Where are you?* I thought, letting the picture fall back on the pile. *Help me find you.*

\* \* \*

Dinner was served at six. The same group of people sat around the table talking as Mrs. Parker set out serving platters heaping with food.

"Did you have a nice day today?" she asked, loading my plate down with mashed potatoes.

What a question. Had my day been nice? Had it been informative? Had I gathered information like I was supposed to? Had I told enough lies?

"Yes, Mrs. Parker. I did."

## Monday, March 20<sup>th</sup>

I woke up with the same knot in the pit of my stomach when the alarm went off. It was seven in the morning. I hated this ritual more than anything. I've never been a morning person. Ever. All I could think was that I'd spent four years in high school, four years in college, and six months in the police academy to end up right back where I started. I had been so tired the night before, I'd passed out after dinner and never had a chance to go over the material on the USB drive. I was falling down on the job already.

I slid out of my nice warm bed and went over to the closet.

Should I wear leggings and boots or the V-neck sweater with skinny jeans? Or the sweater with suede shorts?

I dragged out one of my new outfits and threw it on the bed. Then I pulled out another one. I glanced over at the new notebooks lying on my dresser and shook my head. Back in college. Community college. Welcome to the glamorous life of working undercover.

Grudgingly, I took a shower and got dressed. Mrs. Parker was sitting at the breakfast table with Peter. His mom, Marlene, absently drank her coffee while scrolling through her Facebook feed.

"You're up. I was just going to send Peter." She beamed at me as she set some toast down on the table. "He'll show you where to catch the bus this morning."

"Thanks, Mrs. Parker," I said, sliding into the seat next to Peter's. "Is your school near the college?"

"No," Peter said, drinking his glass of juice. "You go to the big, big school, way down the street from mine."

"Are you nervous, honey?" Marlene asked, looking up from her phone.

"A little. Maybe a lot." At least that was the truth. It was time to find out how good my cover really was. I had fooled everyone so far. This was the real test.

Peter looked at his cheap plastic Avengers watch. "Time to go. 'Bye, Mom. 'Bye, Mrs. Parker. Come on, Shea." Grabbing my hand, he dragged me toward the door. I waved good-bye to the ladies smiling at us from the table.

We had to catch the bus at the top of the street. Peter would go on the yellow school bus, and I had to wait for the shuttle that came down Main Street. According to Mrs. Parker, the county had received some kind of rural higher education grant a few years back that funded the shuttle. It picked up students for the community college as well as for Alfred State College, which was about twenty miles away. It ran from seven to four, Monday through Friday, all day long, shuffling college students in an endless loop.

It was warm for March, and especially muddy. My new shoe boots were already spattered with it, but the sun was shining down on us as we walked up the street. Two other people were waiting at the stop when we got there. One was the little girl named Emily Rose from down the street, the other a girl of about eighteen. Her long brown hair was straightened to perfection, almost to her waist. She was wearing skinny jeans ripped at the knees and a heavy sweat shirt, confirming I was overdressed. She looked at me curiously, earbuds plugged into her head, hiking her backpack higher up her shoulder.

"Kayla, Emily," Peter announced with authority, "This is Shea. She lives with us now at the boardinghouse."

"Hi, I'm Kayla Johnson." Popping her earbuds out, she stepped forward holding out her hand, while Emily just shyly waved.

"Hi," I said nervously, giving Kayla a limp shake. "I met Emily Rose already. She's about the only person I do know in this town. I just moved here and I feel so stupid."

"It's all right," Kayla laughed. "Are you waiting for the Harris shuttle?"

"Yeah, are you?"

"Yes. Everything's right here. Their bus stop, our bus stop. I used to drive myself, but I wrecked my car." She gave me an easy smile. "Anyway, you'll like going to Harris; it's really simple. We're all pretty much on the two-year plan. Two years community college, two years at a university."

"Is that what everyone around here does?" That's what I had done.

She nodded. "Except for a few who don't have to worry about student loans. Our guidance counselor at the high school was big on trying to keep the student loans down. She said she was still paying hers off and she was like, thirty. I think Harris is giving her a cut for all the students she sends them."

I laughed. "If it makes you feel any better, I'm on the two-year plan, too. And I never met your guidance counselor."

Kayla cocked her head to the side. "Where are you from? Portsville?"

Portsville was a slightly bigger town about thirty miles north. "Buffalo."

"Oh no," she said. "You'll probably die of boredom, then."

I looked around. "I hope not. It doesn't seem so bad here."

"I'll show you around campus if you want. I know you probably don't know anyone, right?"

Bingo. Connection made. I played shy. "I don't want to bug you or anything."

"Shut up. Don't worry about it. I'm a lot of fun." Kayla had an outgoing personality and bright eyes. I liked this girl already.

The big yellow cheese bus came rolling along just then. The kids all looked at me like I was some visitor from another planet. Peter got on and waved good-bye to me from his seat up front. Kayla and I stood waiting for another ten minutes, making small talk. What bands did I like? What YouTubers did I follow? Was I on Instagram? Snapchat?

The shuttle, which was thankfully not yellow, rumbled to a stop next to us, and we climbed on. There were a few people already on the bus, all looking tired, books and backpacks piled on the seats next to them, earbuds in, heads down. The ride to the campus was short from our stop. Still, I cursed Bill for not letting me have my own car.

As soon as we pulled into the bus loop, Kayla pointed out a group of people standing by the double-door entrance. "Those are some of my friends. Come on, I'll introduce you. I used to drive the girls, but *crash*, you know?"

Kayla marched us straight back to where they were standing, clustered up, blocking one of the doors, and addressed them all as if she were the mayor.

"Everybody, this is Shea. She just moved here from Buffalo." She pointed around the circle. "This is Rob, Tyler, Maddie, and Jenna."

They all said their hellos to me in turn. "Hey, Shea," Tyler said, while he eyed me up and down.

"Welcome to Kelly's Falls," the girl named Maddie said, glancing over at Tyler, who took the hint and looked away from

48

my chest. She had messy blonde hair with one subtle pink highlight that framed her heart-shaped face. "You just moved here from Buffalo?"

I nodded. "Yeah, I got here this weekend."

Jenna looked at me as if I were nuts. "Why would you do that?"

"My parents died in a car accident, and the chief of police is my uncle, so I came to stay with him," I told them, with just a touch of self-pity to soften them up and make them feel a little bad for me, because I was an evil person who lied for a living.

"I'm so sorry." Jenna put her hand on my arm, and everyone went quiet for an awkward moment.

"How do you like Kelly's Falls so far?" Tyler asked, trying to restart the conversation.

"It's really nice here. I think I'm going to like it."

"The police chief is your uncle, huh?" Rob asked. I could see him looking me up and down, just like Tyler. At home I worked out at the police gym every other night when it was mostly empty, keeping my waist small and my butt from getting two nightsticks wide. I had forgotten what wearing a fitted V-neck sweater could do to accent your upper half. I pulled my jacket closed and tried to smile.

"Yeah, but I'm staying over at the boardinghouse. He doesn't think it would look right, him being a bachelor and all. I guess you could say Mrs. Parker is looking after me."

"Your uncle didn't think it would look right? Look right to who?" Kayla asked, cocking an eyebrow.

I shrugged. "I don't know. To people."

The group began to break up and head into the campus, to my relief. The college was actually multiple buildings spread out over a huge swath of land. One wing of buildings was devoted to liberal arts, another to the applied trades; the south wing was the library and media center. The science buildings were housed on the other side of campus. The building we were standing in front of contained the offices and sat adjacent to the student union. A high-rise in the far corner of the campus that overlooked the soccer fields was the new dorms.

"I'll tell you what." Kayla grabbed my arm before I could disappear into the crowd. "Here's my schedule and my phone number." She started scribbling her classes down on the cover of my notebook. "Text me when you're done at registration. That way I can take you around and stuff."

"Yeah, thanks. I will."

"Come on, I'll show you where the admissions office is." Kayla led me into the large brick building behind us while everyone else scattered.

I took a better look at Kayla as she led me to the registration office. She was rail thin and had long chestnut-brown hair. She looked like she should be in a shampoo commercial instead of a classroom in Western New York. In my brown V-neck sweater and dark leggings, I felt really overdressed compared to the girls on campus, most of whom were locals from Kelly's Falls or the immediate vicinity. They were wearing sweat pants and baggy sweatshirts. People stared at me as Kayla led me down the hall to the office, tucked in the corner by the main entrance.

"I have to go to my eight forty-five class, but remember to text me and we'll try to meet."

"Thanks, Kayla," I called after her. The lady behind the desk looked up. She had her black hair piled high on her head like some huge onyx turban.

"Are you the new girl we got a call about?" she asked in a harsh, raspy two-pack-a-day voice. You could tell she was dying for a smoke.

"I guess so." I walked up to the desk and set my new notebooks down on it.

"Welcome to the Harris campus, honey. We just got your file this morning. You're the chief's little girl?"

"His niece."

"His niece. Well, that's wonderful. Some of us ladies here were afraid he'd up and eloped on us, that you were his step-daughter or something. We are so proud of your uncle around here, I can't even tell you." She went on and on while she handed me my papers and forms to fill out. On the far wall, over another desk piled with papers, was a huge reward poster with the three girls' pictures on it.

It was kind of scary, just then, with those girls staring at me. This was their school. These people were their friends. I was now in their lives. I was touching a part of them that no police file could, no matter what was printed inside it. I took the stack of forms and sat down at a small table in the back corner of the office. The lady behind the main desk started answering phone calls and typing into her keyboard at the same time.

I glanced around the office. There was a huge banner proclaiming that the last day for summer registration was May fourteenth. The spring sporting-events calendar was posted, as well as the sign-up sheet for literacy volunteers. The sheet urged the students to help raise awareness for rural literacy struggles.

Then I noticed another sign-up sheet under the missing-girls poster. I needed to inspect that. I wandered over to it, trying to angle my cell phone on my paperwork to take a picture without the flash. It was for a support meeting for friends of the missing girls. The first name I didn't recognize. The second name on the list was Kayla Johnson. I scanned the rest of it. Joe Styles's name was on it, near the bottom. My phone wouldn't cooperate, so I pulled my little notebook out of my pocket and jotted down a few names.

"Are you finished yet?" the secretary asked, looking up from her computer screen.

I threw my little notebook into my purse. "Almost."

"Good. That was Mr. Beakman, your admissions adviser, on the phone. He wants to see you when you're done."

"Okay." I nodded, heading back over to the desk and finishing the paperwork as fast as I could. Someone had spilled coffee on the desk and only halfheartedly cleaned it up. I tried to keep my stuff off the stains as best I could while balancing the class catalog on my lap.

"Here you go." Handing them over to the secretary, I saw her phone message blotter. There were lots of calls from news outlets for the school administrators.

Noticing me noticing the messages, she turned them over. "Vultures. The media calls constantly. But they're looking for dirt, not the girls." She flipped through my papers absently, making sure all the questions were answered and all the forms signed. "Fine. Mr. Beakman's office is through that door and on your right."

I told her thank you and followed her instructions. Mr. Beakman looked like his name suggested: tall, thin, and birdlike, with a slightly crooked nose. He seemed very pleasant, not like the worn-out, overworked guidance counselor I'd had at North Side High in Buffalo.

"Come in. Sit down." He was standing by the window, watering about twelve little plants he had scattered on a bookcase. He too had a missing poster up on his bulletin board. Finishing with his plants, he settled down across from me, carefully placing his brass watering can on the floor under the desk.

"You've got an interesting file," he said, flipping through it. "Usually we don't accept students so late in the semester, but your personal tragedy with your parents made you an exception."

"Thanks, I guess."

"So you're the chief's niece." He was still thumbing through my paperwork, missing the sarcasm in my voice.

"Yep."

He folded his hands in front of him. "I see here you went to North Side High School in North Buffalo."

"Uh-huh."

"Isn't that the school with the serial-killer teacher?"

I nodded. "Yes. Terry Roberts. I had just enrolled there for summer school. It was so scary when we found out who was doing the murders." That too was the truth.

"Horrible. Just horrible. Now we have these three girls missing." He wiped his forehead with the back of his hand. "I don't know what this world is coming to."

I sat there with a blank look on my face.

"Well, let's get down to business, then. I see here from your file that you want to enroll in the criminal justice program here."

I suppressed a wince. That was Bill's little joke he had thrown into my file. "I was hoping to get into some kind of law enforcement."

"That's fine. We don't get many girls around here looking into that line of work."

"I plan to move back to the city."

He went on and on with his questions about furthering my education and my current schedule.

"I took Intro to Criminal Justice, Psychology 101, and Intro to Corrections during the fall semester. I had a four-point-oh grade-point average." Thanks to Bill Walters for sending my fake transcripts from Erie Community College West Campus. "I just need some electives and stuff."

We argued a little on that point, but in the end I won out. After an hour of baloney, we got everything straight. "Here's your schedule card. I hope you like it at Harris. I think you'll find that even out here in the sticks, we still have wonderful academics."

"Thanks, Mr. Beakman."

I wandered the halls for a while, in no hurry to get to class. I felt like everyone I passed was looking at me, but that was probably just my imagination. Missing posters were plastered all over the school. I found one by the lunchroom with black Sharpie x-ing out the eyes and the words *RIP BITCHES* written underneath. I managed to take a quick cell phone picture of it, since I was all alone in the hall for the moment.

My first class, an English elective on Shakespeare, was already over. I went to my second class, a 101-level art elective. Kayla was also in that class. The professor signed my registration card, gave me the course syllabus, and made me promise to come by his office after two o'clock to go over what I'd missed. I enthusiastically agreed and sat down.

"What took so long?" Kayla asked, glopping some paint onto her canvas.

"My new adviser had to get my life story," I whispered.

"Cool. I have one more class and we can go get lunch at the student union, if you're free."

"Cool," I echoed, sketching out a melting iPad on a boulder. I thought about Kayla's name being on the list. I had to wait a while to bring it up, after I had gained her trust. I had to find out why Joe Styles would sign up to go to a support meeting for a girl he'd probably wanted dead in the first place.

I didn't have a class after my art class, so I got to jot down some notes before meeting Kayla for lunch. I found my way to the library and sat down in the back corner of the room and decided to make the most of it. I hunched over a notebook, making lists of all the things I saw that I thought might be relevant.

People walked by, whispering, but no one seemed to notice or care that I was there.

Lunch was another story. The student union building contained four floors of offices used by the various clubs and groups. The first floor consisted of a huge bookstore, an open cafeteria-style eating area, and a coffee place. You had your choice of pizza, burgers, sandwiches, or Chinese. The center of the room was filled with round tables that stretched all the way to the far back wall. The coffee shop also carried fresh-baked doughnuts. I saw this in my future as I waited to pay for a ham-and-cheese panini. Old habits die hard. *If loving coffee and doughnuts is wrong, I don't want to be right, even if it is a stereotype.*

Kayla and her friends were obviously well-known on campus. That made sense, since most of these people had gone to high school and grammar school together. Everyone was divided into their little groups. Bearded hipsters and artsy students near the front, hockey and basketball players near the back, which was right behind where we sat. Next to the athletes' tables were the burnout tables where all the cool druggies sat. And it was there that I first laid my eyes on Joe Styles.

He sauntered over, munching on an apple. I recognized him from his mug shot. His long brown hair was pulled back from his gray eyes into a man bun. Tall and on the lean side, he had the kind of build where you could see the muscles in his tattooed arm work every time he picked something up. He had on a pair of faded Levi's and a vintage Ramones T-shirt. A black earbud trailed over each shoulder, the cord snaking its way down to the iPhone in his left hand.

"Hey Kayla, Maddie; who's your friend?" He plunked himself down next to me and slid his arm around the back of my chair.

"Joe, this is Shea Anderson. She just moved here from Buffalo," Kayla said in a disgusted voice, as if he smelled particularly repulsive that day.

"Shea Anderson? You sound like a French restaurant."

"Good one," I joked. "I've never heard that before."

Maddie choked back a laugh. He glanced over at her. "It's about time we had some girls around here who actually dress like girls."

"Screw you, Joe," Kayla shot back at him.

"Misogynistic much?" Jenna asked, and Maddie snorted so hard she put her hand over her mouth to cover it.

I don't think he knew what the word meant, so he turned to Kayla. "Don't worry, I didn't forget that night. Ever tell Skyler about it?" he asked, winking at her as he got up. "'Bye now." He waved his apple at me as he went back over to his table, sitting down with his friends.

Kayla was scorching mad. I thought she was going to go over and throat-punch him. "I'm sorry," she fumed. "I just really, really hate him. Joe's going here to get his GED supposedly, but he just hangs out in the student union and sells pot and pills." I had forgotten they had an adult education program on campus. As I looked around, I began to notice more and more older students I had mistaken for faculty.

"He thinks he's such a stud," Maddie agreed, picking at her salad. "I don't know what Skyler ever saw in him. He was nothing but a dick to her the whole time they were going out."

"You know Skyler," Kayla said. "She only likes guys she can fight with."

"Who's Skyler?" I asked, nibbling at my little square of cafeteria panini.

"Skyler Santana," Jenna said, looking up from her nails. She was peeling the gel polish off in big blue strips and dropping them on the floor. "She was a friend of ours. She was one of those girls who disappeared in December."

"They were all our friends," Maddie corrected.

"Those girls on the posters? Does anyone know what happened to them?"

Kayla shook her head. "They just vanished." She started digging around in her purse and came out with her phone. She swiped it open and started showing me picture after picture of her and the missing girls. Them in a bathroom making faces into a mirror. Them at a party. Them with red plastic cups, smiling into the camera while a drunk-looking boy photobombed them from behind.

"Wow," I said, softly taking the phone from her hand to get a better look. "All of you hung around with them?"

"Olivia Stansfield was my cousin—is my cousin," Kayla corrected herself. I could tell she was getting upset, so I tried to change the subject.

"Then Nick must be your cousin too."

"You know Nick?"

"I met him yesterday at the café in town with my uncle. We were having lunch, and he came in. He sat with us and had a cup of coffee."

"I love Nick; he's like a brother to me. He's really taking care of my aunt and uncle."

I handed back her phone. She put it down on the table faceup, with a picture of her and Skyler making a duck face across the screen still showing.

"Nick Stansfield is legit the hottest guy this town has ever produced," Maddie gushed. The other girls nodded in agreement. Maddie, whose pierced nose and pink-streaked hair fascinated me for some reason, opened up his Instagram account and showed everyone the latest picture he'd posted. It was of him and his sister sitting in a restaurant somewhere. Nick still had the menu in his hands as Olivia rested her head on his shoulder, smiling into the camera.

Jenna looked over at me. "I have to go to the bathroom. Come with me, Shea?" I could tell by the tone of her voice that something was up. She got up and I followed her. The bathroom was all the way across the student union. As we were walking, Jenna leaned in and told me, "Olivia and Kayla were like, best friends. I mean, they were cousins and all, but they hung around every day. She doesn't like to talk about it. Me, her, Maddie, Skyler, and Emma were all best friends."

"I'm so sorry. I didn't mean to be nosy."

"No, it's okay." She pushed open the bathroom door with her hip. "You didn't know."

I liked Jenna right away. She didn't seem like the rest of the girls at the lunch table. She seemed a lot more mature. She had long hair like Kayla's, but it was dyed a dark, dark brown, and she wore black-rimmed glasses. As I watched her touch up her perfectly sculpted eyebrows in the mirror above the sink, I realized I was staring, and reached into my purse for some lipstick.

"I watch Morgan James tutorials on YouTube almost every day. My eyebrows were such a mess. You should check them out," she told me, eyeing up the hairy caterpillars I had crawling across my forehead. I'd never gotten into the whole eyebrow thing, but now, looking at hers compared to mine, I was rethinking that position.

As we were walking back to our table, a commotion broke out where we'd been sitting. The hockey team guys were all standing up, blocking our view. All I could make out was a line of Harris Jaguars jerseys and the nervous bouncing that invades bystanders when they're expecting a fight.

We skirted around the guys, back to Jenna's friends.

"What's up?" Jenna asked as we sat down.

Maddie looked over at us, her nose stud sparkling in the afternoon sunlight. "Joe was yelling at Noah Ross for something, and Mr. Davis came over, and now they're arguing."

Standing with arms folded and a smirk on his face, Joe was about ten feet away from us. Mr. Davis, the campus safety officer, was lecturing him unsuccessfully. Joe said something back, Mr. Davis grabbed his arm, and Joe jerked away violently. Mr. Davis motioned to the exit. Joe turned, looked right at me, smiled, and spit on the floor. He then followed Mr. Davis out the door. I could see in that moment why he was considered a ladies' man. If I really had been a college freshman, I think that would've been just about the coolest thing I'd ever seen. It was the old bad-boy image, that smoldering misunderstood rebel in blue jeans. If you were eighteen, he'd be exactly the kind of guy you would want to bring home to piss your parents off.

"What a dick," Maddie said, turning back to her food. My eyes lingered on the doorway. He was definitely something.

\* \* \*

"What did you find out today, Mata Hari? That our local college is a hotbed of criminal activity?"

"Very funny, Chief."

"Roy."

"Okay. Very funny, Chief Roy."

I was sitting in his office making my first official report to him. I understood how he felt about the whole situation, so I tried not to make it worse. He sighed and sipped his coffee. "I'm sorry. Let's try again. How was it?"

"The campus is a lot bigger than I thought it was going to be. I got lost three times."

"Besides the sheer girth of the school, any other first impressions?"

"I met Joe Styles today. Very charming."

He nodded, hands still wrapped around his *Gone Fishing* mug that had a little ceramic rod for a handle. "What did you think of him?"

"I think it's very interesting that someone like him would sign up for a support meeting for a person that was going to put him in jail."

"Joe definitely isn't the sensitive type. But they still saw each other, even after he found out she agreed to testify against him."

"You're kidding."

"Nope. They just couldn't seem to keep away from each other. You know how people are. Sex clouds the brain."

"I think I made an impression on him. What that might lead to, I don't know yet. I think he's our best bet so far."

"So what are you going to do about it?" The chief was looking at my outfit in disdain. Sweat pants tomorrow for sure.

I swung myself around and around in his old swivel chair. If I was going to play a college student, I might as well act like one. He frowned, and I stopped. "There's a party in the woods someplace on Friday night. The hockey team is throwing it. I guess we're all going. Hopefully, he'll be there and I'll get a chance to talk to him."

He took a moment to process that information, then said, "The party. That brings up an interesting question. I'm supposed to break up parties like that. Underage drinking and that sort of thing. Where does that leave you?"

"Well, I've got to go to the parties. I've got to do what college students do. I can drink; I'm of age."

"You are also a police officer, and as you know, drinking at that party with those kids, aside from being morally and ethically wrong, just might constitute endangering the welfare of children."

"I'm undercover. What do you expect me to do? I've got to hang out with them to learn things from them. And they're not children. No one will be under eighteen and no one will still be in high school. How about I just don't drink?"

"It's still morally wrong."

I rolled my eyes. "Duly noted, but I've got to do it. Did you read the FBI's guidelines for undercover operations? I'm sure Bill emailed you a copy. I practically have it memorized."

"Look, Shea—"

"No, you look." I was sitting forward now, gripping the arms of my chair. "I'm undercover. I've put myself in real danger here. If they catch on, whoever they may be, that I'm not who I say I am, who knows what will happen?"

"Aren't you being a little overdramatic?"

I thought back to the Roberts case: the needles, broken glass, and blood. A shiver went through me. "Am I?" I challenged, but he didn't reply.

"Sorry, Chief. Nice talk, but I have to go home and start a couple of papers." On that note I got up, finishing our conference a little earlier and angrier than either of us had expected.

**Tuesday, March 21<sup>st</sup>**

"Guess who asked about you yesterday?" Kayla tried to sound coy as we climbed off the bus.

"Who?"

"My cousin Nick," she squealed, and gave me a pinch on the arm.

"Nick asked about me?" I was trying to play it cool, but I wanted to squeal back. I wanted to do the bouncy up-and-down squeal where you hold on to each other and annoy everyone within ten feet. But I suppressed my wild animal urge.

"Yes, he wanted to know if I had met you yet. I told him yes, and he said he thought you were pretty."

"He did not. Really? He said that? What guy says that?" I was overflowing with an enthusiasm that wasn't entirely faked. Maddie grabbed my arm, hooked hers through it, and we took a celebratory selfie.

"Oh yes, he did," Kayla assured me. "His exact words were, and I quote, 'She's a pretty girl.' End quote."

Maddie stared at her phone. "I'm posting this one," she announced, and hit send. We walked into the main office building, followed the connecting corridors until we got to the south wing, then stood around by the front of the library's huge double doors, where there was a sort of small lounge, waiting for our first classes to begin. It would become our meet up-place during the day.

Jenna came walking up, holding her phone out. "I just saw your picture on your Instagram. Too cute!"

"You are so lucky," Maddie told me. "Nick Stansfield is the hottest guy ever."

"Wait, what?" Jenna asked, shoving Maddie playfully.

"Nick told Kayla he thinks Shea is pretty," she responded. And that, my friends, is how rumors make their way around the world.

"Why weren't you on the bus?" Maddie asked Jenna.

"My mom dropped me off on the way to the bakery," she replied. Her parents owned the bakeshop on Main Street, where she worked as the night manager. She was going to Harris for culinary arts, to carry on the family business. "Are you hooking up with Nick?"

"What? No." I shot a pleading glance over to Kayla. A wave of guilt passed over me for crushing on a victim's family member. It was unprofessional, unethical, and just plain wrong. But so was every single thing I was doing in Kelly's Falls.

Just then Joe Styles came sauntering up to us. "Hey, ladies. Hello, Shea."

"Hi," I replied, hugging my new books to my chest. No more peep shows for the masses.

"I have to lay low from Mr. Davis for the rest of the week, but I'm back," he told us, a little proudly. "Got to get my education on. That's what I'm paying all this tuition for, right?" He leaned against the doorframe, sort of hanging there, staring at me.

"Good for you," Kayla told him abruptly, turning her back to him. "Now go away."

"Don't listen to her, Shea. She's really in love with me. But I'm going to hold out for something new." He winked at me. "See you later." He blew Kayla a kiss and strolled off toward the athletic center.

Kayla fumed as he walked away.

"I think someone else besides Nick thinks she's pretty," Jenna observed, pushing her glasses up on her nose.

"Who doesn't Joe like? I think he's been with every girl in the school, almost," Maddie chimed in.

"He doesn't do anything for me," I said, and that was the truth. Maybe at sixteen or eighteen that type of guy is appealing, but when you get a little older, you realize it's just plain immaturity. Most guys have enough of that without taking it to the extremes, like Joe. Not that he was unattractive. He definitely had that *Sons of Anarchy* thing going for him. And bad can be hot. Real hot.

"He wouldn't for me either if I had Nick Stansfield," Maddie pointed out with a laugh. Maddie was a laugher. Just about anything could set her off, I noticed.

"I don't *have* anything. I had a conversation, that's all." But I was trying to convince myself at the same time that that was all it had been: a conversation. A brief conversation.

It was time to go and Kayla walked with me, since our classes were in the same wing.

"Hey," she said, stopping in front of my classroom. "We're all going down to Freddie's after class today. Do you want to go? It'll be fun."

Freddie's was a little pizza place in town. It had video games and a pool table, so most of the high schoolers went there after school, and even the college-age people, to socialize until it was time to go home for dinner. In a town that small, a good pizza place was bound to be a magnet for the under-twenty-one crowd. What Kelly's Falls really needed was a good coffee shop. If I could have opened a Starbucks there, I would have become a multimillionaire.

I told Kayla I would go. For the rest of the day, the big joke was that I was a Freddie's virgin.

I took some time that day to really look around the campus. There were a lot of people attending Harris, and I couldn't believe how many of them were older students. The one plant in town was rumored to be in financial trouble, and some people were not waiting until it closed its doors to reeducate themselves. In Kelly's Falls you had two kinds of people: the plant workers and the frackers. The frackers migrated across the Pennsylvania border every morning, convinced that their newfound gold rush was going to continue for a long time. The plant workers were praying they made the cut every year, when it came time for corporate to downsize, but taking classes just in case.

After my classes were over, I met up with the girls and we made our way over to the infamous Freddie's. A hipster guy with a less-than-epic beard named Brody was more than happy to cram all of us into his old rusty Impala and drive there. The Impala wasn't nearly as uncomfortable as I'd thought it would be, considering there were six of us stuffed into it.

Freddie's was pretty much a hole in the wall, and you could tell the younger crowd sustained his business, with its concert-poster decor and run-down jukebox that still played old-fashioned CDs. Kayla and her friends sat in the last booth against the wall next to the jukebox. I noticed it had the best view of the door.

On the wall above the counter, next to the cash register, was a huge missing poster. It seemed like the town had gotten used to the idea that the girls were gone, but no one talked about it. Except for the exchange at lunch the day before, I hadn't heard another word about it.

We had been there a total of ten minutes when Joe Styles came strolling through the door with a couple of his followers. "See that girl right there?" Jenna said, pointing to a little bleach blonde who had trailed in after Joe. "That's Amber Wray. She cuts hair over at Desi's salon. She's been in love with Joe for years now. If she even thinks Joe looked at you, she'll go spaz."

"Does he like her?"

She shrugged. "He hooks up with her."

"At least someone's hooking up in this town," Maddie lamented. "Can't you bring some hot guys down from Buffalo?"

Before I could assure her that my well of hot guys in Buffalo was dry, Joe walked right up to us and leaned against the juke-box. That must have been his thing—the Cool Lean. "You sure made friends fast. Here you are at Freddie's."

I nodded and sipped my coffee. "Here I am."

I looked over to see Amber and her friends in the booth across from us. She was staring and talking about me to her friends. I smiled up at Joe. "I don't think your girlfriend likes me."

"She's not my girlfriend. Just a friend. I like making new friends." He looked at me for just a second too long, then strolled over to her and put his arm around her. She was giving me the stink eye.

Kayla elbowed my side. "Looks like you're on a roll." I glanced toward the door to see what she meant. "Hey, Nick," she called to him. She waved him over to the booth.

"Hi, everyone," he said. Absently, he ran his hand through his short dark hair, as if it might have gotten windblown during his walk through the parking lot.

"Nick, you remember Shea, right?" Kayla said, grabbing my arm.

His brown eyes met mine with a sparkle. Or maybe I just hoped it was a sparkle. Maybe he sparkled for everyone and that's why all the girls crushed on him. "Yeah, we met. I'm sorry I was such a downer at lunch the other day."

"That's okay." I think by then I might actually have been blushing. He looked great. I hadn't registered how tall he was, maybe six foot three, and broad shouldered. He had on a navy-blue jacket with the collar up, as if he was using it to block the wind. I've always loved the way a guy looks in worn faded jeans. Not skinny ones. Ones like he was wearing, that hung off the hips and made you wonder if his boxer briefs were peeking out under his shirt. Just looking at him made me feel like I was eighteen all over again. A whole five years melted off my life.

Who was I kidding? Except for almost getting slaughtered by a serial killer, I was no different than any of those girls in the pizzeria. And maybe we even had that in common, with the other girls in town missing.

"Mom's making a huge steak tonight for dinner, if you want to come over, Kayla."

"I'll come over. Have her give me a call, okay?"

"Do you want to sit down?" Jenna asked, sliding across the bench to make room.

"No, I just came in here to get a soda. My truck was acting up, so I stopped at the hardware store to get some stuff."

"Are you going home now?" Kayla asked.

"I have to run over to the grocery store first and pick some things up for my mom. I'll be home in a little while." He got a Coke to go and waved at us as he walked out.

"He is so gorgeous!" Maddie exploded as soon as he left.

"Did you see the way he looked at you?" Kayla asked.

"Get out of here, you guys." My face was bright red, right up to the tips of my ears. We hung around for a little while, Snapchatted with some other people, got bored, and decided to go home.

"See how dull it is around here?" Kayla said as we put our coats on. "We don't even have a Domino's Pizza."

"It's not so bad," I said, following the others out to Brody's car. He had waited for us the whole time, playing pool with another kid in matching skinny jeans.

"Nick!" Kay yelled. He was carrying two big bags of groceries under his arms out of McPartlan's Supermarket. Maddie had informed me earlier that she worked there part-time on the weekends and asked me if I was looking for a job. I'd politely declined her offer to put a good word in, citing my college catch-up workload.

Nick looked like he was the only customer, from the empty spaces in the parking lot. He raised a plastic bag at us. "You guys are still here? Kayla, you want to come with me? I'll drive you home."

"What about Shea?" She grabbed my arm and started dragging me toward his truck. "She lives just down the street from me at Mrs. Parker's place."

"If she can stand riding in my piece of junk. Come on."

"Lucky," Maddie hissed under her breath as we left her to walk over to his pickup.

"How can you call this a hunk of junk?" Kayla asked, pulling open the door. She let me get in first, then hopped in next to me.

"It looks nice, but it runs like shit," he replied. I was wedged in between them. Nick was so close I could smell the warm, clean soap scent of him that made me want to bury my face in his shirt.

"How do you like the campus, Shea?" Every time he reached for the gearshift, his hand would brush my leg.

"It's all right." I felt so stupid. Here I was, twenty-three years old and feeling like a kid because a cute guy was sitting next to me. "It's not much different than the college I came from."

"RIT is massive," he said as he shifted gears again, sending a shock wave up my leg. "I think maybe I should have done the two-year school first. You get lost in the crowd at a big university."

He dropped Kayla off first. "I'll text you, Nick. You too, Shea." She gave me a wink as she got out.

It took all of thirty seconds to drive the rest of the way to the boardinghouse. He pulled into the driveway and turned to me. "I would have invited you over for dinner too, but it's not a real pleasant house to be in these days. I don't want you to think I'm rude."

"You just met me. I don't expect you to have me over for dinner." I smiled at him. "And I don't think you're rude."

He was clenching and unclenching the steering wheel. "I'm sure your uncle, or Kayla, told you what happened."

I didn't know what to say. "They told me a little."

He took a deep breath and let out an even longer exhale, as if he was trying to control his breathing. Like he was relieved he didn't have to explain himself or his situation. "Maybe you could come over some other time, when it's not so bad."

"Sure. Maybe." There was an awkward silence, and I opened the door. "Well, thanks for the ride."

"I'll see you around, hopefully."

I died all the way up the front steps. Mrs. Parker was in the kitchen making dinner.

"Hi, Mrs. Parker," I said.

"How was your day?"

The kitchen window was open, and I could hear shouting coming from the direction of the Gifford house.

"Is that Sarah Rose and Jake?" I asked.

She walked to the window and shut it. "It's not polite to listen to other people's troubles."

"Are they okay over there? It sounds like they're killing each other."

"They do that a lot. It's just yelling. Words never hurt anyone. If anyone had ever heard Richard and me go at it, they would have thought we were prizefighting. Now I'd give anything to hear him yell again."

"If you say so," I conceded, not convinced. I leaned over and brushed some stray flour off the counter into my palm, then dumped it in the garbage.

"How was your day?" I clapped my hands together, causing a little flour-dust cloud to form.

She glanced up from her mixing bowl. "Not as good as yours, apparently. Was that the Stansfield boy?"

"Do you need any help with dinner?" I asked, looking around, avoiding the subject.

"No, honey," Mrs. Parker laughed. "Why don't you go wash up?"

As I was walking up the stairs, she called, "He's a very nice young man."

My phone started buzzing in my pocket as soon as I got into the hallway. I ran to my room and unlocked my door. "Hello?" I asked breathlessly, flopping down on my bed.

"Well? What happened?" It was Kayla.

"Nothing. He said he was sorry he couldn't invite me over to dinner tonight. That was about it."

"That's it? Don't you see, that means he wanted you to come over! I think he likes you. I'll ask him what he thinks of you tonight and call you back as soon as I get home."

"Don't do that. Please don't say anything to him," I begged.

"I have to go. I'll text you later." With that she clicked off the phone, and I knew she was going to run right over to his house and start grilling him.

After dinner I called Bill to check in. He thought that business about the support group was interesting. I also mentioned I was now friends with Olivia Stansfield's cousin and that her brother had given me a ride home.

"Good. Get right in there. Immerse yourself in the town. You've got a great start, but don't try to do everything at once. These things take time."

"Half the time I feel like I have a huge neon sign over my head that says *Fraud!* on it. Like there's no way I'm going to fool all these people. But then I really look at everyone and it's like they're numb. They pretend nothing's wrong, like this hole in their town doesn't exist."

"Small towns can be like that. Especially one that's had such a bad shock. They don't feel safe anymore. Just remember everything I taught you in the Roberts case."

"I'll try."

"How is the police chief handling all this?"

"He hates it. But he's tolerating me as well as he can manage. I guess we'll just have to wait and see."

"Good. I wasn't sure how he'd play along with all this. We practically had to twist his arm to let you come down there."

"I think I'm starting to grow on him."

"Just be careful. Don't alienate him. He's your only backup. Whoever is responsible for their disappearance is, in all probability, a murderer. We don't want you to get caught in a bad spot again. I almost lost you once, kid; I don't want to make the same mistakes twice."

"That was my own carelessness. I never blamed you." That was another lie. I blamed both of us equally.

"I should have been keeping a closer eye on you. On the guys assigned to you. You were my responsibility."

"I'll call you if anything comes up," I told him, trying to get off the line with him. We'd beaten that conversation into the ground. I didn't want to rehash it again.

"No," he said. "You'll call every night. This case is too uncertain. There's too many open ends to be screwing around."

"Good-bye, Bill."

"'Bye."

Maybe it was talking about it to Bill, or maybe it was the role I was playing, but that night I had another one of my nightmares. It wasn't a nightmare, really; it was a memory that I couldn't get out of my head, no matter how hard I tried to push it away.

*I'm at North Side High School again. I'm Shea Anderson for the first time, and I'm investigating Terry Roberts, the popular teacher and track coach I was sent undercover to observe. Bill is convinced Roberts is the one who slit three female students' throats and drank their blood. All were young girls with short brown hair and brown eyes. All were a specific body type: my height, my weight, my build. Today I stayed after school under the pretext of needing extra help in math.*

*I've been at North for a month of summer school. Bill's cover story is that I failed my junior-year trig and need to pass the class to graduate. I've stayed after with Roberts twice before with no incident. I'm convinced Bill is wrong; he's targeted the wrong person. Roberts is kind and a good teacher. There is no way Terry Roberts could have committed those horrible crimes.*

*Time jumps forward, and now I'm running down the hall with a handcuff still dangling from my wrist. I'm desperately looking for a classroom door that isn't locked. My backup is outside, blissfully ignorant of what's going on, parked right in front of the school.*

*I can hear my bare footsteps slapping on the floor. I've lost my shoes somewhere. My steps sound like uneven thunder in the empty school. There's no way I can hide myself. I hear Roberts coming up behind me, but I don't dare turn myself around to see.*

*I stumble up the stairs from the basement, falling at the top, slithering up the wall like a worm trying to stand. I finally get to my feet again and run as fast as I can manage. I can hear Roberts charging up the stairs behind me as I throw my hip into a classroom door that's open a crack. I run to the window, but the bottom half is frosted so the students can't look out, so my backup can't see me. I grab a chair with my hands, a cuff still biting into my wrist, the other dangling in the air like a metal hangman's noose. I swing my whole body around, almost missing the window. One of the legs catches the glass, shattering it. Scrambling up on the radiator, broken glass stabbing into me at a thousand points, I throw myself through the rest of the window.*

*I'm stunned for a second when I hit the ground. All I see is grass and glass. I know I'm cut up and hurt. I look back toward the window and see Roberts in it, climbing out with a knife in hand. I start crawling like a worm over the lawn, glass slicing into my knees, my legs, my elbows, my palms. I hear the voices of my backup, but I can't see them. I hear their feet falling on the lawn as they run toward me, but I can't see them. I hear a shot, but I don't see it.*

I woke up, sweating in terror. My T-shirt was soaked through, my hair stuck to my face. This was a nightmare that would never go away. This nightmare had once been my reality.

I went back to sleep after a million years of staring at the ceiling in the dark, blanking out my mind, thinking of nothing but a white wall, praying not to dream.

## Wednesday, March 22nd

I got up the next morning feeling like I hadn't slept at all. After the Roberts incident, my doctor had put me on sleeping pills to try to relax me. I'd been afraid I would get addicted to them, so I threw them away after about a week. My nightmares were something I'd have to live with or get over; either way, pills wouldn't help.

I pulled a light sweater over my head after my morning shower. My college assignments were ready, tucked neatly into my binder that was stuffed into my backpack. I pulled my hair into a quick ponytail and slipped my leggings on. Kayla was waiting for me downstairs. We walked up to the bus stop together. "I can't believe you don't have Uber or Lyft in this town," I complained, hugging my arms to my chest in an effort to stay warm. The temperature had dropped, and Mrs. Parker had said at breakfast there was even a chance of snow.

"We had one guy, Lucas Wilson, but he got a DWI on New Year's Eve, so that was the end of that."

"I guess there's not much call for ride-sharing here. In the city, you could get away with not having a vehicle. Just hit the app and a car was there within five minutes. Seems like you almost have to have a car in this town." Except for the girls I hung around with. Figures.

"I had my own car," Kayla explained again as we gazed up Main Street for our shuttle. "But I wrecked it the first week of December on the bridge. I was dropping Skyler off, and I hit an ice patch. I spun out right into a pickup truck. Lucky for me, he saw it coming."

"Totaled?"

"Totally. My mom had a fit. I don't know why; I paid for the car myself. I used to work for Dr. Stevenson in his office, until I messed up the files on his new computer system and he had to let me go." Kayla was a little bit of an airhead.

"Does your mom ever let you take her car?"

Looking uneasy, she told me, "My mom has agoraphobia. You know, fear of going outside? I mean, she does sometimes, like to go to the doctor or to Nick's house once in a while to see my aunt, but she stays inside mostly. My parents are divorced, and my dad lives in Florida. My mom got bad after he moved out, with the phobia stuff and her OCD. She needs to have her car. Just in case. Every time I take it, she has a panic attack after a half hour and I have to rush home. Now, with Olivia gone, I try not to stress her out. It's easier to take the shuttle."

"Do you work now?" I asked her, trying to change the subject. I'd had no idea she had such a messed-up home life.

"Work-study in the library fifteen hours a week. That's what I do every day from one to three. It's so boring. There's this one guy that works there—his name is Bob—he's always checking out these semi-dirty books, and he always makes me check them out for him. He's so gross."

"What about Tyler?"

She gave a half shrug. "Tyler's cute. We went to high school together. I don't know. I had hoped college would offer a better variety of men, but it's mostly the same people from my high school, with a generous sprinkling from Portsville and Belmont. A lot of the hockey players are from all over because our team is so good. They get their grades up here and try to get into a division-one or -two school. Most of them live in the dorms." She sighed. "I would love to meet a guy who didn't grow up in a fifty-mile radius of here, you know?"

I knew the feeling. Buffalo was a city, but even there the available-man pool got very shallow, very fast.

The shuttle came rolling up, and we hopped on. I could see she was upset as we slid into the plastic seats, so I tried to change the subject. "Besides the two-year plan, how come you didn't go away to school, if you want to get out of here so bad?"

"Because I majored in cheerleading in high school," she laughed. "My grades were terrible. I was lucky I even graduated. Harris was the only place I could get into."

"Do you like it?"

She shrugged. "It's not so bad. My grades are definitely better. I'll probably transfer to Alfred State when I'm done here."

"For what?"

"Education. I'd love to be a gym teacher."

The shuttle pulled into the campus loop. Those of us who were getting off did; the rest continued on to the transportation hub to jump on the bus that took them all the way to Alfred State.

A girl in my Shakespeare class approached me after class, asking me if I wanted to join the Feminist Student Alliance. She was clutching her books to her chest with a very pleading, hopeful look in her eyes. It was probably hard to attract new blood in so small a school. As sincere as she was, I politely declined. The chief probably would have a stroke if I started joining student organizations, spying on their subversive activities and bake sales.

As I walked to my next class, clutching the paperwork the student had given me, I thought about the three missing girls. Joe was already in my orbit. What I needed was more background on Skyler and Emma. I could tease a lot of what I needed to know about Olivia out of Kayla, but the other two were going to be harder. Sure, their friends liked to say what a bad girl Skyler could be and how evil Joe was, but there had to be more to the story. Same with Emma. Not about her being a bad girl, but about her being the polar opposite. That was going to take more digging, more lying, and more things my new-found uncle would frown on. But hell, I definitely wasn't there to make him happy.

*　*　*

After school I went home to work on a twelve-page paper that was due on Friday. Coming into classes in the middle of the semester was tough. I had a ton of stuff to make up and I had to take tests like everyone else, no matter how much of the material I'd missed.

As I alternated between my iPad and my constitutional law books for my paper, I decided to take a break. I threw them all down on the bed and went downstairs to see if there were any cookies in the cupboard. Henry was in the kitchen making a peanut-butter-and-jelly sandwich.

"Hello." He was glopping grape jelly from a mason jar on a piece of white bread. Outfitted in his official uniform of stained overalls, today he had accented it with a green trucker baseball hat that read *Norton's Feed and Tractor Supply*.

"Hello there. Are there any more of those chocolate-chip cookies left?" I asked, hunting around in the cabinet.

"I think Peter got to them. That boy grows about a foot a week these days. Eats like a horse."

I closed the cupboard door and grabbed two pieces of bread out of the bread box. "I think I'll join you in a sandwich."

He pushed the chunky peanut butter over to me. "Help yourself. Is that Kayla Johnson you catch the shuttle with in the morning?"

"Yes. She said she smashed her car up."

"Did she ever," Henry confirmed. "I remember that car. You could hear it two blocks away, the muffler rumbled so hard. She smashed it up on the Hoyt Bridge."

I smeared jelly across my peanut butter. "That's what she said."

"That bridge is bad luck; always has been. Two guys died building it in the fifties. The work truck they were riding broke through an unstable patch and they were drowned. Then about four years ago, a girl named Carol Losi jumped off and killed herself. They didn't find her body for almost two weeks."

"Two weeks?" I asked, biting into my sandwich.

He nodded and wiped his hands on his overalls, crumbs bouncing to the floor. "She got caught up in some branches and things farther down the river. What a way to die. Tony Bartlett told me she stunk so bad they couldn't even keep her in the funeral home; had to keep her in the morgue until the day of the service. Terrible for the family. They couldn't even see her to say their good-byes." He bit into his sandwich, and a glob of grape jelly oozed out the side. "Closed casket and all."

"That's awful," I replied, putting the rest of my own sandwich down.

"Those things happen," he said. Finishing off his lunch, he put his empty plate in the sink. He walked out into the living room to watch *Jeopardy* reruns, jelly still smeared on his chin. I cleaned up our mess and went back up to my room to finish my studies.

I had to scour the Internet for articles on Van Gogh for Art Appreciation. Unfortunately, I didn't have a printer at the boardinghouse, so everything I found had to be saved to my laptop and printed out at school, which was a major pain in my ass. So much for my love of higher education.

The nights in my room at the boardinghouse were the worst, especially those first few days. I felt cut off from my real life, my real self, which could have been a good thing for me, considering. Bill had expressly forbidden me to confide in anyone, and I held out until that third school night before I texted Karen. I had to talk to someone as myself, not as some character who had been created to fill a role.

I put my iPad on my nightstand and grabbed my cell phone.

*CAN I CALL YOU?*

*WHO IS THIS??* Karen demanded. I realized my new number must be coming up as unknown. *AND WHY ARE YOU YELLING?*

*IT'S YOUR ROOMATE. I ACCIDENTLY LEFT THE CAPS LOCK ON. WHO'S BOTHERING YOU NOW?*

Immediately my phone began to vibrate. I hit the accept button and sat on the edge of my bed.

Karen sighed into the phone. "Connor broke up with me. Now he wants all his T-shirts and sweat shirts back. Only I don't want to give them back; I like to sleep in them. He's been blowing up my phone, sending me text messages, tweets. I mean, who cares about a couple of shirts like that?"

"How many do you have?"

"Eleven, more or less."

"That's his entire wardrobe, more or less," I laughed.

"Possibly. But he broke up with me. He should have taken them home the last time he was here."

"Are you wearing one right now?"

"Of course. But only because it's laundry day and nothing else is clean. But anyway," she continued, changing the subject, "why are you calling me? I thought you were in extra deep, deep cover."

I lay down on my comforter, tucking my pillow under my head. "I needed to talk to a real person."

"Those people aren't real? They stuck you in with robots?"

"No, no, no," I corrected. "I mean someone I'm real to. These girls are more than real. I feel guilty, you know? They lost these people who were so special to them, and here I am, lying to them."

"You're trying to help them," Karen pointed out.

"It's just hard. Keeping the balance, I mean. These are great girls. I'm really not that much older than they are, and I remember what it was like, trying to navigate life during college, trying to figure out where you're going. It's like I'm watching them *become*, you know what I mean?"

"I do. I believe it was me who saved you from having bangs in college, remember?"

Stifling a groan, I rolled over onto my stomach and propped myself up on my elbows. I could see headlights rolling past the house from my window. "This is more serious than growing out my bangs."

"I know that, stupid. I was trying to make you laugh. How's the investigation?"

She'd made me smile, anyway. "It's still so new. I feel naked out here. I thought I'd be okay without backup or a handler in town, but now I'm getting a little nervous, especially since the chief of police doesn't want me here."

"Why the hell wouldn't he want you there? He's not getting anywhere." I pictured her sitting on our sofa, drinking Pepsi right from the two-liter bottle, wearing one of Connor's vintage AC/DC T-shirts.

"Because he wants to be the one that solves this?"

"Ohhh," she said knowingly. "He's afraid your dick is bigger than his."

"I wouldn't put it that way."

"I would." She would. "Anyway, what else is going on? I mean, really, you didn't call to tell me all the girls are wonderful Mary Sues and the big, bad sheriff doesn't like you. That's to be expected. There has to be something else bothering you."

She knew me so well. "I met a guy."

"I knew it! Now we're getting to the good stuff! What's he like in bed?"

"Not like that." I cut her off, trying to slow her roll. "It's one of the missing girls' brother. I just met him, and now I can't stop thinking about him. Am I a horrible person?"

"Yes," she replied without stopping to think about it. "You should keep your mind off potentially murdered girls' family members. How much more cliche could you possibly be? I would think that after the whole Roberts thing you would steer away from emotional attachments. Particularly because you have no backup."

"What's that supposed to mean?" I demanded.

"It means, how do you know he's not a suspect? They always look at the families first, right? He could be this charming serial killer. Banker by day, throat-slashing psychopath by night."

"He's a twenty-one-year-old college student, not Charles Manson. And if there was even a remote possibility he was responsible for the girls disappearing, I couldn't have anything to do with him." The good old FBI guidelines for undercover operatives covered that scenario. The last thing I'd done the night after I first met him was double-check his alibi. He'd been back at college. Plenty of witnesses.

"What???" I could practically see her sitting straight up, remote dropping from her hand, cigarette dangling from her lip.

"A *younger* man? Please, please have sex with him as soon as possible. You need it so much."

"You just called him a serial killer."

"Forget everything I just said. Tell me all about him."

I listed off the reasons he was on my mind so much: great smile, killer body, smelled like heaven, thoughtful. Basically, that he was too good to be true, if only his sister hadn't been a missing person.

"Damn," Karen replied when I was done with my dissertation. "Now I want to sleep with him."

"No one's sleeping with anyone. I've got a job to do."

"How sad," she said, then brightened up. "You know you're going about this whole thing the wrong way?"

"What?"

"These girls. You think they're so perfect and wonderful, but they're not their real selves either right now. They just lost three friends under unknown circumstances. The cops are talking to them, their parents are asking them questions, the media is there. They are on their best behavior. Girls that age have only one currency: secrets."

I rolled that thought over in my head as she went on. "Think about it. Nowadays, if you find out your friend is fooling around with your boyfriend, you threaten to post the dirty pictures she sent him on Instagram for all the world to see. Everyone has a cell phone pointed at each other, so you have to sneak away to do things you don't want anyone to see. In a small town like that, the only thing girls their age own for themselves is their secrets. And they guard them well."

"Why aren't you here instead of me?" I asked, reaching over to scribble the word *secrets* down on the draft of my art appreciation paper sitting on my nightstand.

"One of those girls, or all of those girls, has a secret. You need to find out what it is. Then you'll solve your case."

Footsteps pounded up the staircase. "Shea?"

"I have to go," was all I managed before Mrs. Parker was knocking on my door. I clicked disconnect and tossed my phone on top of my homework, covering up the word I'd written. "Yes?" I called.

She stuck her silver head inside. "Do you need anything before I turn in? I sleep so soundly I might not hear you knock. My hearing isn't what it used to be."

"No thanks. I'm good. But thanks for asking." I wanted to get rid of her so I could chew on what Karen had just said to me.

Mrs. Parker nodded. "Okay. Have a good night."

"You too," I answered as she shut the door.

Looking over at my nightstand, I picked up my art appreciation paper. *Secrets*, scrawled in blue ink, was staring at me. I wondered what secrets my newfound friends were keeping. And how was I going to get at them?

## Friday, March 24th

The week went by fast. I got settled into my classes pretty easily. I saw Joe Styles around every day. He would make it a point to come over to me, say something, annoy my friends, and walk away. I found out Amber Wray wanted to beat me up. I had forgotten how much girls at that age would do for a guy they liked. She worked full-time at the salon, but I would see her around town. When she was with her dirty little friends, she would call me a bitch. Kayla and Jenna gave it right back to her when they were with me. Maddie almost got into a fight in Freddie's with two of Amber's friends over the whole thing. I was glad they were sticking up for me, but I didn't want anyone to come to blows over nothing.

By Wednesday, as soon as I got home, my phone was buzzing a hole in my back pocket. Kayla would text, then Jenna or Maddie. Then it would become a group text. By Thursday they were all borrowing my clothes. Kayla stopped down at seven o'clock in the morning to raid my closet. I marveled at how fast we had all become friends. I realized that, unlike in the city, where everything was cliquish and groups were hard to break into, this town was so small that just being the chief's niece meant I had to be all right, included, one of them.

I really liked these girls. They weren't tough and streetwise like some I'd met in the city schools. They were nice people and they were scared. The missing girls were always in the back of their minds. The sense of security they enjoyed had been destroyed.

I was a little nervous about going to the party because of Amber. She'd been telling anyone who would listen that she was going to kick my ass. I wasn't afraid of her, but if I really had been eighteen and new in town, she probably would have terrified me. After being on the force for a little over two and a half years and going through everything I had gone through, this girl was a day at the beach.

I put my cold-weather gear on, knowing how bitter it gets in the woods. People will do anything to drink alcohol, even brave subzero temperatures. I slipped on my thick knitted gloves with the tips of the fingers cut out for better grip, just in case.

Rob and Tyler picked Kayla and me up at seven. Kayla was kind of dating Tyler. It was one of those on-again, off-again things that seemed more often off than on. He was a member of the hockey team. Most of the players lived in the dorms on campus and they didn't have a house or anything fancy like real fraternities, so a beer blast in the woods was the best they could do. They were all in those twilight years between eighteen and twenty-one, when you're an adult but not allowed in bars.

Kayla was giving me the lowdown on campus politics when we heard a car horn out front. We ran down the porch steps and hopped into Rob's car.

"Are you scared of Amber?" Rob asked, fiddling with the rearview mirror to see me in the back seat. I immediately readjusted my jacket to cover any stray cleavage.

"No," I said. "And I think we're a little too old to be fistfighting over boys."

"Right? And she's just jealous because she thinks Joe wants you," Kayla piped up.

"Yeah, well, she can have him. I think he's gross." What a word: *gross*. I felt ten years younger just saying it.

"I hope I'm not gross," Rob said, pulling away from the curb. "That would be such a buzzkill. Wouldn't it, Ty?"

"Absolutely," Tyler agreed, giving me a little elbow in the arm.

"Shea likes my cousin, Nick." Kayla twisted around to talk to me and Tyler in the back seat. Her seat belt was half strangling her as she hung her head between the seats.

"Shut up, Kayla," I said, pushing her back toward the front with a laugh. "Where is this place, anyway?"

"It's called the Straights; don't ask me why. There's a dirt road off the main street where we park; then you follow the path out to this clearing in the woods. Someone starts a fire and we're all set," Tyler explained.

And that's exactly what it was like. It sure brought back memories, trudging through that muddy path to the clearing in the woods. Getting hit in the face by branches bouncing back from the person in front of you. The smell of pine needles, smoke, and spilled beer. I used to party at a place like it when I was in high school, called the Pitts. I guess every town has its underage party place.

The path led to an oval-shaped clearing with a huge bonfire in the middle. Everyone was huddled around it to keep warm. One guy passed out the plastic cups while another collected five dollars for each, which allowed you to drink off the keg. All the funds were supposed to be for renting a barn on the outskirts of town so the hockey team could throw their next party out there.

A lot of people had brought their own coolers or backpacks filled with beer, though. I think it pissed off the guys trying to fund-raise.

"I'm not drinking tonight," I told Kayla when she went to buy a cup.

"Why not?" she asked in disbelief, like you'd have to be loony not to drink. "Rob is the designated driver."

"My parents were killed in a car accident. If everyone else is going to drink, then I'll stay sober and be a designated driver too."

"Oh, okay." I felt bad because I had made her feel bad. I hated lying to her, but it was necessary.

I spent the next half hour meeting people. Everyone seemed to know Amber wanted to beat me up. Everyone also thought I was going to get my butt kicked. I tried to laugh it off, not provoke anything. It seemed everyone was waiting for her to get to the party, like our fight was going to be the main event of the evening. I thought I might have gotten lucky, because at ten thirty she still hadn't shown up.

But of course, I've never had much good luck.

Someone had brought a Bluetooth speaker and was playing songs from their playlist off their phone. A lot of people were vaping, sucking on their Juuls as they stood around the fire. From inside the tree line, the smell of weed wafted out. I was glad whoever was partaking was out of my line of sight. That was another issue I didn't want to have to deal with.

At five to eleven, Joe came strolling in, Amber and her friends tagging along behind him. I inwardly cringed as Amber and her two besties took up positions directly across from me, eyeing me up the whole time.

Joe was with his buddy, Charlie. Charlie was an older guy, maybe twenty-five. He was short but built wider than Joe, one of those stocky fireplug types. He had a nasty-looking scar under his right eye that twisted over his nose. I had heard he had gotten it from fooling around with fireworks and was missing a finger too. He had gloves on, so it was hard to tell which one. They had brought their own bottle of Jack Daniels and a two-liter of Coke to wash it down with.

Joe made a beeline right to me. "You're not drinking?" He asked when he saw that I didn't have a cup. He wore a heavy flannel under his leather jacket. His brown hair was loose tonight, hanging down to his shoulders.

"No. If someone needs a ride, I can drive. My parents were killed in a car accident."

"That really sucks. I'm sorry. Here." He handed me his plastic cup and twisted the cap off his Coke. "Now you won't be thirsty." He poured in some soda for me. It fizzed and bubbled up, making me stoop in and sip it before it could spill over.

His sweetness kind of shocked me. I looked up into his gray eyes. "Thank you."

"Bitch," I heard from behind me. Joe and I both turned to see Amber standing behind us with two of her girlfriends.

"Really, Joe. I appreciate this." I turned back around, trying to ignore her.

"Don't turn away from me," she said, getting into my face. Her two friends pushed their way through the crowd that had begun to form around us to back her up.

Joe grabbed Amber by the arm. "What the hell are you doing? I was just talking to her. You're not my girlfriend, got it? Huh?" But somehow I think he was enjoying the attention.

"When people are around, you say that, but not when it's just me and you." She shook him off. "You whored around on me with Skyler, and now you want to whore around with her. Look at her," she demanded.

88

"I'm looking at her." The attitude came rolling back in as he eyed me up and down. "She looks pretty good to me." Laughter burst from the crowd, egging her on even more.

She stepped between us, cutting off his line of sight. "She's nothing but a stuck-up bitch from the city."

"You're ridiculous," I told her, throwing my half-full cup into the flames. The plastic crinkled into itself as it melted with a hiss. My friends were trapped on the other side of the fire, blocked by the burning logs and gathering crowd.

"Trailer-park-trash Skyler was ridiculous," she spat out.

"Don't you ever say anything about Skyler Santana ever again," Maddie screamed from across the fire, trying to get over to us. Tyler grabbed her and pulled her back. I could see Kayla trying to push her way through the crowd, but the guys were holding her back, wanting to watch the whole thing play out. All around me people whipped out their cell phones and started filming, including Amber's friends. That's when I realized she had planned this whole thing. Amber had talked up wanting to beat me up because she wanted to make some kind of fight video to post on YouTube or Twitter. She had orchestrated this whole thing so she could make a potential viral video.

"Look," I said, backing up. "I don't want to fight you."

"Maybe I want to fight you," she said, getting in my face again. She was so close I could see her black eyeliner and blue eye shadow sparkling. "Maybe I want to kick your ass." She pushed me, and I took another step back. She was angling me toward her friend's cell phone. I turned my face the other way.

"Really? How old are you? Ten? Grow up," I told her, sounding exactly like my mom. "Who fights people in the woods?"

"'Cause you're so mature, right?" She was so close she was spitting on me when she talked, and it was grossing me out and pissing me off at the same time.

"Amber!" I heard Joe yell from behind. "Stop with your bullshit!"

"I'm leaving now. I don't have time for this," I said as I tried to push past her. One of her friends came up right alongside me, trying to stick the camera in my face, blocking my way. I twisted my body from her, and Amber shoved me with both hands.

The crowd let out a sinister "Ooooooo," and she pushed me again. I had already sized her up as the hair-pulling, face-scratching type. I kept trying to retreat and keep my face off camera.

I guess I wasn't putting on enough of a show, because she kind of pushed me by my shoulder and tried to punch me at the same time. I took one step back, grabbed her arm, and took her—face first—right to the ground. Everyone was screaming and cheering and egging us on. I peeled my gloves off as she got up.

She was so mad, she screamed like a crazed lunatic and tried to rush me. Big mistake. I grabbed her again, using her momentum against her like I'd learned in the police academy, and dumped her in the mud. This time when she fell to the ground, I sat on top of her. Straddling her with my knees pinning her elbows, I grabbed her face. "Now, you listen to me. I don't want your boyfriend. I don't want to fight you. Just leave me and my friends alone, okay?"

I got up. Her friends stopped filming and rushed over as I backed away. Covered in mud, with twigs stuck in her hair, Amber was still trying to come after me. They literally had to drag her away. I could see a nasty mark spreading across her jaw from where her face had hit the ground.

"You're dead!" she screamed. "You're going to be the next one to disappear!"

"Screw you, Amber!" Maddie burst out, and tried to stumble across the fire to get at her. Kayla intercepted her before she could fall headfirst into the flames. A shower of sparks exploded from the logs, making the crowd scatter a little.

With the help of the hockey guys who were throwing the party, Amber's friends managed to get her to leave. Not quietly, but away she went down the path, yelling and screaming.

All around me people were toasting me and clapping me on the back, trying to hand me beer. I waved them off, looking around for my friends, who had disappeared with the distraught Maddie. Thankfully, everyone had put their phones away.

"Where'd you learn to fight like that?" Joe asked, walking up to me.

My adrenaline was flowing so bad my hands were shaking. "Buffalo. And I wasn't fighting. I was defending myself. Shouldn't you be with Amber? Or do you still want to hang out because I look so good?"

"I'm sorry about that, okay?" He grabbed me by the shoulders, hard. "She's not my girlfriend. I just hook up with her."

"Wow," I said bitterly, trying to pull away. "What a nice guy you are."

"I know how that sounds," he said. "But it's true. I can't help it this hellhole is so small she can't find someone else to leech on. I didn't think she'd really hit you."

"You sure stood around and did nothing to stop it."

"Was I supposed to tackle her? After everything that's happened? You think I'm going to put my hands on any girl in this town?" But his fingers were digging into my shoulders as he said it.

"I don't know. I don't even know you, Joe."

"I wouldn't want someone like Amber for a girlfriend." His eyes caught mine. "I'd want someone like you."

I finally shook him off me. "That's a good one. Did you tell that one to Skyler?"

"It's not a line. And I loved Skyler. I'm not as bad as everyone thinks I am." He bent over, grabbed the stuff he must have put down during the fight, then handed me another plastic cup with Coke in it.

"I'm stuck here. Just like you." Standing in the firelight with one hand stuffed in the pocket of his ripped jeans and the bottle of whiskey dangling from the other, he looked like a modern James Dean, or at least James Franco.

I didn't know what to say. The best I could do was, "Thanks again for the soda."

He gave me a halfhearted shrug, like he had just really opened up to me and I'd shot him down hard. Which I guess I had. Then he turned around, slid into the crowd by the fire, and was gone.

I went to find Kayla. She and Jenna were taking care of Maddie at that point, who was drunk and crying.

"No, that's wrong. That is so wrong. I can't even—" She was slobbering all over herself. "If she ever says anything about Skyler again, I'll kill her." She sobbed even harder when she saw me.

"Are you okay?" I asked, putting my arm around her. They had leaned her up against a tree so she wouldn't fall down.

She grabbed on to me with both hands. "Thank you. Thank you. You didn't know Skyler or Olivia or Emma, but thank you." She cried on my shoulder for a few minutes while everyone tried to comfort her. She was a hot mess. Sob after sob racked her whole body. When I finally pried myself away from her, Jenna convinced her it was time to go and took her home.

Kayla suggested we leave. The party had started dying down. Once the battle was over, all the excitement had gone, too. I didn't feel like staying anyway. I was still pumped up from the fight. I felt like I wanted to run three miles, uphill, in a snowstorm.

It turned out that I didn't have to drive at all. Rob had indeed stayed sober and wasn't in the mood to go home yet. He suggested we go over to Freddie's, since it was only eleven thirty. Kayla said she was starving and hopped in the back seat with Tyler after we trudged back to Rob's car.

Freddie's stayed open until one AM on the weekends, and it was packed when we pulled into the parking lot. As we got out of the car, we could hear the band playing in the bar down at the other end of the plaza. Kayla spotted Nick's truck as we were about to walk into Freddie's. "Nick is at Bingo's," she said excitedly.

"So?" Tyler said. "Let's go inside. It's cold."

"Come on, Shea. Let's go say hi to him." She pulled on my hand and started to drag me across the parking lot. Looking back, I motioned to the guys who were watching us from the doorway. "What about Rob and Tyler? They sounded pissed."

"Who cares about them? I wish my fake ID worked here. We have to go all the way to Alfred to go to the bars. Everyone knows us here."

I stood by Nick's truck while Kayla looked for him in the window. I figured I'd let her make a fool of herself first. She finally got his attention by frantically waving to him, and he came outside. I looked down at my shoes, highly embarrassed.

"What are you guys doing here?" he asked. He seemed surprised, but pleasantly so.

"We saw your truck from Freddie's. We stopped by to say hello," she gushed. I wanted to poke her and tell her to calm down and be cool.

"Come on inside, then; it's cold," he said, starting for the door.

"We can't go in there; we're not twenty-one," Kayla told him, as if he was absolutely nuts.

"I know all the guys who work here. Just don't drink, and they'll let you in with me." He looked right at me and smiled. "Don't you want to come?"

I looked over at Kayla and she at me, and we fell into step right behind him. As soon as we walked through the door, the huge bouncer held out his hand. "ID, ladies?"

We both looked at Nick. He leaned over. "They're with me, Jim. They aren't drinking." Jim nodded and with one meaty hand waved us in. From the look on Kayla's face, you'd have thought she'd died and gone to heaven.

Bingo's was small and dark, but actually pretty nice as far as plaza-style drinking establishments go. It had a long, polished wood bar and a big dance floor in front of the stage, where everyone was dancing to the band. The whole place was decorated with hot-air balloons—on the walls, suspended from the ceiling, behind the bar; they were hanging everywhere. Which was strange to me, since it was called Bingo's and not Balloons. But what did I know? Maybe the owner had a hard-on for hot-air balloons?

As I peeled off my layers to get down to my thermal top, it was easy to see that Nick was the big man at that bar. Everyone acted like he was some kind of celebrity, buying him drinks and girls asking him to dance. Nick's friend took our coats and hung them up for us. As soon as we sat down with them, every girl in the place was shooting us the side eye.

Nick introduced us to his equally attractive friend sitting at the table. "Zach, do you know my little cousin, Kayla? And this is her friend, Shea. She just moved here from Buffalo."

"Nice to meet you, Shea." He stuck out a hand, and I shook it.

"Do you go to RIT, too?" I asked.

"Naw, I go to Alfred State. I try to get back to town on the weekends now that I know my boy Nick is here."

"You're a good friend," Kayla said. "Getting him drunk and keeping him busy."

"And what about you, Kayla? Partying with the big boys tonight?" he teased. She laughed, lowering her eyes in a flirty way. I could tell she had a thing for him and it hadn't started just then.

I sat back and took a long look around while Nick ordered some Cokes from the waitress for us. There was one of the huge missing posters hanging in the back room of the bar along with an announcement for a fund raiser to help support the information center at the local church. I was so absorbed in the poster, I lost track of the conversation.

"I thought my little cousin could use some supervision tonight," Nick was saying to his friend.

"I think she's the one who needs it," Kayla laughed, pointing at me. "She almost beat up Amber Wray at the party."

I shot her a look and tried to shush her. "Why'd you do that?" Nick asked, his eyes wide in surprise.

"Because that idiot Joe Styles has been paying attention to her and Amber likes him. So she decided to start a fight," Kayla explained.

"I didn't want to fight her," I insisted. "We're not eight-year-olds in the playground. I mean, who does that? Really?"

"Amber Wray," Kayla answered in a disgusted voice.

"We sure are two lucky guys," Nick commented, taking a sip of his beer, then reached over to feel my bicep. His fingers wrapping around my upper arm felt like an electric shock.

"We got the toughest girls in the bar right here with us tonight. No one better start any shit."

"You got that right," Zach agreed, and they clinked their bottles together. "Absolutely savage. Too bad they're only seventeen."

"Eighteen," Kayla corrected. "And I'll be nineteen in two months."

"So that makes you legal, right?" Zach asked. Nick socked him in the shoulder for talking to his cousin like that.

"Hey man, I'm sorry. And I'm sorry, ladies." He half stood up, leaning forward toward Kayla. "You feel like dancing, Nick's cousin?"

Lissa Marie Redmond

The band was playing a slow eighties metal ballad. "Sure." She smiled so wide I thought her face would crack. Off they went, leaving me alone with Nick.

"I'm sorry if you feel like you're babysitting," I told him, fidgeting with a paper straw wrapper on the table nervously.

"Oh no," he said. "Believe me, I'm really glad you guys showed up. I was hoping I'd run into you again. I've been so busy with my sister. I mean, I really want her back, and I've been going crazy trying to find out what happened to her. She's an awesome person and I miss her." He polished off the rest of his beer in one gulp. "Look, I'm sorry. I can't stop talking about it. She's on my mind all the time."

Apologizing for agonizing over your missing sister? I should have been apologizing for not getting a flashlight and going to search for her right then and there. "That's okay. I understand."

He gave me a sad smile that didn't quite reach his eyes. "You want to dance?"

Taking my hand in his, he led me out to the dance floor. I put my arms around his neck, and I felt his hands fall around my waist. His shoulders were broad and well built. I could feel the muscles work under his striped rugby shirt. "You smell really nice," he said in my ear.

"Thanks," I replied softly. "So do you." Like Irish soap and clean linen. After I realized what I'd just said, I wanted to go jump off a cliff. He was making me lose my power of witty comebacks. And when his rough cheek touched mine, all power of resistance. What the hell was he doing to me? I was turning to mush.

The song ended and we drifted away from each other, but he still held on to my hand as he led me back to the table. Kayla noticed and gave me a look. That knowing holding-in-a-girly-squeal-with-all-my-might look.

The bars in Kelly's Falls closed at one o'clock, so it was almost last call. We got our coats off the pegs and put them on. Of course, Nick helped me with mine. We excused ourselves to go to the ladies' room as the band began to pack up their equipment. The bass player, sporting a sweet, sweet mullet, gave us a wink as we walked by.

"Do you think Rob and Tyler hate us?" I asked Kayla in the bathroom. We were trying to make ourselves look presentable just in case they turned the house lights, aka the Ugly Lights, on at last call.

"Yes, but who cares? I had the best night. This has been the best night since Olivia left." I noticed she said *left* and not *disappeared*. Maybe it was something, maybe not. I was reading into every word, every sentence. I had to remind myself that not everything was a cryptic, revealing clue.

Satisfied that we wouldn't horrify Nick and Zack, we filed out of the bathroom. I followed Kayla to the bar, where the guys were waiting.

"So," Zach said, half jokingly, to Nick. "Do you mind if I take your cousin home?"

"You put a hand on her, and I'll break it off," he warned him.

Zach turned to me. "Sorry, I've only got a two-seater. You're going to have to go with Nick. I know that's horrible and everything, since he's so repulsive, almost squidlike, but it was nice meeting you." Before I could say anything, he grabbed Kayla and walked her out the door.

"Looks like it's you and me," Nick said, taking his keys out of his pocket. I was so nervous, I really thought I was eighteen again. He said good-bye to all his friends who worked there, which was just about everyone, and we walked out to his truck. I hopped in next to him, but now with just the two of us, he seemed like he was a million miles away from me. We sat in silence while the truck warmed up, sputtering and dinging and clanking. The radio had kicked on, the Alfred State station, which played everything from rap to Mozart. A Beyoncé song was playing, his fingers lightly tapping to the beat as he pulled out of the parking lot and onto the road.

"I'm really glad you showed up tonight," he said, finally breaking the silence.

"I had a really good time," I told him, and I meant it.

His eyes never left the road. "Me too, for the first time in a long time."

The ride back to the boardinghouse was over in what seemed like three seconds. Before I knew it, the beast rattled to a halt and we were parked out front. He turned the truck off. "I'll walk you to your door," he said. "Just to make sure you're safe."

He got out, came around, opened my door, helped me out, and then held my hand as he walked me to the porch steps. This guy was unbelievable.

We stopped and were awkwardly facing each other in front of the boardinghouse. "Thanks again," I told him. "I really did have a good time tonight."

"Look." He sounded a little nervous now. "Could I text you tomorrow? Maybe we could go to the movies or hang out or something sometime?"

My cheeks flushed red, and I dipped my head down a little to hide the width of my smile. "Sure. I'd love to."

He fumbled in his back pocket for his phone and added me to his contacts.

"I'll send you a text so you know my number," he said, thumbing the keys.

My phone buzzed immediately, and I saw one word on my screen: *Hi.*

"I got it," I told him, standing there, holding my cell.

He stuck his in his pocket and hesitated for a second. "I felt guilty at first for having a good time tonight, because I still don't know where my sister is. But I did have a really great time with you, and if you don't want to deal with all this, I understand. Hell, I wouldn't be able to deal with it if I were you. So if you really don't want to go out with me, I get it."

I reached over and put my hand over his mouth to stop his ramble. "Nick, I really want to hang out with you."

He put his hand over mine, pulling it away from his mouth, holding it in midair. Before I knew what was happening, he tugged me to him, kissing me. My palm was flat against his chest, feeling the thumping of his heart. My whole body ignited at that kiss, like the electrical shock that had gone through me when he touched my arm earlier.

"Good-night." The word came rushing out against my lips as if he was trying to restrain himself. "I'll call you," he added as he pulled away. I wanted to pull him back, tell him I wasn't done with him, that it was okay, there was more, but I managed to control myself.

He stood on the front walk as I unlocked the door, standing sentry, his hands stuffed deep into his pockets. As I slipped into the hall, I gave him a little wave. Walking back to his truck, it was my turn to watch him through the glass.

What the hell was I getting myself into?

## Saturday, March 25<sup>th</sup>

I sat at breakfast the next morning just waiting for what I knew was coming.

"Was that the Stansfield boy who dropped you off last night?" Mrs. Parker asked casually from her seat at the head of the table.

I closed my eyes and swallowed. "Yes," I replied as pleasantly as I could. "He's a very nice guy."

"A lovely boy," she agreed, passing a plate of bacon over to Peter.

"Nick Stansfield?" The chief raised an eyebrow. "Where did you run into him?"

I glanced around the table uneasily. "At Bingo's."

He stopped chewing his eggs and stared at me. "Can I have a word with you alone?"

I pushed my chair back, and he followed me upstairs to my room. He thrust past me in the doorway and let me have it as soon as I closed the door.

"What the hell do you think you're doing? You are supposed to be eighteen. Do you get that? Eighteen. So what do you do? You go to a bar." He took his baseball hat off and ripped his fingers through his hair, continuing his barrage. "If this gets out, I'm going to catch hell. You are supposed to be my niece. I'm not going to lose my standing in the community because you want to screw around with Nick Stansfield, which is wrong on so many levels I can't even count that high."

I stood there with my arms folded. "Are you done?"

His face got even redder at that one. He continued to read me the riot act. "If you are to continue this farce, or investigation, or whatever you want to call it, you're going to play your part clean. No more bars. Period. Do you understand me?"

I couldn't believe it. I was being grounded. But I figured I might as well give in a little and seem sorry, just to humor him. I didn't want him to blow the whole operation. "I wasn't thinking, okay? I did what any eighteen-year-old would have done. I saw a chance to get into a bar and I went. I didn't drink. Not one. I'm sorry if I made a mistake."

"I just thought you would have had better sense than that, seeing as how you've done this before."

Just then my phone buzzed on the nightstand. I held up my index finger. "Hold that glare, Chief. Just let me answer this." I picked up my cell and answered before he could protest. "Hello?"

"Hello, Shea? This is Nick." A guy actually calling a girl he'd just met on the phone and speaking? Unheard of. I was expecting a text, maybe, that said *Hey*.

"Hi." I hoped he couldn't hear the sound of my nervousness. Or feel the glare of my faux uncle radiating through the phone.

"I'm sorry it's so early, but I have to go with my parents to a benefit for my sister this afternoon, and I didn't know when I'd have a chance to text you. Listen, do you want to go to the movies later, around seven thirty?"

"Sure. That sounds cool."

"Great. I'll pick you up then. 'Bye."

I said good-bye and ended the call. The chief was staring at me. "Seriously? 'That sounds cool'? Are you here to date Nick Stansfield or to find his sister?" he asked.

That did it. I dropped the phone on the bed. "I'm supposed to be a college student. I can't go around asking questions and following up leads like a regular investigator. I'm here to make them trust me, to make them let me in on something they wouldn't tell a cop. You can't do that in a week. It takes a little time."

"These girls don't have time. And once you gain everyone's confidence, eventually they're all going to have to deal with the fact they've been lied to and used."

"At the end of the investigation, I just move back to Buffalo, like I've been saying. Hopefully, they'll never know."

He yanked his hat back on. "This whole situation stinks to high heaven. And now you're getting personally involved with Nick Stansfield. Hasn't he been through enough?"

"He has to go back to school sometime. Maybe he'll leave first."

"Wow." The chief laughed bitterly. "I can see you have a well-thought-out strategy going on here. I'm so glad the FBI talked me into this. Do me a favor: when this all explodes in your face, and it will, make sure you take all the credit."

"Will do," I replied, cutting him off. "Should I tell you now about the fight, or after I get back from the movies with Nick?"

He sighed and sank down into the chair by my TV. "What fight?"

"Amber Wray tried to beat me up last night."

"What do you mean, *tried*?"

"Well." I hesitated. "I defended myself."

"Defended yourself? You beat the girl up?"

I could see his temper starting to flare again, so I explained. "I tried to walk away. She wanted blood. I didn't beat her up. I just restrained her, I swear. I was going to talk to you about her. I think we should add her to our list of suspicious persons."

"Amber Wray?" He was starting to annoy me with his repetitive questions.

"Yes. I went over some of the statements again last night when I got home. One girl at the party said the fight between Joe and Skyler was over "another girl." Rylie Olson's statement also said that the reason Skyler said she was leaving was because of the fight. What if Amber was the other girl? And what if she had something to do with the disappearance? According to the timeline and pictures, she wasn't at the party. But anyone could have found the three girls just by checking their social media accounts that night. It's worth a shot."

Even though my night had ended with Nick, I hadn't been able to get the image of Amber's two friends sticking their cameras in my face out of my head. I'd sat up and poured through the reports I had.

He finally seemed to calm down as he thought about it. "Joe never mentioned Amber in any of his statements about why he was fighting with Skyler. I never considered her because she wasn't at the party." He leaned back in my chair and folded his arms across his chest.

"That's exactly right. Where was Amber that night? Joe said he and Skyler were fighting because he didn't want her to leave. But why did Skyler want to leave the party so badly, if Joe wanted her to stay? And knowing that he was the only suspect in the disappearance, he didn't try to throw the blame on anyone else. When you asked about the fight, he never mentioned any other girl being a part of it, so is he covering for someone?"

"If you're serious about this, take my advice; stop fooling around with Nick and follow up on Amber."

"I would like to, but that's easier said than done. I'll have to go through Joe Styles for information, and Joe would be hard to stomach even if he wasn't involved in all this."

He raised his eyebrows. "Maybe you should be dating him instead of Nick?"

My mind flashed back to the way Joe had been standing, silhouetted by the fire, the bottle in his hand. That look on his face that said I was judging him, just like everyone else. "Insulting each other is stupid. And nonproductive. I'm going to call Bill and explain the situation." I reached for my cell.

The chief put his hand over mine on the phone. "No, don't do that. I know the reason you're here is to help. Maybe I'm just pissed off at you because the case is going nowhere. And you just came up with a plausible lead. Maybe it's my fault. If I were a better cop, the Feds wouldn't have needed to put you in."

"I don't think that's the case. And if it's any consolation to you, this is a very fucked up situation."

"It's no consolation." He seemed a little deflated now. "This is getting tougher and tougher for me. They've been gone going on three months. I see Brandy Santana sinking lower and lower. Emma Lansing's parents and the Stansfields are running themselves into the ground trying to come up with something."

"It's not your fault. You didn't kidnap those girls."

"It just feels like it is. I knew them, all of them. This is a small town." I saw the deep creases of worry wrinkle up his forehead. "I feel like I'm these people's protector and I let them down."

"We're doing everything we possibly can," I reminded him gently.

Nodding, he said, "Let's go back down. They'll think I'm being too tough on you."

I followed him out of my room and downstairs. We ate the rest of our breakfast in silence. Everyone danced around us, figuring he must have let me have it for going to a bar. I really didn't care one way or another if the chief was mad at me. I had done what any college student in America would have done. If I hadn't gone in, that would have been suspicious.

Later that afternoon, as I was watching TV in the living room with Peter, I got another call on my cell.

"Well, I hope you're happy," the chief told me.

"What now?"

"Amber Wray's parents just called me up and want you arrested for assault."

"No kidding?"

"Yeah, no kidding. Can you come up with witnesses to say she hit you first and you tried to walk away?"

"Everyone at the party saw it. And recorded it." I voiced my suspicions. "Amber probably put it on YouTube by now."

"Good. Come on over to my office. The Wrays are on their way now. We have to get this straightened out."

I flipped off the TV and sent Peter upstairs. Tossing my jacket on, I trudged through the slush to the chief's office. It has never ceased to amaze me how parents think their kids are holy angels. That they could never, ever do anything wrong. Even when the kid is caught on video, red-handed, with fifteen prior arrests, the mother will still scream her baby is innocent.

Which is exactly what I found waiting for me at the station house. Amber's mother and father were already there, sitting in some folding chairs. The chief obviously kept the chairs around for just such an occasion, because I had never seen them in his office before. Usually there was just his chair and mine.

"This is Mr. and Mrs. Wray. They want to talk about what happened last night."

Amber was sitting in her own little chair off to the side. She had a huge purple bruise along her jawline. I sat down on the army cot and folded my hands in front of me.

"Not a scratch on her, Chief. Look at my daughter," Mrs. Wray ranted. She was clutching an old black purse on her lap, knuckles white, kneading the worn leather strap between her fingers. "Your niece must be at least three inches taller than her."

"Mrs. Wray, what matters is who started the fight. Shea tells me Amber wanted to fight her over Joe Styles. She told Amber she didn't want to fight, and Amber hit her first." He looked over at her. "Is that true?"

Amber looked at the chief, then at her parents, and burst out, "Look what she did to me! Look at my face!"

"Did she hit you first?" he asked again, patiently.

She folded her arms across her chest and mashed her lips together.

"There were at least forty other people at the party. Why don't we call a few of them up and get their versions? Or better yet, watch the numerous cell phone videos that were taken of the incident."

Mrs. Wray's face clouded with anger, and she slapped her husband on the shoulder with her purse as she got up. "Come on, Amber. It's obvious he isn't going to do anything about this. Come on, Stan." Poor Stan meekly followed his wife out. As Amber was about to leave, she turned and mouthed the words *You're dead* to me.

After they left, I turned to the chief. "Why are people such lunatics?"

He shrugged. "Amber Wray has been bullying girls in this town since I got this job. Now she gets one big bruise, and her parents are screaming for blood. Unbelievable."

"So girls beating up girls is a thing in this town?"

"Don't act so superior." He glanced down at his watch. "You better get going. You have to get ready for your big date."

I ignored the snark in his voice. "Are you going to follow up on Amber as a suspect?"

"I already started." Pulling two huge folders out of his desk drawer, he tossed them down between us. "Here's a timetable of all significant events, as well as the approximate time everyone came and left the party. Here are all the sworn statements." He tapped the fatter file with his finger, then pulled a couple of pieces of paper out of a smaller one.

"I dug out Amber's. Her statement was in a separate file for people not at the party. It seems she and Danielle Dombrowski were at Amber's house until twelve thirty. She sent Joe Styles"— he glanced down at the paperwork—"seventeen texts, two Face-Time requests, and called him six times. She says she dropped Danielle off at twelve forty, went back home, and went to sleep. Claims she was home no later than one o'clock."

"Can we confirm that?"

"We could have, if her parents hadn't been away on a cruise that weekend."

"She was all alone."

"You got it."

I picked up the timetables and leafed through them. Her last call/text message/desperate attempt to contact Joe had been logged in at 12:04 AM. "Could you please email me all of this? Her friends were trying to videotape our fight. Aggressively. I think she orchestrated the fight."

"For what purpose?"

"To be able to film it. And post it somewhere."

He considered this for a second, then waved his hand over the pile of statements. "Make sure you tell Bill Walters about the video angle when you check in with him."

I smiled up from behind the paperwork. "And you said I was useless."

"This might turn out to be nothing, so I wouldn't go breaking your arm patting yourself on the back. My department is still on the case. Not to mention the state police, sheriff's department, families, parents, and friends. You're not the only one investigating this thing."

I dismissed him with the wave of my hand. "I'm the only one who will solve it."

"Oh yeah, James Bond? And why is that?"

I got up, gave him one hell of a smile, and said dramatically, "Because I'm the only one who's in their world."

He rolled his eyes at me as I walked out.

\* \* \*

Nick picked me up right on time. He didn't just honk his horn and have me come running out. When I came down the stairs, he was talking to Mrs. Parker in the hallway, an easy smile on his face, hair still wet from a shower. "Hey," he said when he saw me, the laugh lines around his eyes crinkling.

"Hey," I replied, and Mrs. Parker excused herself.

"Ready?" he asked, and when I nodded, he reached over and held the door open for me. He held the door open for me. A guy under twenty-five actually went out of his way to hold a door open for me. I'm all for equal rights and everything, but it was fantastic.

We went to see a movie in town. He seemed a little more at ease than the night before, although we didn't speak much during the show. Thankfully, it was a Marvel movie and there were no deep issues or sex scenes involved. Afterward he asked me if I wanted to grab something to eat. I said yes, and we made our way over to Freddie's for some pizza. It was still early, and plenty of people were hanging around.

I saw Maddie and Jenna. They waved to us and then gave me the thumbs-up as soon as he wasn't looking. They were talking with some guys I had never seen before over by the jukebox.

Stopping by our table a few minutes later, Maddie leaned in close and whispered in my ear, "You are so lucky."

I knew Nick must have heard, so after she left, I took a sip of my milkshake and teased him. "Does everyone around here have a crush on you? Is some girl you used to date going to come after me now too?"

His face went red. "A lot of Olivia's friends had crushes on me. I think it was just because I played football. But that was a long time ago. Don't worry, you're safe with me."

"I don't think football is the only reason," I told him. He looked absolutely beautiful in his navy-blue sweater and his faded jeans. His dark hair was combed back so nicely over his ears and looked so soft that I wanted to reach out and touch it.

"Seems like a couple guys have crushes on you," he countered.

"I guess we have that in common, then."

"It kind of seems to me like we're both sort of sad," he said suddenly.

That surprised me. "How so?"

"Well, I lost my sister, and you lost your parents for no good reason. I think maybe that kind of pain can draw you to someone."

He was right: damage attracts damage.

At that moment I felt like a total and complete fraud. I could feel the color draining from my face. I put my pizza down and wiped my mouth with my napkin, letting it partially cover my face. What the hell was I doing?

"I'm sorry." He reached over and grabbed my hand. "I didn't mean to upset you."

"It's all right, Nick. Really." I gave his hand a squeeze, but I felt like I was going to throw up. His sister was missing and he was sitting there comforting me? Comforting me over an outrageous lie?

Just then Sarah Rose came in to pick up a pizza. Emily was with her, holding on to her hand. She saw me and waved. As she was reaching across the counter for the pizza box, I noticed a purplish-green bruise the size of a grapefruit on the underside of her left arm. I knew then that her and Jake's arguments were more than just words. She left as quickly as she had come in, without stopping to talk.

To make matters worse, Joe Styles walked in. He and his little flock of followers, minus Amber, sat down diagonally from us. That put us facing each other. He talked with his friends for a few minutes and then sauntered over to where Nick and I were sitting.

He didn't acknowledge Nick at all. "I heard Amber wanted you arrested."

I didn't look at him. "She couldn't have me arrested. You were there. She started it."

He put a hand on my shoulder. "All over me?" I saw Nick tense up when he touched me.

I shook his paw off. "I wouldn't say that. I wouldn't say that at all."

"I'll be over here if you need me. Hi, Nick." Joe gave him a slick shit-eating grin and went back over to his entourage, probably just a split second before Nick could jump up to bash his face in.

"Let's get out of here," Nick said in a low voice. I could tell it was taking every ounce of control he had to let it go.

"He's just trying to get to you," I told him as he held the door open for me. "And me, too."

"I can't be near that guy," Nick said as we walked out to his truck. He hit the unlock button on his fob, and the car blinked twice. "I want to throttle him every time I see him."

"The feeling is mutual." I hopped into his truck. "Where to next?"

He glanced at his watch. "It's eleven thirty right now. I've got to get up early for church tomorrow. If you want, you could go with me."

Asking me to go to church with him? What planet was I on? The last guy who'd texted me for a date in Buffalo had followed it up with a close-up picture of his junk.

"I'll go with you, sure."

He clenched and unclenched the steering wheel. "Is that weird? Is that too serious? Church and all?"

I shook my head. "No. That's fine. I haven't gone in a while. I think I could use it."

He drove me home once again, this time pausing in the driveway. "I hope I'm not going too fast with you with all this. I've been moping around like a zombie for almost three months. I guess you take my mind off everything. The people around here—they're the biggest bunch of gossips. They think they know everything about me. About my sister. All they do is spread rumors. I don't have to worry about that with you." He smiled, and this time it did reach his eyes. "You don't know anyone."

"I really like hanging out with you. Last night and tonight were great," I told him.

"Good." His voice was filled with relief. And maybe hope.

Then he leaned over and gave me a long, sweet good-night kiss.

*   *   *

Back up in my room at the boardinghouse, my brain was in overdrive. The more I thought about the fight and how it had gone down, the more I focused on Amber's friends with their phones in my face.

I pulled up everything Roy and Bill had given me on Amber Wray.

If she hadn't been at the party the night the girls went missing, where had she been?

Flopping on my bed, I propped my iPad open in front of me. I opened Google and typed in *Amber Wray, Kelly's Falls, New York*. Immediately random sites popped up that promised I could *FIND OUT ANYTHING ABOUT ANYBODY! SEE POLICE ARREST RECORDS!* They were all websites designed to give you public information for a small fee.

I kept scrolling.

Jackpot.

On page three of my search results, I found two YouTube channels connected to her, but they were old. One hadn't been posted to in over two years, the other, a year. I clicked on them both.

In the older videos she was doing hair-styling tutorials from her bathroom, showing people how to straighten their hair, how to correctly choose the right product for maximum curls, and what to do about split ends. She was wooden and stiff and kept stopping to correct herself. The lighting was terrible, and at one point in the last video she posted, she burned the tips of her fingers on her flat iron. She had only posted four videos on that channel, with only six followers.

The next channel was more recent, and on that one she rated hair and skin products. Once again, the production quality was crap. She was back in the cluttered bathroom crammed with junk and half-used beauty products.

She'd posted six videos to that channel, gaining only twelve followers and not many likes, but the comments people left were brutal. Someone told her to put a bag over her head, and another wrote that someone should be there teaching *her* how to do her own hair and makeup.

I tried to click on the last two videos, but they'd been flagged and removed for violating YouTube's community guidelines.

The last video she'd posted on that channel was from almost a year ago. She'd kept the videos to herself, maybe trying to build up an audience before telling people around Kelly's Falls what she was doing. None of my friends had mentioned Amber being on YouTube, which they definitely would have talked about, if only to mock her, if they knew. Amber had aspirations of being an online influencer of sorts, but her hair tutorials and product reviews had been a flop. I wondered what kind of videos she had posted that would violate the guidelines. Maybe she'd found more success with that particular content on a different platform. A platform that had no guidelines.

I went back to Google and typed in *Where can I post video content?* Site after site after site popped up. I tried to narrow the search to *fist fight videos*, and I was swamped with pages. No matter how narrow I tried to make the search, it wasn't narrow enough. There was just too much out there.

If Amber was making violent videos and posting them somewhere on the Net, I needed to find them.

But searching the Internet blind wasn't helping. I needed more information.

**Sunday, March 26<sup>th</sup>**

had to refocus and put all that Internet stuff on the back burner. Nick picked me up at eleven o'clock to go to the noon mass at St. Martin's. Mrs. Parker was so happy I was going to church, I thought she was going to kiss me. The chief gave me a disapproving look at breakfast. "Now you two are going to church together?"

"Oh Roy, they're young. I think this proves what a nice young man he is. How many boys his age would take a girl to church?" I could tell Mrs. Parker was all for Team Nick.

"Not many," he agreed, and didn't bring it up again.

So Nick and I went off to church. It seemed like the whole town was there. St. Martin's Roman Catholic Church was a center of social doings in Kelly's Falls. Everyone was christened there, married there, and sooner or later, buried there. Nick's family, like a lot of old families in town, had their own pew. He led me down the aisle, and I genuflected, crossed myself, and sat down. His mother and father were already there, along with his grandmother and great-aunt Elizabeth.

"Mom, this is my friend, Shea Anderson," Nick whispered. Mrs. Stansfield smiled slightly and patted my hand. She looked terrible, like she hadn't slept in days.

"Who is she?" his great-aunt practically screamed.

"You don't know her, Aunt Elizabeth. She just moved to town. She's Nick's friend," Nick's dad explained hurriedly, trying to shush her.

"Are you one of Olivia's friends, dear?" she asked, oblivious to everyone else. She was about five foot one with wild white hair. It was like talking to an ancient dandelion that was ready to blow.

"No, Aunt Elizabeth. She's Nick's friend," Mr. Stansfield replied, trying to control his voice. Mrs. Stansfield's eyes welled with tears, and Nick's dad put an arm around her shoulder, trying to comfort her. I felt very uncomfortable, like I didn't belong there with them. Mrs. Stansfield wiped her eyes halfheartedly.

The mass started, and I tried to concentrate on praying. It's funny, but a lot of cops are close to God in their own way. I guess we have to be.

The priest was younger than I had expected, somewhere in his early forties with graying dark hair. He was a wonderful priest, very powerful and intelligent. He said a prayer at the end of the service for the three missing girls. He pleaded with anyone who had any information to come forward and speak to the FBI or to him. After the mass, Nick took me through the line to introduce us.

"Father O'Halloran," Nick said as he shook his hand, "this is Shea Anderson. She just moved here last week."

"Welcome. I'm sure if you're with Nick, you know all about our crisis here in town."

"Yes, I'm aware."

He shook his head sadly. "It's been a nightmare. I don't have to tell Nick that. Emma Lansing taught Sunday school here. The children are just devastated. It's been very hard on them."

I just nodded gravely. I didn't know how to respond. I almost thought he shouldn't have gone on like that in front of Nick. Father O'Halloran reached around and put his arm across Nick's shoulders. "But we have faith, don't we Nick? We'll find them, I know it."

Nick was trying to control himself. I could tell he was getting very emotional. "You're right, Father. We're going to find them. Listen, I'm going to take Shea downstairs to see the information center, okay?"

"I'll be down in a little while," he replied, turning back to the long line of parishioners that had formed behind us. Nick led me to the back of the church and down the stairwell into the basement.

The church used the basement for bingo games and Sunday school along with the occasional meeting of some organization or another. When I came down the steps, I saw that they had turned the main hall into an information center for the missing girls.

"They've been great here," Nick said, looking around. "Especially Father O'Halloran." He walked over to a desk with a computer, phone, and stacks of flyers on it. Behind, on the wall was a massive whiteboard with magnetic pins stuck into a map of the town. A larger map of the state had even more pins to represent where people calling in had claimed to have seen the girls since their disappearance. There were also maps of the different searches that had been held, and the different types of searches that had been used to try to find the girls, and the ground they had covered. They had brought in dogs, tried massive grid searches, and done aerial hunts with state police helicopters—everything.

He pointed to a woman in her late forties with frosted blonde hair wearing a T-shirt with a picture of the three missing girls on it. She was organizing flyers on a table, stacking some in one pile, sorting others into another, with a look of sheer concentration on her face. "That's Emma's mom. She's here every day," he whispered.

The woman looked up as if she'd heard her name, saw Nick and me, and waved. We waved back, and she returned to her job with the same nervous intensity.

"Someone is here all the time, waiting to see if a lead comes in on the Internet or if anyone calls in with a sighting. At first there were a hundred people here around the clock; now there's only five or six." He looked around. "In another month there'll only be me and Mrs. Lansing, I think. That's the hardest part: realizing that even though your life is at a standstill, everyone else's goes on."

I'd often wondered how people could live with such extreme pain and uncertainty daily. On the street you saw kids abused, dealt with women and girls with cigarette burns, wives beaten almost to death, horrible rapes, talked to the parents of homicide victims. I could never figure out how they didn't just crawl into a hole somewhere and hide. Which is what I'd basically done after the Roberts case. Where did their strength and bravery come from? How did the victims and the mothers and the families have the courage to face the world? Watching Nick struggle with all that pain was enough for me to strengthen my resolve to do whatever it took to find his sister.

Whatever it took.

His mother and father were talking to some people across the room by the ancient coffee maker set up on a rickety card table. Aunt Elizabeth and Grandma had gone home.

"Mom, Dad, I'm going back to the house," he called to them.

"We'll see you in a little while," his dad called back. He looked red-faced and upset. A white-haired woman had him cornered and was going on about something. Nick's mom had her hand to her forehead, her lips puckered as the woman rattled on, oblivious to the reaction she was causing.

As we were about to leave, Father O'Halloran came down the steps into the basement. "Leaving so soon, Nick?" he asked.

"Yeah, I have to get Shea back home."

The priest looked at me intently and took my hand. "It was very nice meeting you. I hope to see you again." He held on to my hand just a fraction of a second longer than necessary. I pulled back uncomfortably from him, but I managed a small smile.

We walked to Nick's truck silently. It was a beautiful day, cold but clear and bright. Another frost had snuck in overnight, and the snow glistened and crunched under our feet as we made our way through the lot. I got in his truck, and he said, "Don't take this the wrong way, but could I just take you home? I always get this way after I go down there. I just want to be alone."

I told him it was okay and put my hand on his leg to try to soothe him a little. He put his hand over mine, squeezing it gently as he drove me home.

That should have been the end of my day, when he dropped me off, but I had work to do.

*  *  *

Doing surveillance on someone without a car isn't just tricky; it's almost impossible to do it right.

Amber worked at Desi's Hair Salon on Main Street, across from Kilkenny's Dry Cleaning. After double-checking online that both places were open on Sundays, I went through my closet and found the only two pieces of clothing I owned that were dry clean only: a pair of tan pants and a little black dress. Hey, you never know when you're going to need the LBD, right?

Both pieces were clean—I hadn't worn either since coming to Kelly's Falls—but I balled them up and stuck them in a canvas tote bag with one of my button-down shirts. Slinging the tote over my shoulder, I walked over to Kilkenny's.

Bells hanging from a red ribbon jingled when I pushed the door open. Mr. Kilkenny turned around as I came in. He had a full head of crazy white hair and was about seventy-five years old. A sign in the window proclaimed that the shop had been serving Kelly's Falls for fifty years. Looking at Mr. Kilkenny's smiling, lined face, that seemed about right. I put the tote on the counter and pulled out the button-down shirt. I'd never been in the shop before, but I'd driven by it enough to see the sandwich board outside advertising that they repaired buttons and zippers while you waited. I'd pulled off one of the buttons on the cuff before I'd come.

He examined the shirt, taking the button from my hand. "Helen!" he called into the back, beyond the racks of clothes hanging from the carousel. "I've got a quick job for you!"

Helen must have been his seamstress. "Bring it to me!" she replied from somewhere behind. Mr. Kilkenny turned with my shirt and button in hand and disappeared behind the clothes.

A small table with two chairs sat in front of the picture window. I slid into one and propped my chin on my fist, watching the comings and goings of Desi's Hair Salon across the street.

Amber's chair was situated right in the front window. She was busy cutting a balding man's remaining hair, bending over in concentration as she snipped away. I sat and watched. I didn't know where she was posting her videos or how this would help me find out, but it was the only lead I had to follow up on.

A girl came from the back, broom in hand, sweeping up the hair from around the base of Amber's chair. I recognized her as one of the camera-wielding girls at the party. She was short, with long blonde hair that hung down straight on either side of her round face. I watched as she bent over with a dustpan, which seemed to piss Amber off, because she stopped cutting and said something to her that made her jump back with the broom. She hung her head and disappeared into the shop with her dustpan and broom.

Of the two girls Amber had been with, she seemed to be on the lowest rung of their social ladder. Amber was on top, with the redhead they were with as her number two.

Dustpan Girl was the one I needed to talk to. You always zero in on the weakest link in an investigation.

I got my shirt back, paid my bill, and walked out. Amber couldn't work seven days a week at the salon. I had to get Dustpan Girl alone. She was definitely the weakest link.

* * *

I walked along Main Street, hands stuffed in the front pockets of my jeans, fingering the pickup receipt for my dry cleaning. Halfway home, I was debating whether or not to pop my earbuds in. I usually don't when I'm walking alone. Almost getting murdered by a serial killer tends to keep you on your toes.

But some things you can't avoid. Like getting pelted by something in the back of the head as a car zooms by, the driver screaming "Loser!" out the unrolled passenger's side window as she blasts her horn.

I stopped dead, hand flying to the back of my skull, expecting it to come away bloody as Amber made a right turn and disappeared.

There was no blood, only ketchup. A wadded-up fast-food bag lay on the ground next to me.

My face burned hot. I wanted to run back to the boarding-house, look up Amber's address in my files, find her, and shove that white paper bag filled with garbage down her throat.

Then reality pushed my revenge fantasy to the side. I wasn't allowed to assault people, cop or not.

I kicked the bag and kept walking. My scalp tingled where it had made contact. The question that kept rolling over and over in my mind was, *Who does something like that?*

And the only answer I could come up with was, someone who would do even worse to the people she thought were getting between her and Joe Styles.

*  *  *

"Who were the two girls at the party with Amber?" I asked Kayla later that night as I sat in my room, trying to heal my wounded pride.

"Oh, them?" I pictured her sprawled out across her bed, skinny legs dangling over the side. "That was Samantha and Danielle, Amber's two minions. Danielle is the redheaded one, and Sam has the long blonde extensions."

"Those were extensions?" I hated playing stupid. You could tell they were fake from a mile away.

"Totally. She got them done at Desi's salon, where she works with Amber. She does nails."

"And the other one, Danielle? What's her deal?"

"She lives with her boyfriend over in the trailer park. He's older, like thirty, and works for Pat Lynch construction. He's got about one tooth left in his head from smoking meth."

"Pat Lynch?" I was confused.

"No, the boyfriend, Brian Higgins. Pat Lynch owns the construction company."

"Oh, okay. Got it." I was taking notes as we talked, trying to keep the names and connections straight.

"They both follow her around like puppies. They have since middle school. It's weird."

After we clicked off, I went over my notes. If Sam and Danielle were willing to film Amber's escapades for her, what else would they do?

**Monday, March 27th**

I didn't hear from Nick at all the rest of that night or the next morning. If that wasn't bad enough, I found out Amber Wray was telling everyone she was going to sue me. Which was hilarious, since she'd assaulted me with garbage the day before. Maddie was still pissed about what she had said about Skyler the night she tried to beat me up.

"Skyler was no angel, okay, but Amber has no room to talk about anything she did or who she did it with," Maddie told me as she copied my Social Psychology notes in the student union. Today she had her blonde hair pulled back in a ponytail, the one dyed-pink strand hanging loose by her cheek.

"Did those two fight a lot?" I asked.

"Yes and no. They never fistfought, because Skyler was Joe's girlfriend. If Amber would have touched her, Joe would never have spoken to her again."

"He may be a jerk and treated her like dirt, but he always really liked Skyler," Kayla agreed. "I mean, they were actually together, you know? Not just hooking up."

"So why did they break up?" I bit into my orange, and juice squirted everywhere. I could see Joe out of the corner of my eye with his groupies across the room.

Jenna shook her head. "After the cemetery incident, I guess. I mean, she was wild and all, but she wasn't into anything sick like that. They only went out about a year straight; the rest was on and off. He smokes a lot of pot and deals a lot of it on campus. Don't get me wrong, Skyler smoked weed, and wasn't happy about Joe dealing it. But meth? No way. No way was she going to put up with that."

Kayla looked over at Joe and absently began drawing a big heart around the name *Zach* that she had decorated her notebook cover with. "He's a player. He cheated on her all the time. That's all they ever fought about."

\* \* \*

We killed all the time we could, then went our separate ways. I waited until I had a break in my classes, and then I called the salon. A cheerful voice answered on the second ring. "Desi's Hair Salon, Annmarie speaking. How may I help you?"

"Is Amber Wray working today?"

"Let me check." I heard pages flipping in the background. "No. She comes in the day after tomorrow. Do you want to make an appointment? She has a few openings."

"No." I hesitated, like I was thinking, then asked, "What about Sam? Is she doing nails today?"

"Yes. Sam will be here from noon to close. Can I get your name and put you in the book?"

"No, thank you." I hung up on Annmarie.

Looked like I was getting my nails done.

It wasn't a lie that my nails needed to be tended to. I'd been neglecting them since I'd gotten to Kelly's Falls, and it showed.

So when I walked into Desi's salon at three thirty after my classes, I actually was a young woman in desperate need of a manicure.

A pretty lady in her fifties with a platinum bob sat behind the desk. She looked up from a fashion magazine when I came in. "Welcome to Desi's. I'm Annmarie. What can we do for you?"

I held my hands out and wiggled my fingers. "I think I need to get my nails done."

Her smile faltered as she looked over my fingertips. "You sure do." She tilted her head back, calling behind her, "Sam! We've got a lady here who needs your help."

A beaded curtain parted in the back of the shop, and Sam started walking through. She stopped halfway when she saw me, one arm holding back the ropes of colored beads.

I feigned surprise at seeing her, and we both stood there awkwardly until Annmarie asked, "Is there a problem?"

"I . . ." Glancing back at the door, I made it seem like I was going to leave. Annmarie's eyes narrowed at Sam.

"There's no problem," Sam chirped, a little too peppy. "Pick out a polish and have a seat here." She grabbed the back of a chair at the nail station closest to the beaded curtain and pulled it out a little. A forced smile was plastered across her face.

I picked a nice, light shade of blue from the rack and walked over to her station, slipping into the chair. "I'll just leave when she's busy," I said under my breath as Sam sat down across from me.

She picked up my right hand and dunked it into a bowl of warm water. "Listen, I'm really sorry about the other night," she said, low enough that Annmarie couldn't hear.

"Sorry enough to record it?"

"That was Amber. She wanted to video the fight." She gently placed my hand on a towel and put my left one in the bowl.

"Why? Why in the world would she want something like that on video?"

She hesitated before answering me, looking around as if she was afraid Amber might pop out of the back room at any moment. "Amber is one of my best friends, and I don't want to talk bad about her, but I never should have let her talk me into being a part of that. Ever since she's been doing this new blog, she tries to post all these extreme videos."

She started to file the thumbnail on my right hand. "She runs a blog?" I asked.

Nodding as she worked, Sam said, "She used to do YouTube videos, but she couldn't get anyone to follow her. Then she tried posting some questionable stuff and got kicked off. She found this blog server that posts all these crazy, bizarre, weird videos and uses that now."

"What kind of questionable content?"

Sam started on my pinkie. "I don't want to talk about it here at work." Her eyes slid over to Annmarie. "But it's bad."

"Is the video of me on there?" I asked, trying to sound horrified.

"No." She started gliding blue polish over my nails. "She didn't want to post a video of her losing a fight."

"Can I double-check?" I raised my voice a notch, just enough for Annmarie to look over at us. "Can I have the blog's address?"

"Yes," she hissed through her teeth. "I'll write it down before you leave. But it's not on there, I promise."

"Don't be offended if I don't take your word for it. I need to see for myself." I made Sam write it down and pulled it up on my phone before I would get up to pay. She sat staring at me, face frozen in a weird grin, not knowing what I was going to do. Finally, I went up to the reception desk and paid. I even left her a tip. She'd actually done a good job. Admiring my nails, I pushed the door open and left Sam stewing at her station.

\* \* \*

I went home and called Bill. I figured I might as well give him an update. I also wanted to ask about something that had been bothering me for a while.

"How did you get the chief to go along with all this? He hates the fact I'm here."

"We threw the idea out to him after we came up with no leads. I explained what we did in Buffalo, and he was hesitant. You know me; I might have put a little pressure on him."

"Maybe a lot."

"Maybe. I could never take no for an answer."

The FBI isn't in the business of solving local crimes. If the local law enforcement people ask for their help with fingerprints or psychological profiles or tire-tread analysis, the Bureau happily provides. Something like what we were doing was more than highly unusual, and all the chief would have had to say was no. That's why I couldn't understand why he was giving me such a hard time.

I told Bill about the recording of the fight and Amber's aspirations of being a viral video sensation. The blog server she was now using had no content guidelines, so it contained the most bizarre, graphic content I had ever seen. And I'd seen a lot. I knew I could dig through her content myself, but Bill literally had a whole cyber squad at his beck and call. I also told him about getting hit with the bag of garbage. "If Amber did something to the girls, if she went psycho and posted about it online, this could be the break we've been looking for," I said.

"Great job, Shea. I'm going to call my guys in on overtime right now. I want them combing through every single video she's ever posted."

I breathed a sigh of relief. "Let me know as soon as you got something."

"You'll be my first call."

I doubted that.

I ended the call and lay back on my bed, staring at the ceiling.

It seemed like I was always waiting for something.

I got sick of waiting for Nick to call me, and I didn't want to engage in any more gossip with my schoolmates, so I grabbed my coat and decided to go for a walk. It was still light out and the weather was warm. I figured I'd get to know my new home a little better. A Western New York spring is a funny thing. When people picture spring, they think blades of green grass shooting up through the last leftover clumps of snow. They think robins and crocus and blue skies. We have those things, but not until May. In March and April it's a mess of muddy snow and gray skies. One day the temperature is in the fifties, the next it's snowing. One day it's raining, the next there's an ice storm. Spring is anticipated around these parts, but that's only because it marks an end to snowdrifts as big as your car and wind so cold it seeps into every crevice of your house, making it impossible to stay warm.

As I trudged along the sidewalk toward Main Street, I thought about what I was doing there in the first place, besides getting hit with garbage. Admittedly, it was better than driving around in a patrol car. At that time of year, our calls were few and far between on the midnight shift, so I wasn't missing any action on the street. I was thinking more about my life in general, about how I wasn't even leaving a boyfriend behind. After a few bad experiences with guys on the job, especially the last one, I'd sworn never to go out with a cop again. Working the hours and doing the things we did on the job made it tough to meet anyone else. I'd been pretty much on my own for a while. And then Nick had walked into my life. I tried to tell myself any long-term relationship was impossible, for very obvious reasons. But at the same time, I felt an intense attraction to Nick that I hadn't felt with anyone for a long time. If ever.

I walked down Main Street, past Desi's salon, past the shops, most of which were closed. I realized it must be past eight o'clock. I stopped in front of the bakery and looked at the wedding cakes in the window. Two little figures perched high up on the top tier of white frosting were looking back at me. I realized I was feeling lonely. I had gotten the same way during the Roberts case. I don't know that many people know what it's like to assume an entirely new life—to leave your old life on hold and expect to pick it back up where you left off. I'd found out that you can't. Somehow what you give up to do something like this stays gone. There's a hole in your real life, missing time that can't be patched up or replaced. I knew I must be crazy to be putting myself through it all over again.

I also knew I was going crazy waiting for something to happen. Now I was waiting for Bill's cyber people to sift through Amber's posts. I couldn't just sit on my ass while that happened.

And nothing else *would* happen unless I pushed the envelope a little. I knew Emma Lansing lived only five houses away from Nick and Olivia. It was a walk, but I needed to *do something*. Sitting in my room waiting for magical clues to appear was getting me nowhere. Getting to Sam was a start, but I needed to do more.

I tucked my head down and walked into the wind. If anyone saw me, I'd just say I was going to pay Nick a surprise visit. Half the girls in the town were hot for him, so why shouldn't I act a little desperate if I had to? Besides, I reminded myself, Nick was not the reason I was there.

I turned down a side street and headed into the neighborhood.

Warm yellow light glowed from the windows. The houses looked so cozy and inviting as I made my way down the sidewalk.

It was actually farther than I'd estimated, and my ears were frozen. I clapped my hands over them until they got cold, then stuffed them in my pockets until they were warm enough to cover my ears again.

Finally, after what seemed like an icy eternity, I saw both Nick's and Emma's houses materialize as I turned a corner.

I must have passed by Emma Lansing's house at least five times, including that first drive around with the chief, but never at night. Now I could see a Christmas tree, complete with twinkling colored lights, front and center in the picture window.

I stopped dead, blew on my hands to warm them, and figured out my next move. And my next set of lies.

Emma's house was designed a lot like Nick's, minus the huge foliage that blocked the Stansfields' driveway from view. I looked down the street. Nick's truck was parked on the road in front of his house.

No cars sat in Emma's driveway, and except for the lights of the tree, the house was dark.

I crossed the street, looking left and right for anybody who might be out for an evening stroll, then turned up Emma's walkway and climbed the stairs up onto her porch.

Making my way over to the window, I peeked in. All the holiday decorations had been left up. A jolly-looking two-foot-high Santa stood next to the fireplace holding a red sack. I could just make out a couple of unwrapped gifts poking out from under the tree: a pair of checkered Vans, new headphones, and some vinyl records.

I leaned in, cupping my hands around my eyes and pressing against the window to get a better look. Pictures lined the mantel, but the light from the tree wasn't enough for me to make out what they were of. My breath fogged the glass, so I wiped it with my coat sleeve.

"Can I help you with something?"

A voice from behind startled me. I jumped back from the window. Standing in the driveway in a housecoat was Emma Lansing's mom, cell phone in hand.

"Oh, I'm so sorry! I saw the Christmas tree and I wanted a better look. I don't know what I was thinking."

"I don't either. I already called the police."

"I'm the chief's niece, Shea." I had my shivering hand to my chest. "I was just on my way to see if Nick Stansfield was home. I'm so sorry I came up on your porch."

"I thought you were the girl I saw with Nick in the church basement, but I wasn't a hundred percent sure." She pulled her housecoat tighter around her against the wind that had kicked up. "I had a security system installed this month. Cameras. Goes right to my cell phone. I was down in the basement when I got the alert."

I started to move slowly toward the steps. I couldn't see her right hand, and for all I knew, she'd gone out and bought a .357 Magnum when her daughter went missing. "I'll just be on my way, then. Sorry to bother you."

"Nick's not home. His mother called to tell me he was taking her to bingo at the fire hall. You walked here?"

I nodded.

"Why don't you come inside, and I'll make you some hot tea before you freeze to death. The temperature really dropped once the sun went down. Not a good night for a walk."

Just what Bill had taught me: lie, apologize, let them think it's their idea to talk to you. "My fingers are frozen. That sounds so good."

"Come around to the side door," Mrs. Lansing said as she disappeared around the corner. I scrambled down the porch and followed her. As she reached for the door, I exhaled a cloudy breath of relief: her hand was empty.

"I'll call back and tell them to cancel the squad car," she said, stepping aside so I could walk into her red-and-white-decorated kitchen. "Have a seat. I'll put the kettle on."

"Thank you." I slid into the rustic-looking wooden chair as she punched some numbers into her phone. The almond-colored fridge was covered in pictures of Emma. Half listening to her tell the dispatcher it was a false alarm, I studied the snapshots. Emma and Father O'Halloran with a group of kids about eight or nine. Emma and an older white-haired man—her grandfather, maybe? Emma wearing a Police Athletic League baseball jersey and hat, holding a bat. Emma on a beach in a one-piece bathing suit with Olivia Stansfield, smiling into the camera. Picture after picture after picture.

Mrs. Lansing noticed me noticing. "That's my Emma. Isn't she beautiful?"

"She sure is," I agreed as she fussed over a sugar bowl and creamer cup. Putting them on a little matching serving plate, she set them down in front of me.

"My husband is going to tell me I'm crazy, letting a strange girl in here after everything that's happened. But you're not really a stranger, are you? You're Nick's friend and the chief's niece."

I smiled. She was still crazy to let me in.

"We're keeping the tree and decorations up until she comes home. She had a newfound fascination with vinyl records. But they say everything comes back into fashion again, don't they?"

Mrs. Lansing tapped her fingers on the granite countertop while she waited for the electric kettle to whistle. The feeling slowly crept back into my face and hands in the warmth of the cozy little kitchen.

Finally, the kettle whistled, and she poured the hot water into the waiting tea mugs. "My mother always used to tell me to let tea steep for six minutes," she said, putting my cup down in front of me. She took a seat across from me and began to bob the bag, up and down, while the steam rose.

I mirrored her with my own tea. "Thanks. This is great."

"Was Nick expecting you?"

"No." I wrapped both hands around my mug while I waited out my six minutes. "I thought I'd surprise him."

"His mother told me he met someone. My Emma had such a crush on him growing up. But I think that was because he was safe, like a big brother. Emma wasn't much of a risk taker."

"No?"

"Maybe that's the wrong word. She was more of a follower. Easily led astray. That was why I worried over her friendship with Skyler. Skyler's mother had a hard time of it growing up; her father was a raging alcoholic, and the apple didn't fall far from the tree." She ran a hand through her shoulder-length frosted hair, only to have it fall back into her eyes. "I tried not to judge Skyler—sins of the father and all that—but it was hard. Especially when Brandy Santana started going with Will Garrette, the father of her little ones. He's bad news, always was. Emma was my only baby, and I always tried to protect her." She gave a bitter laugh. There were deep-set worry lines etched in her forehead and in the corners of her mouth. "Not that it helped."

She picked up her mug and sipped it, and I followed suit. "I'm so sorry."

She waved a hand. "I'm the one who's sorry. I can't stop talking about it, thinking about it. Thinking about her and where she is right now." She took a deep, shuddering breath. "I shouldn't have invited you in just to dump a burden on you."

"Please," I said. "Dump away. Emma's friends? Kayla, Maddie, and Jenna? They're my friends now. They talk about her all the time. Tell me all about Emma." I smiled at her over my cup. "I want to know everything."

**Tuesday, March 28<sup>th</sup>**

I was in a foul mood when I went to class the next day. Bill hadn't called back yet, I was having a bad-hair day, and despite getting a chance to have a fruitful two-hour conversation with Emma's mom that mostly consisted of stories from her childhood but also Emma's anxieties over school, her friends, and her new obsession with records, I was starting to feel like the whole deal could end up being a big waste of time. All my new friends were wearing my clothes and I was starting to get homesick.

"What's everyone doing after classes today?" I asked as we got on the shuttle. I wanted Bill to get me a car. Waiting for the shuttle was cold, windy, and demeaning. I made a mental note to ask Kayla why none of the other girls owned a car out there in the sticks. They always had to borrow their parents'. I'd had my own rusted-out piece of shit by the time I was sixteen and a half.

"We were going to go over to Kayla's and celebrate Olivia's nineteenth birthday," Maddie said. I noticed she now had two pink streaks in her hair. And she hadn't consulted me. Another personal slight.

"We would have asked you to come, but you didn't know her and it's kind of, you know, personal." Kayla was talking softly, playing with the frayed edges of the loose paper sticking out of her notebook.

"Oh, I understand." I wanted to be there and hear those conversations so badly. I sat there stewing, trying to figure out a way to weasel myself an invitation. Emotions would be running high; it'd be the perfect time to fish for information.

As we approached the campus, I could see three huge vans parked along the loop, giant antennae sticking up out of their roofs. News vans. "Son of a bitch," Kayla whispered, leaning over the seat to peer out the dirty window.

"Do we talk to them?" I asked out loud, to no one in particular. Everyone was staring at the trio of reporters with their cameramen, all trying to interview students walking by.

"Yes," Kayla ground out from between her teeth. "My uncle says we have to keep the media interested or they'll forget about them."

"Shit. CNN is back, and I'm wearing the same jeans as the last time they talked to me." Maddie reversed her photo app on her phone so she could touch up her hair quickly.

"What do I say if they want to talk to me? I didn't know any of them." I was panicking. I couldn't allow myself to be filmed and blow my cover.

"I'll talk." Kayla straightened her sweat shirt over her leggings as the shuttle rumbled to a stop. There was steel in her voice I'd never heard before. "We need this. They need this."

Pulling my backpack around, I crisscrossed my arms over my chest, using it as a shield. I let my hair fall forward as we filed off the shuttle, covering my face as much as possible. When the reporters saw the shuttle pull up, they all broke from the sound bites they were doing and converged on us as we disembarked.

"Does anyone want to make a comment on the missing girls?" a tall, skinny blonde asked, holding a microphone out at us.

"I will," Kayla offered, and stepped off to the side with Blondie and her cameraman. Maddie willingly went toward the handsome black reporter, who waved her over to a spot where they could get the name of the college on the side of the building in the shot.

I thought I was home free. I just had to make it to the double doors; surely they'd grab someone else. Then I felt a hand come down on my shoulder. "How about you, miss? Want to talk about how the three girls' vanishing has impacted your life?"

Mustering up every ounce of undercover savvy I'd learned in the last year, I took a deep breath, turned on my heel, and sneezed as hard as I could manage in the young female reporter's face.

"Oh no! I'm so sorry." I wiped my nose with the back of my sleeve while the black-haired lady furiously swiped at her face to get the snot off.

"My makeup!" she wailed, turning to her gruff-looking cameraman, who was trying to suppress a laugh.

"Sorry!" I called, not turning back as I hurried toward the doors. "Sorry!"

Everyone was in a rotten mood for the rest of the day. "I can't believe you sneezed on that reporter," Maddie said as we walked out of our last class together.

"It was an accident," I lied. "I don't know what came over me. I must have got a bug up my nose or something."

"Good thing you did," Kayla said. "I was almost twenty minutes late for my first class. But we have to do it. As much as I hate it, I'll hate it more when they stop showing up."

I hinted and danced around it all day, but I never did get the invite. I said good-bye to everyone and headed out into the parking lot to the bus loop, kicking myself. Kayla was staying after to use the media center for research on a project, and Maddie and Jenna were going to wait for her so they could do the whole birthday thing together. I was missing out on another golden information opportunity.

As I walked toward the shuttle, I noticed a familiar truck in the parking lot. Nick was standing alongside it, hands shoved deep in the pockets of his ski jacket. He saw me and waved.

"What are you doing here?" I asked as he met me halfway through the lot.

"I heard you tried to stop by last night and I missed you." His brown eyes looked mischievous, his smile contagious. "I thought we could go for a ride or something."

I looked around. "A ride where?"

He shrugged. "Nowhere. Anywhere. Where do you want to go? We could be in New York City in six hours. Or Atlantic City. It's less than two hours to Buffalo; we could go there."

I shook my head, laughing. "Why don't we stick around here? What's gotten into you?"

"This place. I'm so full of Kelly's Falls I could vomit. But I refuse to mope today."

Olivia's birthday.

"I'll do whatever you want to do," I said. He was holding the door of his truck open, waiting for me to climb in.

"Really?" His eyebrow cocked as he went around the front to the driver's side.

"Within reason," I amended. Who was I kidding? I would have shelled out the cash for a seedy motel room right there.

"Are you hungry? We could go get some food."

My dirty mind blocked, we went to the little Italian place on Main Street and split a large cheese-and-sausage deep-dish pizza. It was so much better than Freddie's that I wolfed down three pieces. Nick started laughing halfway through the meal.

"What's so funny?" I started wiping my face, thinking I had sauce all over it.

"Most girls hate to eat in front of guys."

"Oh yeah? Not me; I'll eat in front of anyone. With my mouth wide open, chewing like a cow. I don't care who's around."

My phone vibrated in my pocket. I slipped it out. It was a text message from Bill: *Call me.* I put my phone away and took a bite of my pizza.

"That's what I like about you. A lot of the girls at my school are stuck-up rich girls from upstate. They're so fake. At least you are totally yourself."

Pulling a gooey rope of cheese from my slice, I popped it in my mouth. "Who else would I be?"

\* \* \*

Nick dropped me off around seven thirty that evening. Unfortunately, I had scared the pants off Mrs. Parker when I hadn't come home by three o'clock and hadn't checked in at all. She tried not to sound mad as she explained that with everything that had happened, people were on edge. I apologized, trying to look as remorseful as possible, and she seemed to soften. Then she told me she'd left a message taped on my door saying the chief wanted to see me when I got home.

I called Bill first. "What's up?"

"As disturbing as her blog posts are, they actually eliminate Amber Wray as a suspect," Bill said.

My stomach dropped. I'd been so sure this would lead to *something.* "Are you sure?"

"Our computer forensics team determined one of the videos she posted was made during the time the girls disappeared. It was a two-hour-long rant about how much she hated Skyler Santana and Joe Styles, but it was made in what appears to be her bedroom and covers the time period when the girls went missing."

"That's great," I said, swallowing the bitter taste in my mouth. "So we're back to square one."

"Yes and no. There's a lot of disturbing, violent content on the blog. Including the video of her hitting you with the fast-food bag as she's driving. She must have a GoPro on her car. The video doesn't show your face, so we're safe on that end. We're going to monitor the blog and her followers. Maybe one of her crazed fans stepped up for her. I've got my guys on that now."

"What do I do in the meantime?"

"What you've been doing, gathering information like this. You've opened a new investigative path we didn't have before. Believe me, that counts for something."

It sure didn't feel like it.

I hung up with him and called the chief. "I'm sure you heard the news about Amber Wray."

"Bill called about two hours ago. He updated me on everything, including the video of her hitting you with the bag. I can't believe she's got a rock-solid alibi," he said. "Tough break. I thought you might have been on to something."

"Me too."

"If you've got a few minutes, can you come over here?"

"Sure," I told him. "Am I in trouble?"

"Not today," he said, and then amended it to, "Not yet."

I made sure I told Mrs. Parker I was going to the chief's house before I left.

As I walked over, I noticed a newer red four-door sedan parked on the street. The driver's face and the plate were camouflaged by the shadows. The harder I squinted, the more I was convinced that whoever was inside was watching me. I told myself to keep it together—and tell the chief as soon as I got in.

The chief's house was small and boxy, a perfect little brick Cape for a single man. I was surprise at how nice it was for a bachelor pad. "Hey, Uncle Roy, did you notice that red car outside?" I asked as I crossed the threshold.

"Oh that? Yeah, it's been there a while." Roy was standing in the middle of his living room. He laughed out loud at me. "Paranoid much? Followed so many people now you're thinking people are following you?" The living room was very big, decorated in a southwestern theme of blues and grays. It was beautifully done and immaculately clean.

"No," I said quickly, a blush rising to my cheeks. "Well, maybe a little. I did get smacked in the head with a fast-food bag. It's been a long week."

"Sit, please," he told me. He was wearing a Buffalo Bills sweat shirt and jeans. I had never noticed how muscular he was for a man his age. It was pretty easy to see why all the women in town were after him.

"This is a great place," I commented, parking myself on his tasteful gray couch.

"Thanks. I had someone come in and pick out all the colors and drapes. Just because I can't do it myself doesn't mean I don't have good taste, does it? I think it came out pretty well." He clapped his hands together. "Do you want a drink?"

He headed over to the polished wood liquor cabinet in the corner of the dining room.

"Am I allowed to drink?" I asked, a little sarcastically.

"As long as it's not out in public where people could come to question my authority."

"You don't like that, do you? You like to be boss."

"I am the police chief."

"Point made. And made. And made. I'll have whatever you're having."

He raised an eyebrow. "You drink whiskey?"

"Hell no."

"Good. Neither do I." He poured some Baileys Irish Cream and butterscotch schnapps into a couple of rocks glasses with some ice. As he walked over to the couch, he rattled the cubes around in the glasses. "I hope the Irish in you won't come out after drinking this."

"I'm half Irish and half Polish. You never know what you're going to get." I took the glass from him. "I know you didn't ask me here to get me inebriated, so what's up?"

He took a long swallow of his drink. "A couple of things, really. I'm sorry I've been so hard on you since you've come here. You have brought some new perspective into this case, especially in the Amber Wray department. It's just very hard for me. You didn't know them. It was my job to protect them. They were my girls, in a way."

I nodded. "Apology accepted. And I'm sorry I act like I'm some supersleuth."

"I kind of like your confidence; it suits you. Were you out with Nick?" he asked, and took another long sip.

"He picked me up from school today. We went for pizza."

"You're probably breaking every girl's heart in this poor town."

"No," I shot back. "That would only happen if I started dating you."

"I don't think that's exactly the truth." But when I looked at his face, it was tinted red.

"Oh yeah? Look at poor Marlene, pining away for you. She'd sell her soul to get you in the sack."

"Marlene is definitely not my type."

I leaned my head back on the couch and smiled over at him. "And just what is your type? Big blonde bimbo? Rail-thin yoga instructor? You can't tell me there isn't someone special in your life."

"There was once, but it didn't work out." He tossed back the rest of his drink. "I try not to think about it too much. It was a long time ago. There aren't too many women around here who live up to my standards. I'm pretty picky. Chipped nail polish? Gone. Text me twelve times a day? Gone." He picked up the bottle. "Want another one?"

I handed him my glass. "Sure."

He refilled it all the way to the top. "Drinks too much? Gone."

"I guess that's good news for me, then." I sipped my baileys. "Because you are way too short for me."

"I'm five eleven," he protested.

I shook my head sadly. "Undatable."

He laughed and clapped me on the shoulder. I wasn't joking. Anyone under six feet tall, I really considered undatable.

I'm not much of a drinker anymore, ever since I became a cop, for the simple fact that alcohol makes more problems than it's worth. I hadn't had more than one or two drinks in maybe five months. But the chief and I wound up getting very, very drunk together. We also ended up where all police end up: comparing stories.

"You know, Roy, I'm going to let you in on a little secret," I told him from my new position on the rug. How I'd landed on the rug was kind of a gradual slide from the couch.

"I can't hardly wait." He was chuckling into his drink a little.

"I am not a very good cop."

"What do you mean, you're not a good cop?"

"I mean that as far as regular police work goes, I suck. I can't do paperwork. I forget things. I make mistakes—stupid, sloppy mistakes. And as much as I hate to admit it, I'm not cut out to be a street cop."

"I don't believe that."

I sighed. "I'm a creative thinker, which you can't be in our kind of job. Facts. Hard facts are what count, and I tend to read into things too much. If she killed him at ten forty-five, that's it. End of story. I can't think that way, and it doesn't do any good to be like that when you're just a lowly patrolman."

"Do you want another drink?"

"Roy, I want another big drink."

We exchanged police stories and compared our jobs. I was going on about a car chase I was in once.

"We don't get much like that around here," the chief said, downing another one. He was sprawled over his couch, sinking into the overstuffed cushions. "But when something happens, I'm a one-man car. We only have more than one guy working at a time on weekend nights, so there's no backup. I went to this bar fight two years ago, about five people outside the Frog and Skunk out on the highway. I start breaking it up, and I get a beer bottle upside my head. Now I'm calling for help, holding on to my gun and trying to make it back to my car because I can't see for all the blood. It took the state police maybe six minutes to get there. I was totally helpless. When things happen around here, you better hope luck is on your side."

"If you're a cop, you have to make your own luck, or you're dead," I commented from my spot on the floor.

"Is that how you got this detail? By making your own luck?"

"I did that Roberts thing last summer." Bill had informed me that the chief had been told about my involvement as a way to convince him I could be an asset in the missing-girls investigation. So much for a gag order. "Bill Walters saw me one day when I was in homicide with a witness. He was downtown to talk to the lead detectives on the schoolgirl murders. I had the pleasure of finding body number three that day," I explained. "I just happened to walk by, and he came running out of one of the conference rooms and stopped me. He had this wild plan of planting me into North Side High School and trying to nab this teacher. A search warrant of the suspect's house had yielded nothing, and they were getting desperate. It was an election year and the powers that be needed the case solved. They would have brought psychics in if they had thought it would help. Instead, they put me in, and Terry Roberts tried to murder me. Case closed."

"You sound bitter about it," he observed. "I would think you'd be proud."

"I got made a lot of promises about being promoted to detective and things like that. In the end they bumped me back to patrol and forgot I existed, until now."

Propping himself up on his elbow to get a better drunken look at me, he asked, "So why did you take this case? Why not tell them to go to hell?"

"That wouldn't help those girls." I stared down into my glass drunkenly. "I still believe in things like justice and equity and that the system can work."

"Are you kidding?" he asked.

"Stupid, right? Us true believers end up with broken hearts."

"I'll drink to that. To broken hearts." He raised his glass, leaned over, and tipped it to mine.

"Cheers," I said, and finished the rest of my drink. "Speaking of broken hearts, were you working here when that Carol Losi girl took a nose dive?"

He raised an eyebrow. "Who told you about that piece of our little town's history?"

"My buddy Henry. He said they didn't find her body for two weeks."

"What made you say that about broken hearts?"

"What else would make a young woman jump off a tall bridge?"

"Well, for one thing, she was twenty-six, and for another, she was delusional." He got up, steadied himself, and grabbed the bottle off the table, pouring us both a drink before he sank back down into his fortress of cushions. "She'd been in mental institutions from the time she was a teenager. She had convinced herself we were having an affair. She'd left a diary full of crazy things she had imagined and written down with one of her caseworkers. Then she came up missing. Two young boys found her—thought it was a deer because they couldn't get close enough to get a good look because of the smell. We weren't even sure it was her—had to get dental records. It was a hot summer that year."

"And you said nothing ever happens in this town," I said, taking a sip of my new cocktail.

"You hope things like that won't. There was a big inquiry into my relationship with the girl, which was nonexistent. I was humiliated; I almost left the job. I couldn't believe some nutcase could tarnish my reputation like that. I mean, what's a man without his good name?"

"Whatever came of it?"

He shook his head, eyebrows pulled together in a distressed V. "Her mental instability was documented to the point where it was laughable that I'd be involved with her. It's too bad she couldn't find help. That was probably the worst thing to happen to my town since I've been here. Until the girls went missing."

I raised my glass. "Let's drink to the worst things that have happened to us, and hope they stay that way."

He gave a melancholy smile, tipped his glass to mine again, and said, "I'll drink to that."

About two in the morning he helped me across the lawn to the boardinghouse. We were sort of holding each other up, trying to be quiet as we stumbled into the house. "How am I ever going to make it to class in the morning?" I asked no one in particular.

"No more drinking on school nights," he drunkenly admonished me.

"Your fault. I was coerced."

"Good-night," Roy laughed, slapping me hard on the back. "Right to bed."

"Thanks, Uncle Roy," I responded, and stumbled up the stairs, dragging myself along the banister.

I heard him close the door as he left. I made my way to my room and crawled in bed. Learning that Amber had an alibi sucked, but it gave me some drunken clarity, if there is such a thing. I knew that if I was going to figure this case out, I needed to push harder. A lot harder.

I needed to up my game.

That was the last thought I had before I passed out.

* * *

*I'm in a classroom, sitting in front of the teacher's desk, copying notes from a book. A shadow falls over the pages, and I look up. Terry Roberts is standing next to me, kindly looking over my work, smiling. I'm terrible in math class, failing summer school even, and I have to stay after so she can help me catch up. The room is empty except for us; everyone else has gone home. I turn back to my work, at ease, convinced this is not the person. Walters has to be crazy to think this awesome, inspiring woman could kill a fly, let alone a student. She's been nothing but helpful and supportive of me since I started summer school. And there hasn't been one murder since the last body was found.*

*Suddenly, I feel something slip around my neck. It goes tight around my throat and jerks me back and down. I feel my body hit the floor and being dragged. I claw at the nylon noose around my neck. But it tightens and I can't breathe. I feel like I'm drowning, gasping and kicking out at anything.*

*I think I black out, because I feel myself waking up, and now I'm on a table. At first I'm confused because I don't know where I am. It's dark and cold. I look around and realize I must be in the basement somewhere. Roberts is trying to prepare something on a table. My hands are handcuffed and my feet tied with nylon pantyhose.*

*I see her preparing a syringe. She's going to start drawing my blood, slowly, until it's all gone. I'm lying on my stomach, facedown.*

*I shouldn't be shocked, because I was sent in to bait her, but I am. I'm stunned and devastated and scared. At first, I panic, try to scream, not realizing I have a rag stuffed into and duct-taped to my mouth. I can see Roberts preparing tubing and a bucket; she's going to drain all my blood. This woman who managed to gain my trust, who convinced me she was incapable of being a monster, is going to kill me. And she is going to make me watch.*

*I grab the metal ring of the handcuff on my right wrist and pull. The cuff is tight on my wrist, but what she doesn't know is that I am double-jointed and can rotate my thumb inward, flat against my palm. In defensive tactics in the academy, I used to piss off my cuffing instructors because no matter how tight they would put them on, I could get them off. I slip the cuff off and keep it open, like a hook.*

*While her back is turned, I start pulling at the nylons tying my feet together. She sees and jumps on me, screaming. I bash her in the face with the open cuff still attached to my hand, and she falls back. I struggle against the nylons, falling off the table, and they rip open. She jumps on me again, hitting and punching me. I hit back with the metal cuff, opening a big gash across her cheek and another across her forehead. She grabs both my hands and flips me onto my stomach. Terry Roberts is a big woman, close to six foot tall, and outweighs me by about twenty pounds of pure muscle from working out every day. I feel her snap the cuff all the way down into my wrist, as far as it can close, biting into my skin. As she tries to get the other cuff back on, I kick her as hard as I can manage, sending her sprawling into the table and across the dirty cement floor. I stumble as fast as I can out the door.*

And then I woke up.

The sweat had soaked through my pajama top and pants, making them cling to me. I tried to catch my breath and rubbed the scars on my forearms. If you think almost getting killed by a male serial killer is bad for your mental health, almost getting killed by a female one fucks you up far, far worse. Not that I know anyone else alive who could make the comparison. It's just an educated guess.

But as little girls, you're always told to watch out for the scary man in the bushes. Stranger danger is a man who offers you candy. They tell you to run and go find a mom with a stroller to protect you. He's the guy at the bar who puts something in your drink. Not the lady math teacher who tells you that you can do anything you set your mind to. Not the female track coach who encourages you to push your limits and try your best. She was supposed to be a safe haven, not a blood-guzzling killer.

Sitting up, I wrapped my arms around me to try to stop the shaking. Adding insult to injury was the fact that she was trying to claim acute schizophrenia as her defense. I'd seen her acting rationally every day for a month. We knew that she had followed the first two dead students on their way home and intercepted them. She'd changed her MO with me, but was smart enough to knock me out, put me in the subbasement, walk to the front entrance, and say good-bye to the school security guard. She then got in her car, pulled out of the parking lot in full view of my backup team, and managed to loop around to an unused side door, off security camera range, and get back down to the sub-basement, to me. My backup had followed her car, watching her disappear down the back door, trying to figure out if I was still in the school or not. They'd been on the phone with Bill, asking if they should break cover, when they heard me smash out the glass in the front of the building.

Terry Roberts had planned to drink my blood in the basement, then put my body in her trunk and dump me like the others. Like garbage.

She had thought of everything, planned everything, and would have murdered me if I really had been a high school girl. When they made me see a shrink, Walters had made sure it was someone he was friendly with, so the courts wouldn't know just how royally fucked up I really was. *And still am.*

Even in my alcohol-addled state, I knew that was the real reason Walters wanted me in Kelly's Falls. I was damaged goods, and you can't fake that. You could practically feel it radiating from me. And killers love damage.

Damage attracts damage.

I put my head between my scarred knees and cried.

## Wednesday, March 29<sup>th</sup>

I wish I could say I was still drunk when I woke up at seven o'clock that morning. My nightmares had burned off any alcohol residue in my system. I peeled myself out of bed and puked my guts out in the shower. I debated going to class, thought better of it, and went back to bed. My poor stomach was doing cartwheels. Dreaming about Terry Roberts just reinforced the fact that I was totally and completely fucked up from surviving a female serial killer. I don't know if it was the hangover or my frazzled nerves, but eventually I passed out.

I woke up at three thirty when Kayla texted me to see why I hadn't been to classes. Mrs. Parker had slipped a note under my door saying she would make me a light supper, seeing as I was sick and hadn't gone to college. After I responded to Kayla, the whole gang group-texted me to see why I'd missed classes and to fill me in on what had happened on campus. Nick called at about five o'clock, and I told him I was sick.

"What's wrong?" He really sounded concerned. I didn't want to worry him because he told me he had been at the information center all day, cataloging leads with some of the volunteers. He had enough on his plate without worrying about me.

"I've got a stomach flu or something. I'll be better tomorrow."

"Do you want me to bring you anything? Like ginger ale?"

He wanted to bring me ginger ale. This guy was unbelievable. "No, I'm fine. I just want to sleep it off." Boy, was that the truth.

I found out the chief wasn't feeling so hot himself. We were both like zombies when I finally dragged myself down for supper. "Looks like you two have the same bug," Mrs. Parker said, passing out the bowls of homemade chicken soup.

"I guess so." The chief had huge bags under his bloodshot eyes. He waved away the soup but kept the oyster crackers.

"What time did you come in last night, Shea?" Henry asked, shoveling his mouth full of mashed potatoes. "I heard that front door slam at two o'clock."

"I fell asleep watching a movie over at my uncle's. When I woke up, he was asleep too. I already felt horrible, so I came home."

"That's too bad," Marlene chimed in. She reached over and patted the chief's hand. "You really need someone to watch over you. A woman's touch."

A shudder ran through me as a flicker of Terry Robert's face flashed before my eyes. She used to say things needed "a woman's touch" all the time. It was one of her favorite expressions.

"I'm sure I'll live, Marlene. Right, Peter?"

"Right." Peter was making a mashed-potato mountain.

"Well, at least you're spending time together," Mrs. Parker said. "You two are all you have now. If you don't have a family, you don't have anything."

We exchanged glances, but neither of us replied. If we were all we had, we both knew we were in serious trouble.

I went back upstairs and tried to sleep it off. I kept waking up, thinking I was hearing noises. I got up around ten o'clock to try to puke again, and I looked out the window. A car was parked across the street from the boardinghouse. It was running but the lights were off. When I moved the curtain to get a better look, it sped off, without turning the lights on. It happened so fast I didn't get a look at who was driving. I got on the phone and called the chief.

"You're overreacting, Shea. Again. Who would be out front two days in a row?"

"It was a man—I know that—in a big car. Four doors. I couldn't see anything else."

"Why would someone want to park in front of your house? Are they looking at you, or is it Marlene's mad rapist she's always afraid is going to come and snatch her up?"

"That's not funny. Not when three girls are missing. Not ever. Guys don't have to worry about shit like that. Women do. Every day."

"I'm sorry. That was stupid of me to say. Was it the same car from yesterday?"

"I don't know."

"I'm right here, Shea. No one is going to try to hurt you while I'm right here."

I hesitated. "Maybe I am being paranoid." I'm sorry.

"Don't be sorry," he said. "Go to bed."

"I'm going." I started thinking maybe I *was* wrong, but I couldn't shake the feeling of someone watching me. I considered the fact that I might be losing my mind. That was always a possibility. And at that point I didn't want to rule anything out.

That would be a real inconvenience to Bill, if one of his operatives cracked. He would really regret the day he put me on the

Roberts case then. I closed my eyes and let a deep breath out. My shrink had told me I might have flashbacks. She just didn't say how often.

But it happened often.

*It's the day I stood over that body. The day I met Bill. The day my whole life got pulled out from under me like a tablecloth in a bad magic act.*

*I'm working the night shift, nine at night to seven in the morning, with my partner John Krause. He was at a family picnic all day and smells like he rolled in beer. I'm driving, of course. We're working in Delta District on the West Side. It's a warm Friday in late May, and everyone is out for the night. The streets off Grant and Ferry are packed with groups of kids walking around, looking for something to get into, itching for summer to start.*

*As I cruise down Elmwood Avenue by the college bars, I glance at John. He is fast asleep, with a newspaper pulled over his head. I smile slightly as he rustles under the sports page next to me.*

*All I can think is that at least I'm off probation.*

*I slap him on the arm. "Get up, Johnny."*

*He jumps up, whacking his head on the ceiling of the patrol car. "What? What? We get a call?"*

*"No, we're going to the coffee shop, and you're going to wake up. I can't do this solo tonight; there's too many people out."*

*"All right, just take it easy on me; no capers. My wife was on my ass all day today. I try to talk to her, and she screams at me. I try to spend time with my kids, and she asks me where was I the whole time we were living together. I tell her I was working so she could get her nails done for thirty dollars a week, and to send the kids to hockey, dance lessons, and drum lessons." He shakes his head and huffs, "Women."*

*"Yeah," I agree sarcastically. "Women."*

*I pull into the Coffee Hut on Elmwood Avenue and get us two house blends. He is still awake when I come back to the car, which is a good sign. I hand him his cup and plop down in the seat next to him. He runs his hand through his jet-black hair to get it out of his watery blue eyes. He takes a sip from the paper cup and lets it drop, resting on his expanding waistline.*

*"I should have married someone like you," he goes on. "A career woman, who makes money of her own, who doesn't need to be taken care of."*

*"I'd have shot you dead in a week." More like one day.*

*"That's not the point. The point is I was young and foolish and should have considered all my options."*

*"Sharon was pregnant when you married her."*

*"That's still not the point."*

*"Whatever." No woman could be expected to be married to John and be happy. Happy isn't his thing. He revels in his misery.*

*We answer a bar-fight call at one of the dives on Congress Street. A bunch of the locals are outside yelling and hollering, but none are actually swinging. When we show up, a few more idle threats are thrown around, and then everyone scatters. John has his trusty nightstick out; he's crabby and in no mood to break up fights manually. After the combatants wander off, he tucks his stick under his arm, we jump back into our patrol car, and John clears the call.*

*"Delta 451, I got one that just popped up."*

*"You're killing me, Ralph." Ralph is a civilian dispatcher, but years ago the two of them worked together at the General Mills plant making Cheerios.*

*"Four-five-one, head on over to the foot of Ferry Street. See a man at the entrance there. He says he wants to show the police something. Be advised, 911 says the man sounds extremely intoxicated."*

"Clear," John mumbles into the mic. He shoves it back into its clip on the dash and gripes, "Why do they even put these calls out? Some nut wants to show us his flying saucers."

The foot of Ferry Street is a small park against the river. People fish off the break wall and park in the lot to smoke pot or make out. It is dirty and dark but always full, even at night. On a night like tonight, it's especially true. There have to be about ten cars in the lot, some dimly lit from within, most parked and quiet.

A guy is standing near the mouth of the entrance, propping himself up with a fishing pole. I pull up next to him, roll down the window, and ask, "Did you call the police?"

He grabs on to my door to steady himself. "Yes, I called. Officers, I know I'm not real reliable right now, but I was down here with some of my friends drinking and fishing and stuff. They're still down on the break wall. I came back to the car to get more beer, and I saw a person pull up in a blue car. They pulled a garbage bag out of the trunk and dragged it over in there." He points to a brushy wooded area that leads back up toward the street. "I know it sounds stupid and I've had a lot to drink, but it looked funny. The car flew out of here so fast. I just wanted to see if you might check what he dumped; it looked—funny."

I glance over at John, who rolls his eyes, but I believe the kid. He is in his early twenties, wearing his fishing vest, only there are beer cans stuffed in every pocket. "I'll go take a look," I tell him.

"I'll wait here," John says, sinking down in his seat. He leans over me and tells the kid, "He was probably just illegally dumping some trash."

The caller shakes his head with drunken certainty. "No, it wasn't garbage. It had bulges."

John cocks an eyebrow. "Bulges?"

"Bulges."

*I get out and head to the general area where the kid pointed. It's overgrown with weeds and littered with junk. I kick around in the bushes, sending some rats scurrying. It is dark and wet and smells like other fishermen have relieved themselves there recently. I point my flashlight in the direction of a thick pile of garbage someone dumped far into the thicket, almost near the fence that separates the park from the bridgeworks that stretch over the river. An old couch is tipped over onto its side, spilling yellow foam over some broken chairs.*

*I step around a black puddle of who knows what and pull the couch toward me. It tips back, exposing a green plastic garbage bag, the contents of which are also spilling out.*

*Inside is a teenage girl, her head and neck exposed up to the shoulders. She has short brown hair wetly plastered to her face, her eyes mercifully closed. Her head is turned to the side, toward the river, exposing a dark gash that stretches from her ear along her jawline and across her throat. There is no blood, not a drop, despite the gaping tear that spreads across her throat like some second sick, twisted smile. I know she hasn't been dead long. Her face is a strange ashen color, her lips almost white.*

*Since I've been driving, I don't have a portable, and a wave of panic seizes me. I do not want to leave this little girl all alone while I go back to the car to radio for homicide. I stand there in the dark with my flashlight like a statue until I hear John coming up from behind.*

*"What the hell are you doing? Looking for snipes?" John comes crashing through the bushes next to me.*

*"It's a girl," I say softly. "She's dead."*

*"Oh hell." He immediately goes to touch the body, reaching out to feel for a pulse, but I grab his hand.*

*"No, it's another one. We have to protect the scene. Remember what they said about the first two they found? Don't touch the body; the FBI is handling it." I realize I'm almost babbling.*

He shakes his head, as if to clear it. "Right. You're right. You stay here with her. I'll go grab that kid who called and get the troops in." He turns to look at her again before he heads back to the car. "She's just a kid. Son of a bitch."

I end up standing there in the dark with the body for maybe five whole minutes before anyone else shows up. It seems like five hours. I can't take my eyes off her neck. The cut is clean, like it was made by a razor blade, but the wound is jagged, like he stopped every inch or so to admire his handiwork. She looks to be about sixteen, but she has a solid, athletic build. In life she probably looked like a fierce pixie, with her short hair and sharp features. In death she looks like a broken doll.

I don't hear the guys from homicide come up behind me; I am fixated on the girl. "Officer, is this how you found her?" one of the detectives asks, surveying the scene.

"The couch was tipped over her. She wasn't visible when I walked up."

"Good job, kid. Most people would have blown that drunk guy off," an older black detective tells me as he bends down over the girl. "You or your partner touch the body?"

"No."

"Good job," he repeats. "You're going to have to bring the guy who called to the homicide office pronto. We're going to need statements from all three of you." He pulls some latex gloves out of the pocket of his gray trench coat and puts them on.

His forty-year-old female partner carefully makes her way to the body, trying not to disturb the scene any more than we already have. She bends her blonde head with its dark roots close to her coworker's and says, "Those FBI guys are going to have a field day with this. What's your name?" She squats down to get a better look at the body.

*"Shea O'Connor."*

*"Well, Shea O'Connor."* She tilts her head back to peer up at me. *"She looks just like you."*

And Bill Walters must think that, too, when he chases me down the hall later that night.

## Friday, March 31st

I took a mental health day on Thursday, turning off my phone and letting the text messages and voice mails pile up. I binge-watched sitcom episodes on Netflix and tried to get my brain straight. I told Mrs. Parker if anyone was looking for me, I was still sick in bed, which was at least partially true. I was sick in the head in bed. My shrink had told me I'd need blank days where nothing happened. Turns out, except for letting Bill know I was alive, I could be exceptionally blank.

My return to campus on Friday yielded the scoop on the big birthday celebration. As we sat around the student union during the only twenty-five minutes we were all free at the same time on Fridays, Maddie, Jenna, and Kayla informed me that Joe Styles had shown up at Kayla's house drunk. Kayla was still fuming about it.

"I can't believe he stood there on my lawn and told me how much he loved Skyler and that we really didn't even know her."

Maddie agreed. "We should pay someone to come and kick the shit out of him. Do you know anyone in Buffalo who does that stuff?"

I had been listening while doing some makeup work from the day I missed, trying to let them speak as if I wasn't there. "Oh, what? No. I don't know anyone who would do something like that.

I could see him watching our table from across the room, incensing them even more. "He's just trying to piss us off," Jenna piped up, looking over at him. He raised his little milk carton at us and smirked.

"Dick," Kayla muttered, and turned away.

That was when I noticed the bandages. All three of them had little white squares taped to their forearms in the exact same spot. "What's this?" I tapped Kayla's with my pen.

"We went to Wicked Ink out on Route 19 last night," Maddie said, leaning over and peeling back her bandage. "I got a flower, Kayla got a heart, and Jenna got a butterfly." The simple line drawing was done in black. In the circle center of the flower, the missing girls' initials were inked in script.

Kayla and Jenna showed me theirs as well. The skin around the tattoos was still an angry red, the black ink raised and glossy with the greasy stuff they give you to put on new tats.

"Wow," I said, touching Kayla's gently with my fingertips. "These are really amazing."

"We just wanted something, you know? Something to remind us of them until they come home." Jenna retaped the bandage back in place.

"Mine itches like crazy," Kayla said, rubbing around, but not on her heart.

"That's because it's your first one," Maddie said, slapping her hand away. "You're not used to it yet." Maddie had an entire poem in French script down one shoulder and an infinity symbol in white ink across her left wrist.

"Do you have any tattoos?" Kayla asked me, trying to dig under her tape with a fingernail.

"No. Not yet," I admitted. I had almost gotten one two years ago at the Delta District summer picnic after drinking all day. Three of the guys brought me to Midnight Ink on Elmwood Avenue so I could get the Superman symbol tattooed on my bicep, except I wanted a *D* where the *S* should be in the middle. Thankfully, Andre, the artist, refused to do it because I was so drunk. I came by on my next work night and thanked him profusely.

"I want to get another one on my calf," Maddie told me. "You can come with me when I go. You know they can cover up scars, right?" She pointed to the nasty red line peeking out of my long-sleeved T-shirt at my wrist. I tugged the sleeve down, covering it. I tried to hide my scars from my new friends, I guess with only mixed results.

"What did your mom say when she saw it?" I asked Kayla, changing the subject. "Did she freak?"

She shrugged. "What can she say? I'm eighteen. It's not like I got a huge skull plastered across my chest. I think it's pretty."

"It is," I reassured her. "I just didn't know how your mom would be about it." *Since she rarely leaves her house and all that,* but I didn't say it.

"My mom has three tattoos. So she really can't say anything, you know?" Maddie pointed out. "I got my first one last year with Skyler when we graduated. Joe was even there with us. He got one, too. Sometimes, when they weren't fighting, they were a riot to hang out with. They were up for anything." She looked over at Joe's table. "That's why it sucks so bad that he turned out to be a total douchebag."

\* \* \*

Nick called me as soon as I got home from campus to see what I was doing. I told him I was going to the movies with Kayla and the girls but I could meet him after it was over. He told me okay, that Zach was in town and that they would come and get Kayla and me at ten o'clock. I asked him what he had been doing Thursday night, while I was busy blanking out. I had to make up investigative time as well as schoolwork.

"Father O'Halloran came over unexpectedly. He wanted to talk to my mom. She made me entertain him for a while. He didn't leave until almost ten o'clock. I just wanted to sleep."

"What did he want?"

"Actually, he didn't want anything. He just wanted to know if the chief had any news or if we'd heard from the Feds at all. He's been really good to my mom, so when he drops in like that, we usually indulge him."

"You have to indulge him?"

"I know, right?" He blew out an exasperated breath into the phone. "You would think he lost a kid sometimes."

"Well, don't be late tonight, no matter who shows up, okay?" I told him.

"I got it, boss," he said, and clicked off.

The whole way to the show, Maddie kept reminding me and Kayla of how lucky we were. "They are so hot. I cannot believe you two are going out with the two most attractive guys this town has ever spawned."

"I'm not going out with Zach. He texts me, but he hasn't even called me once. Not like Nick, who calls Shea every day."

"He doesn't call me every day," I protested.

"Almost."

The theater was packed. There just isn't anything else to do in Kelly's Falls on a Friday night. We went to see a new horror movie, but I didn't pay much attention to it. I was too worried about seeing Nick. I was beginning to really like him.

A big problem I have with going to the movies is that if I drink soda, I have to go to the bathroom multiple times during the show. The movie had about ten minutes left when I got up for the fourth time.

"Again?" Jenna crabbed, getting up so I could get out.

"Remind me to let you sit on the end next time," Maddie told me as I pushed past her.

The lobby was deserted except for a few kids playing video games over in the corner. I went to the bathroom, fixed my hair and makeup, and came back out. Joe Styles was standing there in the lobby smiling at me.

"What are you doing here?" I asked, trying to brush past him.

He stepped over and blocked my way. "Looking for you. I was in the movie and I saw you get up."

"Well, I want to see the end, so why don't we go back?" I was still trying to get by him.

"Why do you act like I'm going to hurt you or something? Why do you always give me a hard time?"

"Because you annoy me."

He smiled. "Maybe." He was coming toward me, backing me up until he had me effectively pinned. He straightened one arm out, blocking me in, leaning heavily against the wall. "But maybe you think I kidnapped those girls like everyone else thinks? Maybe you think I had something to do with it too?" he said softly, tilting his body toward mine.

"No," I said, squaring up with him. I wouldn't let him intimidate me. "That's not what I think."

His voice was quiet and strong, but he was smiling. It was almost hypnotic. I couldn't take my eyes from his. I had to stay, to listen. He was telling me something important, the only way he knew how.

He put his other arm out, palm to the wall. "Maybe I did do it. Maybe I kidnapped those girls. Maybe I took them into the woods and sucked the life out of them like a fucking vampire." His face was an inch from mine. "Maybe I hurt them one by one, then maybe I strangled them and watched their eyes as they died, and I got off on it."

I braced my hands against his chest. I wanted to shove him away, he was too close, but I needed to hear this. When he leaned forward, his face was so near mine that I thought he was going to kiss me. His breath washed through my mouth.

Then he jerked away and put his lips to my ear. "But maybe I didn't have anything to do with it at all. Maybe I'm the one getting screwed."

I saw a hand come down on his shoulder and spin him around.

It was Nick, coming to pick me up. He bashed Joe in the face, Knocking him onto the lobby carpet.

Joe looked up, a trickle of blood coming from his eyebrow, and laughed at him. "You didn't have to do that, man. I was done with her anyway."

Nick looked at me, then back at Joe, and walked out of the lobby. I chased after him. Zach was out in the parking lot, waiting in his ride. "Nick!" I called as he charged away from me. "Nick, please!"

Nick walked over and told Zach, "Grab Kayla. I'm going home."

"What's wrong?" Zach tried to open the door, but Nick pushed it shut.

"No," he told him. "I'm gone."

"Please," I pleaded. "Please talk to me." I followed him to his truck, and he finally turned around. His face was twisted in fury.

"I was starting to trust you. And I come here and find you with the guy that probably killed my sister."

"Please listen to me. It wasn't what you think."

His hands were balled into fists at his sides. "I think I saw him practically kissing you in the middle of a movie theater."

Now I had him by the arm, pulling him back to look at me. "Just listen to me. Please." He stopped, his breath coming in ragged huffs of rage. "Please."

Sitting together on the bumper of his truck, I told him exactly what had happened. I was still holding on to his arm, but he was sitting as far away from me as he could. I tried to explain the way Joe had tried to get into my head. The more I explained, the more the gap seemed to lessen.

"I'm going to kill that kid. I mean it, I'm going to kill him."

He still wouldn't look at me. Hands clenched in front of him, between his legs, Nick was staring straight ahead into the parking lot.

"Are you mad at me?" It sounded so weak and immature, like a little girl asking for forgiveness for stealing a cookie.

He exhaled and looked up at the starless sky. "Yes. No. I don't know. I can't say what you can do. We barely even know each other. But I hate that guy. And I won't go out with anyone who hangs out with him too."

"I'm not hanging out with him. I don't want to. I'm so sorry about what happened, but it wasn't my fault. I wouldn't be here asking if that wasn't true."

"You don't have to ask." He put his arm around me and took a deep breath. "Just don't play games."

My self-loathing hit a new all-time high. I was playing the biggest game of all.

I could hear Kayla and the rest of the gang come pouring out of the movies looking for me. I watched Zach pull his truck up alongside them right outside the big double doors and motion to them.

"Get in," Nick told me, helping me off the back bumper. We hopped into his truck and took off before anyone could question us. After driving around for a while and listening to the radio in silence, he parked by the Hoyt Bridge. We watched the river rush by in the moonlight. After what seemed like an eternity, he said, "I'm sorry I hit Joe. Well, not sorry I hit him, but sorry I made a scene like that. You can be with whoever you want."

"Nick, I told you it wasn't like that. He was just—messing with my head. I don't know how to describe it any better than that." I wanted to say Joe was telling me that everyone was looking at him when they should be looking somewhere else. That no matter how many times he said it, no one listened, not even me, until right then.

"Olivia used to tell me what he used to do to Skyler, hitting her and making her do things. I couldn't believe a girl would go out with a guy who would treat her that way."

"You'd be surprised what some girls put up with."

"The funny thing is, I'm more mad at myself for caring so much." He laughed and made a helpless gesture. "I've only known you for what? A week and a half?"

I reached over and grabbed his hand. "I like you too."

He kissed me, and pretty soon I thought we were going to go a little further than I'd planned. But Nick was a gentleman and stopped short of anything particularly exciting. When we finally pulled away from each other, I lay in his arms with my feet curled up on the seat. I could hear his heart beating and feel the soft cotton of his shirt against my skin. The one thought that kept going around in my mind was that he didn't even know my real name.

"Tell me about your sister," I said, putting my head on his shoulder. The wind had picked up outside, and it was getting chilly in the truck.

"Olivia is something else." Even though I wasn't looking at his face, I could tell he was smiling. "She's so smart; she was number one in her class. Smart and pretty. All my friends at school wanted me to set them up with her. I never did, though. I always thought she'd marry a doctor or a lawyer just because she is the type that would impress them with her class. She had a lot of friends. Hell, they're all your friends now. She and Kayla were really close, like sisters almost." He started to twirl a strand of my hair around his finger as he talked. "Emma was her best friend, though. She wouldn't say two words to anyone, that Emma. She'd see me and clam right up. I guess that's why her and Olivia were friends. She was someone Olivia could trust. Emma would take a secret to the grave. But Skyler"—he paused and looked at me, like he wanted me to understand—"she was always trouble. My mom didn't like Olivia hanging around with her. Maybe it was because of Joe and the things he was into. Maybe she thought Skyler would drag her down."

"That's a mom thing," I said. "My mom was convinced my best friend in eighth grade was into the occult because she brought tarot cards down into my basement."

He laughed, a real laugh, not the strained bitter chortles he'd been choking out. "Maybe my mom was too hard on Skyler. But the three of them, with Kayla, Maddie, and Jenna, were inseparable. Those six have been friends since preschool. I just thank God Kayla didn't come home with them and stayed at the party. That's why I don't believe they ran away, because Kayla would have gone too."

"You'll find Olivia," I told him. "You will."

"I remember when I was about ten and she was eight. We were playing in the backyard on the swing set. It was one of those big plastic ones with the fort on top. I chased her up there, pretending to be a monster, and she wouldn't come down. I was so afraid my parents would get mad at me because it was almost dinnertime, and she was sitting up there crying because I scared her. Finally, I crawled up and sat with her. We stayed there together until my mom came out looking for us, and we both got in trouble for being late." He wiped his sleeve against his eyes. "It's still there—the playground, way in back by the trees. I keep looking in the top part, like maybe she'll be there. Hiding. It's stupid. I know."

"It's not stupid," I told him. "It's hope."

We sat there in silence, listening to the wind for a while. His fingers interlaced with mine as he stared ahead, not blinking. I wished so many things for him. That he knew what had really happened. That he knew his sister loved him too. That I could help him heal, in some small way.

He took me home before it got late, walking me to my door, waiting for me to lock myself inside. Watching him pull away from the curb, all I could think was that I had to help him.

I had to.

I stayed up and thought about everything that had happened that night. Joe's sick assertion of innocence and what Nick had told me about Kayla. That whatever the reason the girls had been taken, the only reason Kayla wasn't was that she hadn't been with them. Whether the kidnapper had wanted one girl or all three, Kayla might know why, whether she realized it or not. I knew from very recent experience that the girls in this clique told each other everything and kept secrets from everyone else. If this was not a random crime, if someone had a reason to kidnap them, Kayla might be keeping that secret.

**Saturday, April 1st**

I called Bill first thing in the morning with my new idea about Kayla. He had had the same idea himself. "I brought that up in the beginning of the investigation. In all of her interviews, she denied any knowledge of anything that would lead to their disappearance. That was one of my main reasons to send you in. I figured they wouldn't talk to us, so we'd see if you could make them talk to you." I could hear him shuffling through papers on the other end of the line. "I'm looking for one of Kayla's personal interviews right now. Okay, here it is."

He paused to go through it. I could hear him flipping through more papers.

"Well?" I prompted him.

"Interesting. There were so many interviews with friends and relatives and schoolmates that hers didn't stick out in my head, though I suppose it should have. I asked all the girls that hung around with our lost ladies this, and I quote, 'Was there anything that happened recently or was said, even if it was a rumor, that might make you think someone might want to abduct or hurt any of these girls?'"

"What was her answer?"

"Joe Styles. Actually, the bulk of our respondents that knew of the situation said the only thing they could think of was the graveyard incident involving Joe Styles."

I took a long sip from the homemade iced tea I had grabbed from the fridge earlier. It was warm now, but still good. "He didn't do it."

"What?"

"Joe Styles didn't have anything to do with it." I told him about our little incident at the movie theater. I was still lying in my bed with my pajamas on. I propped myself up on my arm and related the whole story to him. "I think he really loved Skyler, in his own warped way, and I think he did that to tell me he didn't do it. Like he's got to prove it now."

"He's got a pretty sick way of proving it," Bill countered.

I rolled over onto my back. "You had to see him, to hear him. Everyone thinks he has something to do with it. I think he knows he's being used. I know he knows it."

"You think someone is setting him up?"

"No, no, no. Not like that. I think someone likes that the attention is diverted onto him. He's got an alibi. Everyone at that party saw him passed out, and yet everyone still thinks he's in on it somehow."

"So did you, at first."

"I know."

"What now, kid?"

"Can I have the files? I mean everything."

"Everything includes hundreds of statements, reports, background checks and the like. Everything takes up a lot of space."

"Is any of it on disks?"

"I can't believe you just asked me that. No, we send smoke signals now."

"I mean, can you put it all on one or two thumb drives and send it to me? Or burn it on a disk, or better yet, put it in the cloud for me? Including your offender profile."

He paused, seeming to consider my request. "Not everything, and you can't have the profile. I sent you there to see what you could dig up, not to try to fit a person to my offender profile. Look, I'll copy what I can and send it to you, but I think I gave you the most relevant information in your initial package."

"I know, but those were compiled and gone over by strangers. I might connect with something they missed."

"I'll go along with that. It will take a couple days, and don't expect miracles."

I hung up with him and called Kayla. She wanted to know what had happened when I didn't come back to the movie theater, and then in the parking lot when me and Nick took off. "I must have sent you a hundred texts," she huffed.

Actually, it was fourteen, but I went over the whole ordeal again just for her.

"I can't believe Joe did that to you. And I can't believe Nick punched him out. Nick never loses his shit like that." She was gushing into the phone. This was obviously hot material for the gossip tree.

"I had to do a lot of explaining and groveling. I mean, if I were him, I probably would have just said 'Forget you' and left me there."

"I'm glad he listened to you. I think he really likes you." She bit into something crunchy, filling my ears with the sound of chewing. "What are you doing tonight? Maddie and Jenna want to go to Bella Fisher's house. She's having that big party. You want to go?"

"Sure. What are you going to wear?" I always liked to throw something like that in. Insecurity and uncertainty were very hip among my new friends.

"I don't know yet. I'll probably swing over and grab something of yours. Maybe your black tank with my red bra. Or your purple bra."

I should've seen that coming. Half my wardrobe was on loan. But I was going to have to start drawing the line at lending out my underwear. "Okay."

"You know." She paused, and I knew she was checking to make sure her mom wasn't around. "I should stay over at your house tonight; that way we can stay out late and bring the guys back to your place."

"Sorry, no overnight male guests. It's one of my rules."

She made some comment about me never getting any as long as I lived. I just laughed; I hadn't been getting any prior to my teenage return.

"Are you going to ask Nick to go?"

"I don't think he'd want to hang around anywhere Joe might show up."

"You never know. Just mention it to him. And mention to him to bring Zach. I'll text you later. I have to go and eat now."

I said good-bye and hung up with her. Nick called, but he didn't want to go to Bella's. He said he was going to Alfred State to party with his friends.

"Don't forget about me for some Alfred girl," I warned him.

"I don't think I will, but thanks for suggesting it."

"When are you going to be home?"

"Tomorrow. I have to go to church. My parents have a cow if I don't go with them, so I better stay sober tonight. Well, partly sober, anyway."

I told him to give me a call when he got back. I really was kind of nervous that he'd hook up with some sorority girl. I was feeling jealous, possessive, and insecure—the college-years trifecta. Especially because of the show Joe had put on at the movies the night before. And that was not me at all.

Kayla had her mother's car for once, so she picked me up for the party, but not before she and Maddie raided my closet. I made sure to hide anything that might give me away before they came over. While they were pouring through my clothes, I heard a knock on my door. It was the chief. He glanced over my shoulder at the girls. "Can I talk to you in the hall?"

"Sure, Uncle Roy. You remember Maddie and Kayla, don't you?"

He nodded. "Of course. Hi, ladies. I just have to steal her away for one second."

They waved some clothes at him and turned back to my closet. I closed the door behind me and followed him out into the hall. "What's up?"

"You requested the whole case file? Arrest records? Why didn't you ask me?"

"Bill called you."

"He wanted some of my paperwork. Look, why didn't you come to me with this first?"

"I just hadn't seen you. I didn't see it as so immediate. Relax."

"I want to know everything. Everything. Don't skip over me. Do you understand that?"

"I got it."

He looked over my shoulder at my door and said, "We'll talk about this in the morning. Go out and have fun with your girlfriends."

"We'll hug it out tomorrow, I promise," I told him. Henry poked his head out of his room, looked at the both of us, and popped it back in.

"Tomorrow," the chief told me sternly. "I mean it." He turned and went down the stairs.

I walked back to my room and opened the door. Kayla and Maddie were both wearing my clothes.

I put my hands on my hips. "Are you guys done pillaging my wardrobe?"

"I love your outfits. We have got to go shopping in Buffalo soon. I mean, like, next week." Maddie was looking at herself in the full-length mirror on the inside of my closet door. She had on a pair of my jeans and one of my nicest bell-sleeved sweaters.

"It costs a lot of money to dress this good," I informed them, hoping they'd take the hint. Kayla was pulling on a pair of my favorite black leggings. She had my high black boots stacked next to her.

"Do not scuff those," I warned as she zipped the left one up over her calf.

"Where'd you get all the money?" she asked.

"My parents' insurance." The best way to change the subject was still to bring up my supposedly dead parents.

"Did Jenna get the beer?" Kayla asked Maddie.

She whipped out her phone. "I'll double-check." Thumbs flying, she texted Jenna and got an immediate reply.

"We're good. She got it."

I went into the bathroom to change so they wouldn't see my scars. I'm so self-conscious about them; I never wear anything sleeveless or a tank top without a sweater to cover my arms. I hadn't worn shorts or a skirt without opaque tights since I got sliced up. The girls had seen a little, but nowhere near all the damage I'd sustained.

I put on an old Notre Dame sweatshirt and a pair of my favorite ripped jeans because they were wearing all my good clothes. I really didn't care how I looked because I knew I wouldn't be seeing Nick.

Bella lived over in Nick's neighborhood. We had to stop and pick up Jenna, who had our twelve-pack of beer, before going over to the party. "Hi guys," she told us, struggling to get the beer into the back seat with her.

"How much do we owe you?" I asked, fishing into my back pocket for money.

She waved her hand. "My uncle left this in the fridge out in the garage last weekend. My parents totally forgot he even brought it."

"You didn't get to use your fake ID?" Kayla took a bottle, then handed one to me. "She has the best fake ID. She got it in Toronto."

"Yeah, but I have to drive two towns over to use it," she complained. "Everyone knows me around here."

Bella's house was on a dead-end street set way back, almost into the woods, making it the perfect party spot. It was pretty cold out, but people were outside, all over her lawn, smoking or vaping. We parked our car and strolled in.

Joe was there, with his usual crowd of hangers-on. He was sitting on the stairs in the hallway so he could watch who was coming in.

He was drinking a beer, leisurely slouched back as if he didn't have a care in the world. Wearing his trademark black leather jacket with sunglasses, he tipped them up at me with a smile as soon as I walked in, revealing a nasty-looking black eye. "Hi, Shea."

"Go to hell," Kayla growled, and pushed me forward. We filed into the living room, where the main bulk of people were hanging out. Maddie went to get ice from the kitchen so we could keep our beer cold. Kayla was still fuming about Joe.

"I'm glad Nick punched him. He deserved it."

"Don't let him get to you. He's just trying to get attention," I told her, turning sideways to maneuver through the crowded hallway.

"What I don't understand is why it doesn't bother you. He doesn't leave you alone."

"Jerks like that want you to hate them," I pointed out, ducking under some really tall guy's arm. "It gives them power over you. Look at you—all he has to do is smile at you and you go nuts."

She stopped, leaning up against the wall. The rest of us filled in around her. The house was too crowded, too hot, and noisy. "It's been like that since the night Olivia and the rest disappeared. He and Skyler got into a fight, almost a physical fight, because he said she picked us over him. But I say friends are more important over guys any day."

"They almost got into a fight?"

Jenna nodded, her black glasses slipping down her nose. "If Kayla hadn't stepped in between them, Joe would have punched her. I was so scared. Then I thought he was going to hit Kayla. He was that drunk and mad."

"While we were arguing, Skyler, Olivia, and Emma snuck out. Joe ran around the house looking for them, then crashed on the couch. I went home with Jenna, and the rest is freaking history."

Kayla grabbed her yellow plastic cup filled with ice from Maddie and dumped the rest of her beer in. That kind of put an end to my other-woman theory of the argument. It also confirmed my belief that it was only an accident that Kayla hadn't been with them. Or Maddie or Jenna, for that matter.

Amber showed up, but she stayed at a distance, hovering around Joe. "Look at her," Kayla sneered. "She works in a salon, and her hair looks like she stuck a fork in a light socket."

"And someone should tell her there's a fine line between smoky eye makeup and raccoon face," Jenna joined in. Maddie and I snickered into our beer. Ah, the bitchiness of women toward other women.

The party ended around one thirty when my fake uncle busted it.

Everyone was yelling that if they had to go, so did I. The chief walked up to me and said in his sternest voice, "Go home now, Shea. I'll talk to you in the morning. It's late."

He glanced around the room and added, "That goes for the rest of you. The party is over." There were groans and hoots and catcalls, but everyone went.

The girls dropped me off at the boardinghouse. I couldn't sleep, so I sat up making notes on the case. I came to some conclusions. I needed to see the crime scene. I needed to see the inside of Olivia Stansfield's house. And I needed to get some answers from Kayla. I just didn't know how to ask the right questions.

## Sunday, April 2nd

I slept until noon, when the chief woke me up. He wanted me to come over to discuss this new angle I had. I was tired, so I told him I'd try to make it over after dinner. I went back to bed and was loving every second of my extra sleep when Nick called around one.

"How was your party?" he asked.

"How was yours?" I countered.

"Okay, I guess. Typical college party." Then he asked what he really wanted to know. "Was Joe Styles over at Bella's house?"

"He was, but I didn't talk to him and he didn't talk to me. He's got a big, juicy black eye, in case you were interested."

"Good."

It was my turn to expose my insecurities. "Did you meet any sleazy sorority girls experimenting with their newfound sexual freedom?"

He laughed. "There were plenty of those. Zach hooked up with some girl he met. Don't tell Kayla; it'll break her heart."

"And what were you doing while he was hooking up?"

"Honestly? Fending off this six-foot-four German exchange student who would not leave me alone. I kept going to the bathroom to get away from her, but she'd wait outside. It was horrible. I had a rotten time. I couldn't drink because I had to drive back early today. Zach left me with Helga the Horrifying, while he got lucky with some chick into tattoos and body piercing."

"I almost feel sorry for you."

"Yeah, I thought so." It was good to hear the easy way we had fallen back into step. "Do you want to come over for dinner tonight?" The reason I ask is we're having turkey, and I thought of you."

I smirked into the phone. "Amusing. What time?"

"I'll pick you up at six."

When we were done, I had to call the chief back and tell him I had to cancel our meeting. He just about had a kitten.

"Don't you think this is more important than a date with Nick? Aren't you getting your priorities mixed here?"

"Gee, Chief, I've got a chance to go to the crime scene tonight. When were you going to provide me with that opportunity? When are you going to knock on their door and ask, 'Do you mind if I troop my niece through your lovely home so she can get a real good look around?'"

He was silent for a moment. "Okay, you're right on this one. I didn't think of it that way. I'm anxious to hear what you think you've got on the case."

"It can wait one more night. I have a feeling I'm getting really close to something." I didn't want to let him in on my theory that Kayla might be holding out on vital information. He was likely to drag her into his police station, and then we'd get nowhere.

"As soon as you feel like you can squeeze me in, I'd love to hear this new theory of yours."

"I told you, tomorrow. We'll get together tomorrow, I promise."

I hung up with him, took another nap, and got up around five. All that getting-up-for-college crap was really cutting into my sleep.

I put on a white cotton shirt with tiny embroidered flowers on the collar and sleeves and a pair of relaxed-fit dark-washed jeans and my black shoe boots. I wanted to look sweet, the way mothers like, so I put my hair in a ponytail and went easy on the makeup. I knew she had seen me at church, but church can make anyone look good.

Nick pulled up exactly at six. I was waiting in the hall while everyone else sat around the dinner table. "Have a good time," Mrs. Parker yelled out to me.

"Be home early," the chief added happily. Apparently they were having beef stew, his favorite. And he didn't have to deal with me, also his favorite.

I ran down the walk and hopped into Nick's truck. He leaned over and gave me a kiss hello. "I've got something for you," he told me.

"Oh yeah? What?"

"I got this for you at Alfred." He opened up a paper bag on the seat between us and pulled out a sweat shirt. He handed it over and I held it up. It had *ALFRED STATE* in paisley lettering across it.

"I love it. Thank you, Nick," I squealed, and threw my arms around his neck. I gave him a quick kiss.

"Hey, hey," he laughed, untangling himself from me. "It's just a sweat shirt, but I'm glad you like it."

"I love it," I repeated, staring at it. And I did love it. I sank back into his seat, clutching the shirt. "So how was church this morning?"

"It was church. Same old, same old. Father O'Halloran asked me about you today. I thought that was kind of odd."

That was odd. "What did he ask about me?"

"If I was still seeing you. I thought that was a weird question to ask."

"He's probably just curious. I know he worries about you," I told him, and he dropped the subject.

We drove to his house with me hanging on to the sweat shirt like it was the Hope Diamond. That little gesture kind of proved to me that he really did like me. I suppose I should have been worried, because I knew I was starting something I couldn't finish. I guess I was pushing away the fact that someday soon my detail would be over and I would go back to Buffalo. And no one here would ever know who I really was. Nick would never know who I really was. But at least for a little while I could enjoy my role and be happy with Nick.

All that shifted into my mental notebook as soon as we drove up. I realized as we pulled in that we were parked pretty much how Emma's car had been parked, so I was seeing the house as they would have seen it.

The Stansfield house had one unique property to it: the hedges around the lawn from both sides made it impossible to see a car parked in the driveway unless you were directly on the street in front of it. The house and the porch were perfectly visible but not the driveway, which would explain why no one saw the car the girls drove off in.

Nick led me down the driveway to the side door and into the kitchen. His mother was taking dishes out of the microwave. She wiped her hands on her jeans and smiled. "Hi, Shea. It's nice to see you again. Do you want something to drink?"

"Don't worry about us, Mom. I'll get it," Nick told her as he walked over to the fridge. There was a small copy of the girls' missing poster stuck to the front of it with a magnet.

"It smells great, Mrs. Stansfield. Can I help you with anything?" I asked.

"Oh no. Why don't you two go into the living room until it's ready and keep Nick's dad company?"

She took a sip from a wineglass she had perched on the windowsill above the sink.

Nick handed me a glass of soda. "She likes to be the Napoleon of our kitchen."

"Go on," she said, waving us out. The kitchen opened up to the living room through a set of saloon doors. The first thing I noticed was the huge picture window and the view overlooking the street.

"You have a beautiful home," I said, looking around. Mr. Stansfield was sitting on the armchair in front of the TV. He had taken off the tie and jacket he had worn to church and was lounging in his shirt sleeves and stocking feet.

"Thank you," he replied, sitting up a little. "Make yourself at home, please." I sat on the couch next to Nick. The room was a shrine to the Stansfield kids. There were football pictures, scholastic awards, cheerleading photos, and newspaper articles everywhere. Over the fireplace, across from the window, was a family portrait taken a few years earlier. Nick's hair was longer and he looked thinner. Olivia looked happy, smiling out from the frame. I tried not to stare at the photo, but the more I looked around, the more the perfect house betrayed itself. On the coffee table were papers and pamphlets from different missing-children's organizations. On the mantel, a small silver-framed picture of Olivia, maybe her senior portrait, had a yellow ribbon tied around it.

"How do you like Kelly's Falls?" Mr. Stansfield asked. I could tell he could've cared less what I thought of Kelly's Falls but was trying to make polite conversation.

"It's a lot different from Buffalo, but I like it. I've made some good friends."

"Nick says you hang around with Olivia's friends. They're a nice group of girls."

I nodded. "They've all been really nice to me since I've moved here."

He ran his fingers through his gray hair with a strained gesture. "I always liked Olivia's friends. All of them except that Skyler—"

"Dad," Nick cut in sharply.

"She's always been trouble. If Olivia had just stayed away from her—"

"Dad, you promised. I'll leave."

Mr. Stansfield held up his hand. "No, you're right. I'm sorry." He looked at me. "I'm sure you didn't come here to go through this mess with us. It's very difficult." He swallowed hard, his Adam's apple bobbing up and down in his throat. Nick stared straight ahead. I reached over and grabbed his hand, letting him know I was there for him.

"It's fine, Mr. Stansfield," I told him. "Really, I understand."

"Stephen, will you help me with the turkey, please?" Mrs. Stansfield called from the kitchen. He got up and went to help his wife.

"I'm sorry," Nick said in a low voice. He was sitting stiffly on the couch next to me with my hand between his. I could feel the tension coming off him in waves.

"Nick, you can't pretend nothing is wrong just because I'm here."

"You don't understand. We walk around like zombies, jumping at our phones. My mom cleans the whole house, every day. She scrubs the floors, everything. She'll get up in the middle of the night and clean out the oven. Except Olivia's room. No one can even go in there. When the FBI guys went through it, she had a hysterical fit. My dad just blames everyone, especially himself.

He thinks if only she hadn't been with Skyler; if I hadn't been at school; if he'd been home instead of out."

"You just want Olivia back and you miss her, that's all," I whispered, trying to keep my voice low so his parents didn't hear.

He seemed to think about that and smiled sadly. "Like you, how you don't talk about your parents. You try to be so strong. Sometimes I wish you'd talk to me about them. Maybe just so I'd know I'm not the only one who's ever felt so helpless."

"Dinner!" his mom called. I exhaled a silent breath of relief, glad to end the conversation there.

Dinner started out pleasant. Mrs. Stansfield went on and on about the talk of the town, current events, just about anything that didn't matter. I got the feeling she was close to hysterical half the time. My suspicion was confirmed when she served dessert. Nick went to grab the piece of chocolate cake she cut for him and dropped his plate, smashing it on the floor.

There was a horrible silence.

Mrs. Stansfield stood up, screaming at Nick. "Look at that mess! Look at it! My best china ruined. It's all ruined." She grabbed her napkin and tried frantically to wipe the icing off the floor. She was ranting and raving, sending pieces of cake and broken plate everywhere. "Everything's ruined."

Mr. Stansfield dropped down beside her and grabbed her by the shoulders. "Alice. Alice!"

She seemed to snap out of it and burst into tears. Mr. Stansfield wrapped his arms around his wife and held her. Nick got up from the table and ran out the kitchen door. Not knowing what else to do, I ran out after him.

"Nick, wait," I called after him as he got into his truck. He opened the passenger's side door and let me in. Jamming his foot on the gas pedal, he sped off.

"I have to get away from that house," he said in a high, angry voice.

"Do you want to go to my house? You could come upstairs and calm down. I'm a little scared for you right now."

\* \* \*

Every Sunday night at eight, Henry, Mrs. Parker, Marlene, and Peter watched a movie together on Netflix in the back room. They didn't hear us come in. I had Nick park down the road, and we crept up the front staircase. Henry's room was closest to mine, but he was half deaf, so I didn't worry about being caught.

Nick paced the room. "I can't take much more of this, Shea. They're driving me crazy. I just want to know where Olivia is. I don't care about anything else. I just want to know what happened to my sister." He sank down onto my bed, burying his face in his hands. "I'm so sick of being perfect. My whole life my parents have orchestrated these perfect personas for me and Olivia. The perfect son, the perfect daughter, in the perfect house in the perfect small town." He looked up at me. "I'm not perfect. All the gentleman crap I do? Holding the door, taking you out; don't think for a second I'm not trying to figure out how to get into your pants."

"You don't have to—"

"And neither was Olivia. She was gay, you know."

"What?" I couldn't even begin to try to mask my shock.

"That stuff I told you about not wanting to set her up with my friends? It was because she was gay. I was the only one who knew. That's why she went so far away to school. To get away from here and finally be herself."

"None of her friends knew?"

He shook his head. "No way. It was hard enough being the only Asian girl in town, let alone the only gay Asian girl. She didn't want another label. She was tired of being perfect, too. We used to Skype, when she got to school. She was so happy. She was finally meeting people that accepted her for who she really was. She was making new friends, going to art galleries, plays—all the things she dreamed about. As herself, and not the version my mother constructed."

"And you never told the police when she disappeared? That she was gay?"

"Why would I? No one around here knew." He gave a bitter laugh. "And even here I doubt someone would kidnap her and her friends for being gay."

I wanted to say that people get murdered for less all the time. I wanted to jump up and grab my phone and call Bill. I wanted to ask if she'd ever dumped a guy who might have suspected. That's what I wanted to do. Because I'm a horrible person who hears someone they care about spill their most personal secrets and gets excited inside, because I think I just found a clue.

Instead I sat down next to him and put my hand on his leg. I could at least pretend to be a decent person.

"I'm so sorry, Nick. I don't know what else I can say except that I'm so sorry all this happened to you."

"I should just go back to school. The semester isn't even half-way over. I can worry there just as much as I can here."

"Your parents need you here. Even if you're pissed at them."

He nodded helplessly. "I know, I know. I'd love to just grad-uate in June and take off. Me and you could hop on a plane, go to India or Hong Kong or Australia." He looked up and caught my eyes. "But I forget sometimes how young you are. How you still have three years of college left. I forget because you help me, I think. I'm glad you're here. I really think I care about you a lot."

He leaned in, kissing me so softly it sent a chill down my spine. Easing me down onto the bed, his hand slipped up the back of my shirt, fingers tracing my spine, while the other cupped my face. I tugged his shirt out of his jeans and up over his head. His hands came down on either side of me, suspending him above me in the moonlight. I could see every muscle in his chest tensed, anticipating, as I ran my hand along his abs to his thigh. He leaned back, drinking me in with his eyes. "You're so beautiful," he whispered.

I was filled up with Nick, with his eyes and his lips and his voice. My whole body was responding to his touch, like an ache only he could heal. He slipped my shirt off, dropping it to the floor next to his.

I shivered as his naked chest brushed against mine. He kissed my neck, trailing along my collarbone, down, down, down. I arched my back against the onslaught, but the invitation just aroused him more. His body was flush with mine; the only thing between us was his boxers and my thin panties. He couldn't hold himself back anymore. We were both too far gone for that. My white panties slid down my thighs as his boxer briefs fell off the side of the bed. He fumbled getting his wallet out of his jeans, pulling a condom out, ripping the package open with his teeth.

It seemed so natural. We just melted into making love as if we were two heartbeats, one after the other. I couldn't tell where I ended and he began.

It was so insanely intense, he had to kiss me hard on the mouth to keep me from crying out, over and over. Gripping his back, trying to pull him in deeper, I heard a low moan escape from the back of his throat. His whole body shuddered, and he seemed to collapse on top of me, both of us trying to catch our breath.

In the silence, I lay in his arms, and we watched the minutes go by on my alarm clock. The whole house was quiet. Everyone had gone to bed.

"I didn't come up here with this in mind," he told me softly, twisting a lock of my hair around his finger, like he had when he held me in his truck. He chuckled a little. "Even though it was true what I said about wanting to get into your pants."

"I'm not sorry it happened." *I wanted to get into your pants too*, I wanted to add. "I just hope you don't think I do this a lot."

"No, I don't think that. But I wouldn't mind doing it more."

"Give me a second to catch my breath?"

"No, I didn't mean it like that. I'm sorry," he corrected quickly. I snuggled closer. "That's okay."

He traced one of the scars on my elbow with his finger. "I couldn't help notice all the scars," he said hesitantly.

Time for the biggest whopper of all. "I was in the car crash that killed my parents."

"I'm so sorry." He pulled away from me a little. "I had no idea. Oh, Shea."

"I don't like to talk about it." *Because I'm going straight to hell.* "It's too hard. Too soon. Please."

Nick was silent for a long minute. "If I asked you not to go out with anyone else, would you? I know I haven't known you very long, but I really want to hang out with you. But just me. Every time I think of Joe's hands on you, I want to kill him. Is that normal?"

"To want to kill Joe? In this town? I'd say yes."

That made him laugh. "I just don't see two people at the same time. I'm old-fashioned, I guess."

"I don't think that's old-fashioned." I propped myself up on my elbow. "I think it's honest and fair and a lot less drama." I ran my fingers through the fine, dark hair on his chest. I couldn't stop touching him. I didn't want to. "There's no one special at RIT?"

"I dated a couple of girls, a month here, a month there, hookups and stuff, nothing serious. I studied a lot, unlike most of my friends. What about you? Did you ever have a serious boyfriend?"

"A couple of guys for a few months here and there, like you. But not in a long time."

He pulled me up against him again with a playful growl. "You never answered my question."

I'd hoped he wouldn't notice that. I wanted to tell him yes with all my heart, but I couldn't. How could I tell him I'd be with him if I was going to be leaving in a couple of weeks?

Unless I told him the truth, which I could not do, I had to tell him no.

"I don't want you to think you have to ask me that because of what we just did," I told him.

"I know I don't. That's not it."

"I would rather have you ask again, when we're not naked, for instance, so that I know you really meant it."

"I really mean it." His lips were just a fraction of an inch from mine.

I could feel his breath on my face, his arm around my back, pressing me against him.

"I would just feel better, okay? Can you understand?"

His other hand was lightly traveling up and down my hip.

"I want you to be sure." I could barely speak.

"I understand." His lips dusted mine. "As long as I know you'll say yes."

I angled myself underneath him. "I think you'll know what I'll say."

After round two, we drifted off to sleep together. It was five in the morning when I woke up. I started shaking Nick. "Wake up. You have to go now, before everyone gets up."

He rolled over. "What time is it?"

"It's a little after five. I have class in a while."

He pulled me close. "Skip it. We'll go somewhere for the day."

"I can't. I missed all my classes on Wednesday."

"Okay, okay," he grumbled. He got up and started getting dressed. I watched him pull his jeans on over his boxer briefs. I couldn't help gobble him up with my eyes. Nick was so damn delicious. He had an amazing body, lean and muscular at the same time. I wanted to pull him back in bed, let him have his way with me again, then have my way with him, but I had to be responsible. Damn it.

It was still dark out, so he fumbled around for his boots, making enough noise, I was sure, to wake up the whole neighborhood. But then again, if we hadn't with all the aerobics that had gone on earlier, I was pretty sure we were safe. He leaned over the bed as he put his jacket on. I was still naked, so I had the covers pulled up around me. He pretended to try to peek down the sheet, and I slapped his hand away playfully.

The hazy dawn light cast shadows across his perfect face. "I'll pick you up from school, okay?"

"Don't you have that fund raiser at Bingo's tonight?"

"No, it's Wednesday, and you're going with me. Screw your uncle if he doesn't like it. You just won't drink." He kissed me good-bye, and I watched him creep out the door. I heard the front door as it slowly opened and closed. I waited until I heard his truck drive off before I fell back asleep.

## Monday, April 3rd

That day on campus was hell. I was so tired I passed out in my Art Appreciation class.

Kayla woke me up at the end of the lecture in a puddle of my own drool. I was highly embarrassed. Then I went to my English elective and got my paper back on *The Taming of the Shrew*. My teacher had given me a C on it. I had gotten an A on the same paper when I used it at SUNY Buffalo.

Kayla wanted the lowdown on dinner. "It was all right," I told her while we were having lunch in the student union.

"It must have been better than that. My Aunt Alice called my house looking for Nick at three o'clock in the morning. She said you two took off together. She was worried sick. My uncle almost had to take her to the hospital."

"What did she say? Did she ask for my uncle?"

Kayla's face lit up, and everyone else smiled because she had obviously already enlightened them. "My mother told her not to worry about Nick because he was over at your house."

"What?"

"She could see his truck from our front window. She's not stupid. She told his mom he must have slept over at your place."

I was in shock. "Oh my God." I buried my face in my hands.

"I thought you couldn't have anyone sleep over," Maddie teased, turning the stud in her nose around with her fingers.

"Well, I wouldn't say no to Nick Stansfield, would you?" Jenna asked. She too was taking pleasure in my humiliation.

"So what happened?" Kayla asked, poking me in the side. "Did you get lucky?"

"Nick's mom is going to think I'm a whore," I groaned.

"So you did get lucky!" Maddie squealed, clapping her hands together.

I looked up. "Give me a break, please. I am so embarrassed. I'm going to have to leave town now. I can't believe this."

Jenna nudged me. "Just tell me one thing: was it worth it?"

I sighed, smiled, and said, "Yes. Absolutely yes."

Kayla squeezed my arm. "Olivia would have totally approved of you and Nick."

"I love you and Nick as a couple," Maddie said, "You two are relationship goals."

I left everyone at the student union to talk about my sex life behind my back and went down to the library. I had to print up one of the articles I was required to read for Art Appreciation. I parked myself in one of the computer carrels and fired up the library's beast. Wi-Fi in this town was so sketchy, it was better to use the school's desktop than my iPad or laptop and risk losing my work.

I wanted to think on the information about Olivia being gay before I acted on it. On one hand, it could very well be a motive for murder, but on the other, there was no indication she had been the intended target. Was it worth sharing her sexual identity when it probably had nothing to do with the girls' disappearance? Even to Bill?

I decided to keep it to myself for a while, to see what else came up, before I let a missing girl's biggest secret out of the bag. A secret she'd probably been about to share, since she was feeling confident at her new school. Even the word *secret* seemed wrong. In this day and age, it was just no one's business. How and with whom she chose to share her life with was up to her.

My teacher wanted us to research a major event in art that had happened right there, in Kelly's Falls. Apparently, about five years before, some freshmen at Harris Community College had made a sculpture that some of the other students had found offensive. There was a big battle to get it removed from campus, and when that failed, some activists destroyed it. I had to look up an article in the student newspaper about it on the Internet, then write a paper about the impact of art and its censorship.

As I flipped through the Google search results in my little booth, something jumped out at me. The headline read *Local Girl Found Dead in Apparent Suicide*. The article itself was pretty basic, but it was the last paragraph that interested me. It quoted Father O'Halloran as saying her death was deeply disturbing to him and members of their church, as she had been volunteering there and seemed to be getting her life together. I filed that piece of information away and found the article I needed for class.

Nick picked me up from school, to the obvious delight of my friends. Kayla leaned into his truck and told him, "Next time you two want to be sneaky, don't park so close to my house."

He laughed and pushed her out of the truck. We drove up to Freddie's for lunch. I asked Nick about his mom after we ordered. "She let me have it this morning when I came in. Her and my dad. They said I scared them to death and if I wanted to spend the night at a friend's, I should call and let them know."

"Kayla told me what happened. I could just die. Every time I see your mom, I'm going to think I have a big sign over my head that says, 'Hey, I slept with your son!'"

"My father sat me down after my mother took a sedative. He just told me to be careful, because we're both still in college, and basically try to keep it in my pants."

I could feel myself blushing. "Now your parents think I'm a slut."

"My mom found a condom wrapper in my jeans when I was a senior in high school." He laughed. "You should've heard that conversation. They know I'm not a virgin, so what difference does it make?"

Now my whole face was burning. "It makes a lot of difference to me."

"We are equally guilty, and I have no regrets." He reached across the booth and held my hand. "Have you thought about what I asked you last night?"

I was saved from answering that question by two things. The first was that the chubby waitress set our food down, and the second was that Joe Styles walked in. He was still wearing sunglasses over his black eye. He and Amber sat in the booth across from us, but not before he gave a friendly wave. "Hello, Nick. Hello there, Shea. How are you two?"

Nick didn't look at him. I could tell by the expression on his face that he was trying hard to control himself. I squeezed his hand and tried to smile. Amber was staring at me but talking to Joe.

We pretty much ate in silence. Nick kept glancing at Joe and crushing my hand. "Maybe we better leave," I suggested softly.

"Okay, let's go," he agreed in a low voice.

As we were walking out, Joe called to us, "Good-bye now, kids. Nice seeing you again, Nick."

"That son of a bitch," Nick exploded as soon as we got into his truck. He punched his dashboard a few times.

I grabbed his arm. "Stop it before you hurt yourself."

"I'd like to hurt that little weasel." He threw his truck into gear and drove me home in a silent rage.

He parked right out front. "I'm sure everyone in town knows I slept here last night, with the way my mother was carrying on. I'm not hiding anything anymore. Let them talk."

"I guess I'm the town slut now."

He shook his head. "No." He kissed me. "You're my girl."

I wanted to laugh out loud at the irony of that statement. He didn't even know my real name. "I suppose you won't be coming over for dinner tonight?" I asked him.

"Nope. Don't want to see your uncle. Now get out. My mom is probably calling in the National Guard. I'll talk to you later."

I gave him another kiss and got out. He waited until I ran up the steps and opened the door before he drove off. Mrs. Parker was waiting for me. Her hands were folded across her chest and her mouth was set in a straight line.

"You and I have to have a little talk."

I followed her into the front room without a word. I sat down next to her on the couch. She sat, wringing her hands together staring at them, as if she was trying to phrase her words just right.

"I was young once too and in love. I don't feel as if I have the right to lecture you, being eighteen, but I made a rule and you broke it. Now I can't trust you to keep it. I don't want to embarrass you, but I have to tell you, last night was the last time this will happen. This is a small town. If you don't care about your reputation, think of your uncle."

I waited a second, to look like I was truly taking her words to heart. "I'm sorry. It won't happen again. I don't know what I was thinking. Nick's mother freaked out, and he didn't want to go home. I know it's no excuse—"

"You don't have to explain to me." She patted my leg. "Just don't forget the rules. Respect the other folks who live here. You can have your girlfriends over, but no boys, not anymore. Not even for a visit."

Then she snapped right into hostess mode, as if the conversation had never happened. "Now go wash up for dinner, I'm serving roasted chicken tonight."

I thought it was very hip of Mrs. Parker to react that way. I went to my room and tried to take a nap. I got a knock on my door around five thirty. It was the chief. "Can I come in?" he asked.

I opened the door for him, gesturing inside. "Come in and sit down." He strolled over to the chair by the window and took a seat.

I braced myself for what I knew was coming next.

"Did you have a good time last night?"

"Good news travels fast in this town," I said, stretching out across my bed and propping myself up on my elbows.

"I got a frantic phone call at about three in the morning from Mrs. Stansfield. Seems her son was missing, last seen with you. I took a wild guess and walked outside and saw his truck down the road. By the time I called her back, Kayla's mom had already filled her in."

"There was a scene at Nick's parents' house. He was upset, so I brought him here. It got late and he spent the night."

He nodded slightly, mulling this over in his brain. Then he zeroed in for the burn. "And it doesn't bother you that someday soon this guy you're fooling around with is going to find out you're just using him?"

Wow.

"You can go to hell," I spat at him. "I didn't ask for your approval, Mr. Morals."

"Yes, I am Mr. Morals in this town. I was elected to protect the morals of this town. Don't you forget that." He paused, brushed some imaginary lint off his jacket, and then said, "Now that that's out of the way, because I really, really don't want to hear about your sex life, why don't you let me in on your new theory?"

Feeling extremely hostile toward him at the moment, I sat up, Indian style, on the bed. He was the last person in the world who was going to hear about my sex life.

"Okay, how's this? Joe Styles didn't have anything to do with it."

"How can you be so sure?"

"Joe pretty much conveyed to me he thinks he's been set up."

"What? That crap in the movie theater? He was trying to cop a feel."

"No, he wasn't. Are you going to shut up and listen to me or what?"

"Sorry, go right ahead, Sherlock."

I let that slide, mainly because he was a really sucky Watson. "Whoever took the girls was somebody they knew. Not necessarily someone they liked particularly, but someone they'd open the door for at one thirty in the morning. I noticed from Nick's front window that you can see every car that pulls up. If the girls were in the front room watching TV, they saw the kidnapper pull up."

"Brilliant. We deduced that almost three months ago. It should be on page one of the FBI report."

"I never saw those reports, you asshole. That's why I asked Bill for them. They sent me in practically blind, to see what I could find out without any preconceived notions. That was the whole point. All I got was some background on the girls, time frames, and some notes on the crime scene. I want to go over the rest of the reports."

"You really think you're on to something?" he asked, raising an eyebrow.

"The girls leave the party, go to Olivia's, call a few people, put on the TV and the stereo. Anyone on Instagram knows where they are. Someone pulls in; they see who it is. It's not a stranger, because they open the door. Whoever it is pulls a weapon, makes the girls put their shoes on, and marches them out to the car. It had to be something big, because you had three girls to drive around with, so maybe a van or a big SUV. Maybe something where they could lie down, so they couldn't jump out or grab the wheel. He drove them to a second location, killed them, and then went about his business like nothing happened."

"Which is what your FBI report is going to say. This is not new, not to me. And I have a few questions with that scenario. Number one, where are the bodies? This happened on December twenty-eighth; the ground was frozen. We combed the woods with dogs. We dragged the river and every pond and puddle that wasn't frozen solid for twenty square miles. Number two, we made over half the people in town account for their whereabouts. And do you know what everyone said? They were sleeping, watching TV, or, if you were under twenty-one, at the party the girls were at. It'd be easier to work backward by process of elimination, by determining who didn't do it."

So much for the spirit of cooperation.

"Look, I can see that you're not interested in what I have to say, so I'll just keep the rest to myself. Just don't blow my cover, and I promise I'll be good and won't embarrass you anymore," I assured him.

"Well, I probably won't have to worry about that much longer. If you were wondering why I didn't hit the roof about last night, I have some news for you. I talked to Bill Walters today. Your status here goes under review next week. If there is no discernible progress after this week, you're out."

"They told me it was indefinite."

"Everybody answers to the man, Shea. Bill can't keep you here forever without results."

I was a little shocked at that one. "That doesn't give me much time."

"One more week, maybe two, maybe less, if that theory is all you've got. I'll be leaving now. I have to look into the disappearance of three young girls. I'd ask you to help, but you've probably got a date." He stood up and brushed off the front of his pants.

"I'm sorry you think so badly of me," I told him, shaking my head in mock disappointment. "It's starting to affect our working relationship."

"You know," he said as he headed for the door, "this isn't personal. Actually, I really like you as a person; you're funny and feisty and relentless. You probably are a good cop. Maybe even an exceptional one. But this was just a bad idea from the start. It isn't your fault." With that he slipped out the door, letting it fall closed behind him.

He was gone, but that last remark ticked me off more than anything else. I didn't want his pity. Or his friendship. Or his mock admiration.

I called Bill to confirm what the chief had just told me. I then told him our working relationship had deteriorated to the point where it was nonexistent.

"Don't get so bent. He's the king around there. The law, period. Everyone answers to him, and he always makes everything all right. Now he can't and maybe you can, and he can't deal with it. I've come across it before. It's his ego talking. I'm personally pleased with the angles you've come up with."

"So why are you pulling the plug?"

"You know how these things work. The pressure is on me from my end to produce, too."

"I know that. I'm sorry. Did you get me those files?"

"Yes, and I was waiting for your call. There are two pieces of information you should know. This just came in to me on the NCIC computer from Quantico. One of our field agents ran some names through and came up with Garth Freid as wanted for rape and assault in Texas."

"Who is Garth Freid?"

"Garth Freid, aka Will Garrette, is Skyler Santana's mother's boyfriend."

"You just came up with this now?"

"It was an error. Our guy only ran a statewide check on Garrette because he was supposedly out of town at the time of the disappearance. His real name cleared. It was when one of his initial statements put him in town the day after the disappearances that we put him through nationally under his aliases too. This investigation is continuing in the traditional manner while you're there, you know."

"I know, sometimes I forget." But I didn't forget Mrs. Lansing's comment about him when we were having tea. "Where is this guy now?"

"Nobody knows. We have him marked for questioning, if we can find him. He has a history of assault, drug dealing, a real hard-ass. We've got a pickup order on him as of this morning. I'm surprised the chief didn't tell you."

"I'm not surprised. Our love/hate relationship has tipped more toward the hate side."

"Don't alienate him. He's your only backup. You need to keep him close."

"We should concentrate on Garrette now?"

"Yes, I'd say so. Put your ear to the ground, see what you can come up with. A car registered to him got a parking ticket last Saturday night on Main Street. He could be in town; he could be on the run. Just be careful—he's a real tough guy."

But I knew just where to find such a tough guy. Joe Styles was a junior badass. It seemed to me that he and Garrette would be acquainted, especially since Joe had dated his girlfriend's daughter.

It was time to stop dicking around and make something happen, instead of waiting for clues to magically come to me. Bill wouldn't like it and Roy would hate it, so I decided not to tell either of them. I called Kayla and made plans to go to Freddie's with her after classes on Tuesday.

## Tuesday, April 4th

It seemed like everybody in town knew I was officially hanging out with Nick. That elevated me to almost celebrity status. Before, I had gotten attention because I was a new face, the new girl. Now I was my own somebody. I had a label: I was Nick Stansfield's girl.

Kayla had her mom's car, so we all piled in and made our way to Freddie's. Tuesday was the best day to go because they had large pizzas half-price, and it was mobbed. We sat in our regular booth. The rest of the girls were eating while I watched the door.

"Are you waiting for Nick?" Jenna asked, pushing a piece of her hair out of her pizza.

"No. I don't know who I'm waiting for, but I hope they get here quick."

I had just started picking at my food when Joe walked in with Amber, Charlie, and a little ratty-looking guy named Carl. I ate my slice, finished my soda, and got up. "I'll be right back."

"Where are you going?" Maddie asked as she licked pizza grease from her fingers.

A thin rope of cheese was draped across her chin. I reached over and plucked it off. "Nice. Thanks for telling me I was wearing my lunch," she admonished the rest of the group, who were giggling into their Cokes.

Wiping my hand on a stray paper napkin, I told them, "I've got to talk to Joe for a second, and Kayla, you will not tell Nick, got it?"

Kayla's eyebrows knit in confusion. "I got it. What's up?"

"It's really nothing. I have to ask him for a favor," I said, leaving them to speculate among themselves as I crossed over to his table.

"Joe, I have to talk to you," I said, breaking into his conversation.

"Get the f—" Amber began, half rising in her seat.

"Shut up," Joe snapped at her, cutting her off, then looked at me. "About what?"

I wanted to bounce something off Amber's head, but my eyes never left his. "It's personal."

"Okay," he shrugged. If he was surprised, he didn't show it. He threw his slice down on the paper plate in front of him and followed me outside, much to Amber's dismay. We walked around the side of the building. When we got to the dumpster out back and I knew we were out of sight, I stopped. Joe leaned up against the brick wall, sliding back his sunglasses. "This is interesting. Bored with Nick already?"

I went all in.

"Can you get me some pot? Not a lot, just enough for me."

I think I shocked him a little. "I thought you were little Miss Respectable," he snorted, wiping his arm across his face, like he was trying to keep a belly laugh in.

What I was doing was dangerously skating the line of entrapment, according to the FBI guidelines set forth for undercovers.

The only thing that would save me, possibly, was that what I really wanted was information and not drugs. That and the fact that I had no intention of actually making a buy or arresting anyone for possession of drugs or intent to sell them. I just wanted to find Will Garrette.

"Look, can you or can't you?" I demanded, sliding my eyes around as if I was nervous we'd get caught talking. "I don't want anyone to know about this. I only indulge once in a while, and you're the only person I know around here who would know someone."

He nodded, suddenly serious. "I know some people. Is that all you want is pot? No coke, pills, or anything? I can get my hands on some gummies. Girls seem to like the edibles lately."

"Maybe. I haven't for a long time."

"You don't seem the type," he said. I could tell he was on the fence about helping me out.

"We all have our secrets, right?"

He crossed his arms over his chest with a nod. "Right. Even you."

"Even me." I tried to add a note of desperation to my voice. "When can I have it by?"

"We could get some now, if you wanted to." He smiled at me, like he was trying to reassure me. "But what would your friends say if you left with me? What would Nick say?"

"This is between you and me. If you can introduce me to your hookup, I'd really appreciate it."

"Can you afford to dabble?"

Time to play the fake-dead-parents card. "My parents left me a lot of money."

His face screwed up, as if the sun was in his eyes, and he hit me lightly on the arm. "Hey, I'm sorry. I forgot. I can get some later, tonight maybe."

His sincerity shocked me. For a second I didn't know what to say. "Okay," I agreed. "But I know how it is. I don't want to have to text you every time I want a joint."

"I'll check with my friends, but you never know with these dudes. It should be cool. I'll come around to your place at eight thirty, so be ready. I ain't waiting."

"Thanks, Joe." I actually breathed out a sigh of relief. He gave me an odd, sad smile, and we walked back around the building. Opening the door, I held it for him and then followed him inside. Parting ways, we sat down at our separate booths without another word.

"What was all that about?" Maddie asked.

"It was nothing. I just had to talk to him about something. Don't anyone go spreading any rumors back to Nick." It came out harsher sounding than I had intended.

They all glanced at each other and kept on eating. Kayla didn't look up from her food; she just mumbled, "We won't. In this town, spreading rumors can make you disappear."

I sat back stunned, waiting for elaboration, but everyone started talking about the new young economics professor. No one had ever made a comment like that before. They made it clear to me the subject was closed.

Kayla dropped me off at home a little while later, acting like nothing out of the ordinary had happened. I wondered if any of them had dabbled in drugs since the girls went missing. If private talks with Joe were now the norm with my little group of friends.

When Nick called, I made up an excuse about writing a paper for not being able to see him. I dressed myself in an old pair of Levi jeans and a brown T-shirt with a Buffalo Bills hoodie pulled over it. I also shoved a five-inch switchblade I had taken off a drug dealer down the back of my jeans. Because I wasn't there officially, I couldn't carry a gun, but I'm not stupid. I hadn't told

Bill about the knife; I didn't want a hassle about it. I figured what he didn't know wouldn't give him migraines. Just like the entire expedition I was about to embark on.

At exactly eight thirty, Joe pulled up in an old beat-up Camaro. It was primer gray and rust colored with a patch of blue here and there. His friend Carl, whom I affectionately thought of as Rat Boy due to his rodentlike features, was driving. I ran out the front door and hopped in the back seat, trying to avoid the wicked wind that had kicked up. Actually, I squeezed into the back while Joe impaled himself on the dashboard trying to pull his seat up for me. It smelled like a sewer.

"Carl, you know Shea Anderson, don't you?"

Carl turned his long, thin face my way. "I've seen her around. How you doing?" He revved the engine once and pulled away from the curb.

"Fine." I'd had enough of the small talk. "Did you talk to anyone?" I asked Joe, leaning forward between the seats to get a better look at where we were heading.

"Yeah, everything's fine. You want a beer?" He held one up for me to see. He had a cooler on the floor between his feet.

"No, thanks. I just want to get this over with."

He put the beer down. "That's cool. I understand."

"Where is this place?" I asked as we cruised down the darkened Main Street.

"Right here," Carl said, pulling into a parking lot. "It's above the Laundromat."

He parked his beast of a car, and I looked around. It was a brick building on the lower end of Main Street, with the storefront facing the street. Joe held the door open for me as I managed to extract myself from the back. After eight o'clock on weekdays, Main Street became a ghost town, shops all closed, everyone gone home.

I followed Joe and Carl behind the building. Fire escapes snaked their way up the side of the alley. A few garbage totes sat against the brick wall, overflowing with trash. A white plastic bag tumbled down the alley before getting caught on the mouth of a drainpipe, where it rippled and snapped in the wind.

For a second, I thought I was back in the projects, with the rats and the roaches scuttling around. Joe pulled open a dented steel door that led to a narrow hallway. We climbed about fifteen steps to a landing, and he knocked on the door. I stood behind the guys, trying to see in the dim light. A washed-out-looking bleach blonde with black roots opened the door. Her skin was ghostly white except for her makeup, which was pasted on in patches across her face.

"Is Rick here?" Joe asked her.

She looked me up and down disapprovingly. "Yeah, come on in." She stepped aside.

I've seen a lot of scummy apartments in my day as a cop, but this one took the cake. The dingy little kitchen we walked into had dirty dishes in the sink piled almost to the ceiling. A mangy dog was chewing on itself in the corner, and from the smell of the place, it seemed the dog also used one of the rooms in the apartment as a toilet. Joe pushed me along, his hand on the small of my back, into a living room, where three guys—all around the age of twenty-seven or twenty-eight—were sitting on the floor with another older dude, smoking a water bong. A little girl, about four, played with her Barbie doll in front of the TV screen. She seemed oblivious to everything around her, like she was the only person in the room.

The guys stood up when we came in. One in particular stepped up and clapped Joe on the back. "Hey, Joey. What's up?"

I could see the resemblance right off: same lean frame, same pale-gray eyes, even the way they spoke, slow and deliberately.

"Nothing, man. This is the girl I told you about." He stepped back. "Shea, this is my brother, Rick."

He shook my hand. "She sure is a pretty one, Joe. You get all the hot ones. Ain't that right, Carl?"

"It sure beats the ugly ones," Carl agreed, and took a long pull on the beer he'd brought up.

Two women sat on a torn-up love seat together, interrupted from their cell phones by our entrance. They eyed me, still holding their phones, and one whispered something to the other. They too were bleach blondes, like the chick who'd answered the door, and stoned out of their minds. Both were incredibly skinny and covered in tattoos that snaked up their track-marked arms and shoulders, like twins in a freak show. The one closest to the wall had a beer tucked between her knees.

"You want to make a deal, little girl?" the huge man sitting on the floor by the couch asked, rolling a joint in his fat fingers. Some pot dribbled out as he tried to lick it shut, collecting in his dark beard.

"Yeah, she's the one I told you about," Joe said.

The bearded man shot him a look. "She can speak for herself. You want something? Honey, you gotta ask me for it."

"I just want a couple of joints, for myself," I said nervously. I stuffed my hands in my back pockets, to keep them closer to my knife.

"That's it? Shit, I could have given those to Joe for you." He turned to Joe. "Are you stupid? Bringing her here for a couple of joints? Why don't you two just drive to frigging Canada and sit in a nice cannabis café together?"

"I may be looking for something harder, if you can get it," I added quickly.

He stroked his beard, dislodging the stray weed, which now accumulated on his beer belly. "Darling, if it's out there, I can get it. I got everything you need."

Joe was on the defensive now. "You always say everyone deals through you, Mike. I didn't want to cut in on you and Will."

"Smart thinking on that," the enormous Mike said, "but Will's out of the action for now. He knows they're looking for him."

"Hey, I know you," the emaciated blonde girl without the beer said, suddenly sitting up straight. "You're the police chief's daughter. You came to live with him a couple of weeks ago."

I hooked my right thumb into the back waistband of my jeans. Not that one knife would do much good against all those people.

"I'm the chief's niece," I corrected. The whole room went silent as Mike stared first at me and then at Joe. Then he sprang up off the floor and slammed Joe against the wall.

"Are you insane, bringing that bitch here?" he screamed. What I'd taken for fat was bulky muscle. He banged Joe's head against the wall with every syllable.

Rick rushed forward and got between them, grabbing Mike's arms. "You better step off, man. If Joe says she's all right, then she is. You better calm yourself."

Mike ran his sleeve across his mouth and stepped back. "Screw this. I ain't selling her shit."

"That's fine. But you just sit your big ass down," Rick warned. He was a lot smaller than Mike, but his tone was deadly serious. The other guy with the bong was still sitting against the wall, eyes closed, singing softly to himself.

Rick's head swiveled toward the broken-down love seat. "And you, Brenda, you better learn when to keep your junkie ass mouth shut over things that don't concern you, or else I might have to knock the rest of your teeth out."

"Whatever, Rick." She folded her arms across her sunken chest and sulked, wanting to rebel in some way, but also wanting to save her remaining teeth.

"The problem with these girls is that they get jealous when they see a real lady," Rick remarked, putting a hand on my shoulder. I smiled appreciatively up at him. Guys like him like to play the badass hero sometimes. Better to act like a docile girl still trying to score than whip out my knife and try to back my way out of the apartment.

"Well, where is Will now? Maybe he'll take our money," Joe asked, trying to straighten out his clothes. "I know he'll hook me up."

"Last I heard he was over at Whitey Dugan's place. He ain't dealing right now. He has other problems. Anyone want a beer?" Rick asked, going back into the kitchen.

"Naw," Joe called. "We got our own." I think he sensed how uncomfortable I was. I was dying to get out of that place. And keeping my hand near my knife, just in case.

Peering around for exits, I noticed they must have had a cat somewhere as well, because it was using the half-dead potted plant in the corner for a litter box.

"Can we go now?" I asked Joe.

His eyebrows knit together in concern for me, like he was sorry to have brought me into that whole scene. "We're taking off, Mike," he announced. "Thanks for nothing."

Mike nodded, his face still screwed up in anger. I followed Joe through the kitchen, Carl at my back. No one in the living room said good-bye or acknowledged us leaving, not even the little girl with her Barbie doll.

"Take care of yourself, little bro. Stop over more often," Rick called after us.

We made our way down the stairs together. We didn't say anything to each other until we were crossing the parking lot. I finally let my hand fall away from my knife when we got to the Camaro.

"Sorry about that," Joe said, opening the car door for me to get in. "Mike's really paranoid now that they want Will. He's in some serious shit."

"Who's Will?" I asked innocently, trying to wedge myself back in the car.

"A friend of my brother's. He's older. He goes out with my ex-girlfriend's old lady. He's a good guy; he would have sold to you. I better take you home now. If I can find him, I'll get you what you need. I can spot you a couple joints right now, if you still want them."

I shook my head. "Forget it. I'll import my own from Buffalo. I don't like those people."

He laughed. "Were you scared back there?" Joe was looking back at me in the rearview mirror as Carl drove down Main Street.

"I've dealt with worse." I shrugged. "They aren't my kind of people." Which was going to be my reason not to buy from them if they had wanted to sell to me—that I didn't trust them or their drugs. I had planned to pull Joe off to the side somewhere and give him a whole litany of excuses I'd prepared. And I had two hundred dollars cash in my pocket just in case I had to buy my way out.

Carl pulled into the driveway of Mrs. Parker's house. Joe got out and pulled the seat up for me so I could get out. "Thanks, Carl," I told him. "Sorry tonight was such a bust."

"No worries," he said, giving me a little wave. "We should hang out again. Maybe at my place next time. Less drama."

"Sounds good." I tapped the hood of his car and turned toward Joe. "And thank you for trying."

"I gotta tell you, I never would have thought you would do drugs, not even pot. You always try to come off as so classy and cool."

Classy and cool—that's me, all right. "Yeah, well, there are lots of things we don't know about each other, right? I'd never touch the really hard stuff like heroin or meth." I started walking to the door, with Joe following.

"That's smart. I tried meth twice and lost my mind the second time. Got thrown in jail. Never touched it again. Mike said I got a bad batch, but I think there's no such thing as a good batch." He climbed the steps in tandem with me, like he didn't want me to get ahead of him. "And you saw how skinny and pretty those hypes were. At least there weren't any needles laying around the apartment this time."

"I'll never get addicted to heroin," I assured him. "I hate needles."

"So when are you going to go out with me?"

I stopped dead and turned to him as he leaned against one of the white porch pillars. "You're asking me out? When you know I'm seeing Nick? I appreciate you trying to help me out tonight, but why would you do that?"

He shrugged. "Because I like you. And because I also know you're full of shit."

My gut froze. "What do you mean?"

I could see his breath under the porch light in the cold night air, coming out in puffs. His pale-gray eyes zeroed in on mine. "We're two of a kind, me and you. Bullshitters. I just want to know what you're bullshitting about."

I dug my key out of my back pocket, almost causing the switchblade to fall out of my jeans. "Thanks for everything," I told him. "But I'm with someone. I'll see you around, okay?"

"Not okay." He shook his head, his long hair whipping around his face in the wind. "I guess I'll just have to try harder."

"You know what, Joe?" I laughed. "I don't think you could try any harder. But you are pretty smooth for a country boy."

"You like me, too." He wagged his finger at me with a grin. "Nick or not. I know you do." Then he stuffed his hands in his pockets and walked back to the car. I watched him the whole way. I have to admit, as much as he wasn't my type, I loved his swagger.

I closed the door and went upstairs. I didn't wait for him to pull off like I had with Nick. The whole house was quiet except for Henry's snoring as I passed his room.

The first thing I did when I got in my room was call the chief.

"It's me. I know where Will Garrette is."

"How do you know about Will Garrette?"

"Bill told me all about it." I sat down on my bed and pulled my shoes off. I tried to drop them on the side of the bed as softly as I could.

I could hear him blowing out an exasperated breath on his end of the phone. "So where is he?"

I stashed the knife in my nightstand drawer. "Listen, here's the deal: you can't bust him. The FBI has to."

"Why?" he demanded.

"Because I went somewhere with Joe Styles tonight. The people I met knew I was your niece, and I don't want them to put two and two together."

"Where were you?"

"Someone's apartment. I couldn't even say for sure whose it was. I didn't get many names. Joe's brother Rick was there. Some people there said Will Garrette was at Whitey Dugan's place."

There was a long pause. I could hear him scribbling something down in the background.

"Whitey owns a motorcycle chop shop over off the highway. Are you sure he's there?"

"That's what these people were saying. I think it's definitely worth checking out."

"What were you doing with Joe Styles?"

"Following up. I'll never figure this out going on dates with Nick, right?" I added for his benefit.

"This is good work. Anything else you'd like to share?"

I paused for a second, then decided I didn't want to give him a heart attack over the phone. "Nope."

"I'll contact Bill tomorrow morning. I'm going to try to set up surveillance over at Whitey's. Maybe we can grab him on the road if he tries to leave. I'll be at Bingo's tomorrow evening for the big fund raiser if you're worried about blowing your cover."

"I'll see you there. Nick asked me the other night. I hope you don't mind. I promise I won't drink and I'll be a good girl."

He chuckled into the phone. "It'll give us a chance to act like a family."

"Great. I'll get overly emotional, tell you you're not my father and that I hate you."

"That sounds about right. You know," he went on, "I get the feeling I wouldn't like the situation you were in tonight."

"Yeah, I got that feeling too, so that's why I would never dream of telling you about it."

**Wednesday, April 5th**

The college let out for spring break after classes were over for the day. Because Easter came late, we got off all the way up until the day after, which was April sixteenth. When I was a college student in my real life at SUNY Buffalo, we'd always had off ten days in March. Spring break at Harris Community College seemed so late to me, but I guess each school is different.

Everyone blew off their last classes. Most of the students were going somewhere for the vacation, but Kayla was staying in town. Obviously, she was going to the fund raiser too. I was glad of that because I wanted someone to hang around with besides Uncle Roy. Nick would be busy working the crowd, thanking everyone, and trying to convince people to keep volunteering at the church. I couldn't expect him to stand by my side and keep me company.

Nick texted me at five o'clock saying he wanted to spend some time together before the function. He knew once we walked through the doors, he'd be busy for the rest of the night.

"I'm a little nervous about tonight," I told him as he climbed the front steps. I'd been waiting on the porch for him to pull up. "I'm afraid to see your mother again."

He stopped in front of the door. "I already told her not to get goofy about it. She said she wouldn't bring it up. Hopefully she'll be too busy playing hostess to worry about my sex life."

I fiddled around with the hem of my sweater. "I hope the outfit I picked out is okay. I don't know what to wear to something like this."

"I don't care if you wear a hula skirt. All I care about is that we get enough money to keep the information center open. You wouldn't believe how much something like that costs to keep operating."

I felt stupid for making the clothes comment to him. How shallow could I possibly be? Poor Nick had to beg people for money to find his missing sister. "I know everyone will come out for this," I reassured him. "Everyone wants to help find Olivia."

"Right now. But as time goes by, people forget. If we can't come up with something soon, I'm afraid everyone will just give up."

"Don't think like that," I said, but I knew he was right. Time was not on our side.

He came into the boardinghouse and sat with me in the front room for a while. We held hands and talked about nothing and everything. Every once in a while when he was speaking, he'd clamp down on my hand a little. I could tell he was trying not to break down about the benefit and what it meant that they still had to have one. After an hour, he reluctantly had to leave to help his family set up at the bar. "I'll pick you up at eight." Leaning down, he kissed me lightly on the lips, giving my hand one last squeeze. I went up to my room to watch some Netflix on my iPad to kill time.

Mrs. Parker made some iced tea and cookies and brought them up to me.

"The chief told me you both would be eating at the party tonight. I brought you some cookies to tide you over."

215

"You didn't have to do that." I set the tray down on my little table by the window. Mrs. Parker was looking at the dress I had put out. It was pink and flowered, very springlike.

"You're going to look just lovely," she commented, running her hand over the material on the sleeve.

I felt myself blushing a little. "Thank you."

"Shea, honey," she said seriously, turning toward me. "I didn't come up here to compliment your wardrobe. The truth is, I'm worried about you and your uncle. I know it's hard, but could you just try to see things his way? I see you two every day at breakfast and dinner, not saying a word to each other. It's breaking my heart. He's not used to raising a teenager."

I paused, thinking about how I was going to go about getting off that subject. "Mrs. Parker, it's not easy taking orders from someone who's practically a stranger to you."

"I know," she agreed. "But you are all each other has. He may not act it, or say it, but I know he's glad you're here. That business that happened the other night with Nick just didn't sit well with him. He's on such an ivory tower in this town, he doesn't think anyone would breathe if he didn't allow it."

I thought that speech was very caring of her. Which made me feel like a dirty liar once again. I told her I would try to do better. I'd try to spend more time getting to know my uncle. She seemed satisfied with my sincerity and exited, leaving me the tray.

I started answering the million and one texts I got every day after classes. Kayla texted to see what I was wearing. Maddie texted to tell me not to forget to come over to her house the next night for a little get-together. Jenna texted to see if she could borrow my silk tank top. Nick texted to remind me to be ready at eight.

Kayla walked down to the boardinghouse around seven to finish getting ready at my place. "I just love this room. It's like having your own apartment," she marveled from my bathroom, where she was applying my makeup to her face. "Me and Jenna are looking for a place now."

"It's nice to have my own place, but it gets lonely, though. My uncle and I haven't been getting along. I think once I graduate, he's going to tell me to go back to Buffalo."

"All by yourself?"

"Well, I'm eighteen. He's not obligated to support me."

"I'll miss you if you leave. So will Nick."

"I was planning on going to the University at Buffalo in the fall anyway." My all-purpose handy-dandy cover story lie for leaving town.

"Maybe I should apply, too. We could get an apartment in the city together."

The cover story didn't include tagalongs. "Maybe."

Nick and Zach pulled up in Nick's truck. Kayla and I came down the stairs to see Mrs. Parker taking pictures of the guys in their suits. Nick was wearing a gray suit that really highlighted his brown eyes. He had some pink roses clutched in his hand.

"These are for you," he said, offering them to me. Three pink roses for the three missing girls. His hand was shaking a little. I held the flowers against my chest, wrapped my free hand around his, and smiled into the camera.

Marlene had come down from their room and was cooing to Peter about how handsome the guys looked. Zach handed Kayla a single white rose, while Mrs. Parker continued to catch it all on her phone camera. Zach had on a blue suit with his blond hair combed back. Kayla hadn't been expecting Zach to be there, much less bring her a flower, so she was ready to explode with joy.

We finally got out of there and drove over to the fund raiser. Nick sat in the front seat with me, holding my hand the whole way. He seemed stressed and tired, more so than I'd seen him since I'd been there.

The parking lot at the shopping center was almost full. It looked like everyone in town was at the party. As soon as we walked in, people started clapping Nick on the back and shaking his hand. I smiled and nodded and let Nick thread me through the crowd. Someone had blown up huge pictures of each of the girls, propping them on easels in the corners of the room. People were writing on the pictures, bent over with black Sharpies, things like: *Come home soon!—the Bystrycks* and *Miss you and love you. OXOXOX*. Nick's mom and dad sat at a table up front, by the stage, with Emma Lansing's parents. Mrs. Lansing gave me a wave and a smile when I came in. Kayla's mom was with them, braving being out in public for the sake of her niece.

Skyler's mom was sitting over at the bar, clearly drunk.

Nick went over to his parents, but I stayed at the bar drinking my Coke. Mr. and Mrs. Stansfield waved to me and I waved back, blushing like crazy.

The chief made his way over. "Shea," he said, pulling me aside, "your information checked out. We got him. I'm making the announcement in a few minutes."

"Is he a suspect?"

He leaned in so only I could hear. "Let's put it this way: there was blood all over the inside of his trunk. We've already got samples being sent to the state crime lab."

Nick walked over to us. "Hey, Chief," he said, spotting him. "I heard you have an announcement to make."

He nodded. "In a minute. After Father O'Halloran says a few words."

Just then Father O'Halloran got up on the stage and tapped the microphone a couple of times. "Can I have everyone's attention, please?" Like a switch being flipped, the noise of the crowd dimmed to a hush. The whole room seemed to hold its breath. The priest cleared his throat. "We all know why we're here tonight. It has been a long and terrible time in our community. When something like this happens, it seems a test of faith, and we question why. What happened to them? Where can they be now? And it pains us more that there are no answers to our questions."

He paused, took a long, deep breath, and wiped his eyes before continuing. "Apparently, the chief of police, Roy Bishop, has some information for us. Maybe some answers."

The chief patted my arm and made his way through the hushed crowd, up onto the stage. He wasn't wearing his usual uniform but rather a dark-blue suit that made him look more like an undertaker than a policeman. He shook hands with the priest and adjusted the microphone.

Everyone was tensely waiting for this news of his, including me.

"Hello, everyone. And thank you, Father O'Halloran." He paused to collect himself for a second, holding on to the microphone stand, looking out over the crowd. "At six fifteen this evening, acting on an anonymous tip, the Federal Bureau of Investigation arrested Will Garrette in the Town of Belmont. They have announced that he is a suspect in the girls' disappearance and are holding him for an outstanding warrant while forensic tests are being done on evidence seized in his vehicle."

There was a second of stunned silence.

"Did they find any bodies?" someone shouted out.

The chief's voice was strong and steady and calm. The voice of someone holding the town together by his sheer will. "No bodies have been found. The FBI promised to keep me informed."

"Is he under arrest?" another person yelled.

"He was wanted on felony charges in another state, so yes, he is under arrest, but has not been charged with the girls' disappearance yet."

"He didn't do this!" Brandy Santana cried out drunkenly. She sprang up from the bar, knocking over an empty beer bottle, which exploded on the floor, sending green glass flying. "They took my baby girl away, and now you want to take my old man away too!" She was accusing the crowd now, backing up toward the door. A lady with a big teased hairdo tried to calm her down.

"You just want someone to blame." She pointed a bony finger at her neighbors. "I may not be the mother of the year, but I won't let you pin this on Will. This town has so many dirty little secrets—get off of me!" Two biker-type men grabbed her by her arms and pulled her toward the door. She seemed to crumple a little, sagging under the weight of her grief. One of the men propped her up, half carrying her out the door. A couple of tattooed ladies followed. The angry rumble of motorcycles filled the bar and they were gone.

All around me people were standing in stunned silence. Then Nick's mom's sobs pierced the crowd.

Kayla turned to me, wide-eyed. "If they arrested someone, they must be dead." She started crying and shaking uncontrollably. I grabbed her and hugged her as she wept.

Father O'Halloran was trying to comfort Nick's mom and dad as well as Emma Lansing's parents. Emma's mom was sitting bolt upright, staring straight ahead and mutely still. Her husband was pleading with her to speak to him.

"Nicholas," Mrs. Stansfield called from her table. He ran over to her, and she threw her arms around his neck. She clung to him like a drowning woman, gasping for breath.

"No more questions, folks. I don't have any more answers." The chief stepped away from the microphone. He came down off the stage, cutting through the throng to get to us.

Kayla turned to him. "Are they dead? Are they?" she demanded.

Roy hung his head a little. "I don't know, honey."

She totally broke down then. Bending in half with tears, trying to catch her breath.

Zach tried to talk to her, putting his arm around her, but she wailed harder. "Let's get her some air," he said to me. I nodded, unable to think of a better idea. I felt so helpless. As Zach and I made our way through the crowd with Kayla to try to calm her down, we passed by Father O'Halloran, still comforting the Stansfields. He saw Kayla and tried to reach out to touch her hand. She drew it away like he was a snake about to bite. I was a little surprised by that and looked at him. My eyes locked with his, and then he turned back to Nick's mom. I couldn't process her reaction to him.

The rest of the night was a depressing disaster. Everyone seemed to know that this arrest meant that the girls weren't runaways and that they weren't coming home. A lot of people had been clinging to those hopes, people like Nick's mother. Mr. Stansfield and Kayla's mom had to help her out to their car after the announcement, and they left. Nick felt obligated to stay and Kayla wanted to be with us, so we calmed her down and went back inside.

Needless to say, the party was over. The chief had left, and so had Father O'Halloran. We stuck around until the last person departed, around eleven, and made our way over to Kayla's house. Her mom had gone to Nick's to be with Mrs. Stansfield.

Kayla gave us all a beer from the fridge as we sat around the living room floor. Her eyes were red and swollen from crying.

What surprised me was Nick's calm. "Have you got anything stronger?" he asked her.

"In the cabinet, in the dining room," she told him. Nick got up, went into the dining room, and poured himself a glass of straight whiskey. He pulled out his cell and made a phone call. I could see him pacing in front of the china cabinet, talking in a low voice to someone. He came back into the living room a few minutes later.

"They've admitted my mom into the hospital. She's having a breakdown, I guess. Your mom said to stay here with you, Kayla. She's there with her."

Kayla didn't say a word. Zach put his arm around her and gave her a hug. She leaned her head on his shoulder, and tears rolled down her face.

Nick sat down with me sitting between his legs and wrapped his arms around me. "I hope they execute him. I hope they fry him," he said, his calm facade starting to crumble.

"It's kind of a relief too, you know?" Kayla said, wiping her eyes. "The not-knowing part—that was the worst part. Maybe he'll tell the police where they are. I just hope it was quick. I just hope . . ." She trailed off into sobs, and Zach held her.

"I just want to know why," Nick said suddenly, his voice rising in anger. "I just want to know why someone would kidnap my sister. She never had a chance at life. None of them did. What kind of person does this?"

"A monster," I said quietly.

"I want to know where she is. I want to know, right now, where the hell she is." The look on Nick's face was sad and hurt and angry, all at once. The reality that his sister was dead was almost too much for him to process. His whole body was tense, but I could feel him trembling slightly beneath his shirt. I put my hand against his chest to try to help calm him; his heart was racing, thudding against my palm.

"I wish you could have known her." The tears came now, streaming down his cheeks. He made no move to wipe them away.

"I wish I could have known her too."

*　*　*

Kayla's mom came home around one thirty that morning, looking as wretched as we did. She told us Nick's mom had to be heavily sedated and that Nick's dad was going to stay with her at the hospital. She wrapped her arms around Kayla, and they made their way upstairs together. Zach had left twenty minutes before, at Kayla's insistence. She appreciated him being there for her, but she just wanted her mom once she'd texted Kayla that she was on her way home.

Nick asked me to stay at his house with him. "Not for sex or anything like that." His eyes were rimmed in red as we walked to his truck. "Just to have you there. I just want you to be with me."

He clicked the fob, and the door unlocked for me. I got in the passenger's side and watched as he got in and tried to get the key in the ignition. Nick was shaking so badly, it took three tries. "If you want me to, I will. Do you want me to drive?"

He shook his head. "I got this." The truck rumbled to life, and he pulled it onto the road with a jerk.

His house was still and quiet when we got there. The living room was a wreck. His mother had gone crazy and torn the place apart. The cushions from the couch were scattered around the floor, the mirror on the side wall shattered. Two fat drops of blood were drying on the floor underneath, like some sick semicolon.

He led me by the hand up the stairs to his immaculately clean room. There were football trophies on a shelf over his bed and a picture of him and four friends at the prom in a little frame. They were posing in their tuxedoes in front of their high school. Next to that was a picture of him and Olivia. He had his arm around her and she was making a face. It looked recent, maybe from the summer just past.

"That was last August at a pig roast in Belmont," he told me when he noticed me looking at it. He picked it up and studied it for a second. "I really miss her." Sinking down on his bed with the frame in his lap, he started to cry again. His whole body was racked with sob after sob. I held him as tight as I could. His hand clenched the back of my shirt, wrenching at it. Wrenching at the pain. He cried for a long, long time, and I cried too. I cried for him and I cried for his sister. I cried because if the case was over, I was gone. And he would never know what had happened to me either.

We must have passed out on the bed together. I woke up when his father came home in the morning, Nick's arms still wrapped around me, on top of his bedspread. Nick went downstairs to talk to his dad. When he came back upstairs a few minutes later, his expression was grim. "I'll drop you off. I have to go see my mom."

I tried to straighten out my wrinkled clothes. "Does your dad know I'm here? Did you tell him nothing happened?"

Pulling me back into his arms, he kissed the top of my head and said softly, "I didn't tell him anything, but I think right now he could care less if you're here or not."

When we came down the stairs, Nick's dad was nowhere around.

"He's probably in the basement," Nick told me, making sure the front door locked behind him. "He spends a lot of time down there." His truck was freezing in the early-morning light, my breath coming out in clouds as the engine warmed. Thankfully, he didn't have to use the ice scraper; he just draped his arm around me and pulled me close until the heater kicked on.

"I'll call you if anything happens," he told me as he pulled up to the boardinghouse.

"I'll be right here." I leaned in, grabbing the front of his shirt, and kissed him. "You know that, right?"

He nodded into my kiss, pulling away and letting our foreheads touch. "I know."

I slammed his truck door shut and felt his eyes watching me until I was safely locked inside the boardinghouse. Behind me I heard his tires squeal on the street as he pulled out. I walked up to my room deep in thought. Nick should have filled my every thought, but it was Kayla who was on my mind. She'd been crying like it was a shock that the girls might be dead, like she'd really believed they were still alive somewhere. I remembered the way she'd pulled away from Father O'Halloran. He was her priest too; one would think she would want his comfort. I lay down on my bed and turned off the ringer on my cell phone for everyone but Nick. I wanted to concentrate. Something was not right with Kayla.

## Thursday, April 6th

called Bill as soon as I woke up. I didn't realize how late it was until I saw my alarm clock on the nightstand. It was eleven o'clock in the morning and Bill was wide awake, answering on the first ring. "What's up with Will Garrette?" I asked. "Did he do it?"

"I'd say no at this point. I think it was very premature of the chief to make that announcement last night. He's got an alibi. An illegal one, but it checks."

"What's his alibi?"

"He was making a drug buy in Pennsylvania. He had come in from Texas, with a stop in Philly, before coming back to your lovely town. On the night of the disappearance, he received a ticket from the Philadelphia police for speeding at eleven forty PM. I already talked to the issuing officer, who confirmed it was him driving. Seems he remembers a tattoo on his hand that was so new it was still bleeding. That checks out. Will Garrette got a snail with the words *slow time* tattooed on his left hand in Houston two days before. I think I'd remember that too. A freaking snail. But there's no way he could've made it back to Kelly's Falls by car in two hours."

"What about the blood?"

"We haven't gotten the report back from the state crime lab yet, but the guys up there are saying it's some sort of animal blood. Garrette says he hit a deer in Texas, threw it in the trunk, and he and some drug addict friends had a little venison barbecue. Unless we come up with something else, I can't find a reason to charge him."

"Great. This whole town thinks the case is solved."

"He's going to be held until someone from Texas comes to get him. See what else you can come up with, okay? You grabbed one felon; let's see if you can grab another one. You're close on this now, I can feel it."

I let him go and went downstairs for lunch. Everyone was talking about Will Garrette. Marlene was convinced; if Chief Bishop said it was so, then it was. The chief sat there at the head of the table like he was king. "I'm glad we finally caught him. It's such a relief to me to know everyone in my town is safe again," he said, picking up his ham sandwich. He took a big bite and set it down again.

"That's if he did it," I added.

He didn't bite back; he was feeling too righteous. "We've got the right man," he assured everyone. "Will Garrette is a criminal through and through."

I excused myself before I said something to the chief that I'd regret and went back up to my room. I needed time to think. It kept coming back to me that Kayla was the key. No one seemed to know why Garrette would kidnap and murder those three girls, unless they were involved in his drug dealings somehow, but there was no evidence of that. People needed a suspect to blame. But my gut was telling me Kayla knew something that would point to someone else. It was something Kayla either didn't realize was important or was so scandalous or terrible that she couldn't tell.

I popped the thumb drive into my laptop and went over the pictures and videos from the party again. There was Kayla with Olivia. There was Kayla in the background of someone else's selfie, arms folded, looking pissed. There was Kayla coming out of the bathroom with Skyler and Emma on someone's live feed on Facebook. The drunk girl posting was rambling on about how she'd had the best Christmas ever, and how this was her new friend Drew, and look at her tank top, she was freezing. All the while in the background Skyler was motioning to Olivia, who joined them in a huddle by the base of the stairs. Kayla was with them. She knew what was going on, and it was pure luck she hadn't gone back to Olivia's house.

I decided what I was going to do. It was time to find out what had really happened the night the girls vanished.

Nick called me from the hospital around dinnertime. His mom had gotten worse. He decided to stay overnight with her and told me he'd call or text me the next day.

I sat around my room, trying to decide what my next move was going to be. My time in Kelly's Falls was running out. I knew that even if they never charged Will Garrette with the crime, everyone would still believe he'd done it. It was easier that way. It put things to rest without any bodies or a trial to cast doubt. The town felt safer, but was it?

I opened my window to get some air. It was a little after seven thirty, and the dusk was giving way to dark. I'd just sat down on my bed to start reading one of my textbooks for my art elective when I heard glass shatter. I ran to the window and opened the screen, sticking my head out. Two doors down, the Giffords were battling again. I craned my head out to get a better look and heard another, bigger crash. This time glass sprayed over the porch of their small white house. One of the front windows must have shattered.

I could hear Jake screaming, cursing, and ranting. Enough was enough. The police station was practically across the street and the chief lived three doors down, but everyone turned their backs on it. You see it a lot on the job: husband beats wife, you arrest the husband, wife turns on you. The next day they're back together. But this should have been personal to them. These were their friends and neighbors. It was personal to me. I saw little Emily waiting for the bus with Peter every day. I had watched Sarah Rose getting her flower beds ready, with the baby playing in his playpen set up in the driveway so she could keep an eye on him. Her husband, Jake, was a big guy, six foot tall and muscular. I would see him walking over to the volunteer fire department on the next corner almost every night. He was a volunteer firefighter there and would have a beer or four or five at the bar inside the station house basement. Then he'd come home and all hell would break loose. She was no match for him; it was not a fair fight.

I pulled my hiking boots on and grabbed my jacket as I ran out onto the porch. I marched up to the chief's door and pounded on it. "What?" he asked, pulling it open. He was wearing an old ratty sweater and jeans.

"Don't you hear that? He's beating the crap out of her again, and you're just sitting in here watching the late news."

"Listen, if Sarah Rose wanted the police, she would call us. They do this all the time. She never presses charges."

"So this is okay with you?" I pointed at their house, the shouting still audible. "As long as she doesn't press charges?"

"Don't you put words in my mouth. It's not okay. She never admits to being hit, and he's smart enough not to leave bruises."

"But he does leave bruises," I countered, remembering the one on her arm I'd seen at Freddie's. "Maybe you just don't want to see them."

Just then little Emily came outside and sat on the front steps in her nightgown. She had her hands over her ears and was sitting on the glass-strewn porch, crying silently.

The chief looked at her and then at me and said, "Let me get my gun belt on and call it in." I made sure to stand watch on his front steps as he adjusted his belt to his jeans and called one of his guys at the police station.

"Jeff Darton is going to walk over. Let's go."

We walked down to the house without waiting for Darton to meet us. The porch was covered with glass from the front picture window. There was a jagged hole in the middle of it and the curtains were hanging out, limply caught on the jagged edges. I put my hands on Emily's shoulders, and she hugged me. Darton came jogging over from the police station and joined us.

Jake must have heard something, because he came to the front door. "Roy," he said, looking from him to me and Officer Darton as he stood in the doorway. "I didn't call you. We don't need you."

"You're smashing out windows. Emily is terrified. Where's Sarah Rose?" The chief squared up to him on the porch.

"My wife is in the house."

"Can I talk to her?"

"No."

"Why not?" The conversation had turned from polite to tense in that split second.

"Because you're not coming into my house."

"Then bring her out here."

"No. I don't want you talking to my wife and I don't want you here. I don't want him here." He nodded toward Officer Darton. "And I have no idea what the hell your niece is doing here. Get off my property now."

"I'm only going to tell you this once, Jake, so listen good. In New York State we have a pro-arrest policy for domestic disputes. That gives me the right to come into your house, and it gives me the right to lock you up without her signing a complaint if I have cause. If she's hurt at all, and I mean a scratch, me and you have a serious problem. Now step aside."

The chief was right up on him now, eyes locked with his. Darton was behind him, his pepper spray already in his hand. Jake gave the chief a rough shove. "Get off my prop—" He hadn't even gotten the words out when Roy reached up with one hand and grabbed him by the throat. Jake tried to punch at him, but the chief charged forward, still holding on to his neck. He pushed Jake all the way back into the living room, up against the far wall.

"You may think you can punch your wife around, but you will never put your hands on me, do you understand?" Jake's face was turning purple. "I will come into your house. I will come into your bedroom. I will come, and you will not stop me." The chief was squeezing his throat with his right hand while Jake was desperately grabbing at his arm, but the chief had a stranglehold on him. I came forward, gripping the chief's shoulder, and that seemed to snap him out of it. Finally, Roy let go and Jake fell forward, clutching his neck, coughing. Darton came in from behind and put the cuffs on him.

"I got him, Chief," Darton said, patting Jake down as he scrambled to take a breath.

I heard soft crying coming from the other room. I followed it to the downstairs bedroom. Sarah Rose was weakly going around the room, trying to clean up the broken items scattered all over the floor. Her lip was split and her left eye was starting to blacken as she frantically tried to tidy up. She wiped her face with the back of her hand, smearing a dark-red streak across her cheek.

Blood stained the front of her blue shirt, and wide drops of it dotted her jeans. "Sarah Rose?" I asked softly.

She turned to me, and I could see she was cradling her left hand in her right. "Shea, what are you doing here? Honey, it's late. I had a little accident and I was trying to clean." She sounded on the verge of hysterics.

"What happened to your hand?"

"Oh, it's nothing. I had an accident. It's nothing, except that now—now I can't move my fingers." With that she burst into tears.

Jake had grabbed her, she finally told me, after she tried to defend herself when he got mad about the water bill being so high. I cradled her hand in mine. It didn't take a doctor to see he had broken all the fingers on her left hand.

We could hear Jake screaming he was going to sue as they took him out of the house. I stroked Sarah Rose's hair as she buried her face in my shirt, crying softly. "This is not how it was supposed to be," she repeated over and over. How do you comfort someone whose world, good or bad, has just come to an end?

Officer Darton had taken Jake to be booked, so the chief drove Sarah Rose to the hospital in his squad car. He wanted to call an ambulance for her, but she begged him not to. I had to stay with the kids at Sarah Rose's house. Emily watched me clean up the broken glass. She didn't say a word the entire time; she was used to cleaning up after her dad's temper.

I took her by the hand when we were done and led her to her room to put her to bed. Looking up at me, she said, "Maybe I can come live with you at Mrs. Parker's house."

I pulled her ruffled pink covers up to her chin. "Don't you want to stay here with your mommy?"

She shook her head. "No, because my daddy is mean to Mommy. He yells and breaks things. I hope the police never bring him back."

I kissed her forehead. "Try to sleep, angel." I tucked her in and went to check on the baby. He was lying in his little bed, sound asleep. He had never even woken up, he was so used to the fighting.

The chief got back a little after eleven. He had called Sarah Rose's parents, and her father was up at the hospital with her.

Her mother came to get the kids. She stood in the living room, surveying the damage, a grim look on her face. "I knew it," she told the chief. "We all knew it. I'm just glad someone finally had the guts to do something about it."

Sarah Rose and the kids would all be staying with them for a while. When Jake got out in the morning, he would be coming home to an empty house.

The chief and I walked back to Mrs. Parker's house together. The night was warmer, the winter chill fading away, a harbinger of things to come as spring crept in. Stopping in front of the porch steps I asked, "How's she doing?"

"Her hand is pretty busted up, but she seems relieved to be going home with her parents. I hope things work out for her."

"If by work out, you mean he stops beating her ass, then I hope so too."

Under the porch lamp he suddenly looked sixty-eight instead of thirty-eight. All the cockiness of Will Garrette's arrest had drained out of him. "I had no idea things were this bad. I want you to know I never would have let this go on."

I nodded, but I had my doubts. "I thought you were going to kill him in there."

"I'm sorry I lost my temper, but I don't like men who are cowards, and I don't like people challenging my authority." His voice was tight. "I think you know that by now."

I gave a bitter laugh. "I do know that." But I also saw how much talking it had taken for him to go over there in the first place. If Emily hadn't come outside, would Sarah Rose still be picking pieces of broken glass out of her face while her eye swelled shut?

I looked over at the white porch in the moonlight, the painted rockers still, red and yellow tulips just starting to bloom in the flower beds in front of the house. It looked so idyllic and serene, like an old-time country portrait painted on a ceramic plate in a roadside gift shop.

"I have to go to bed. I'm not tired, but I do have class tomorrow." Starting up the steps, I paused at the top, turning back to him. "I thought this town was supposed to be sleepy and quiet."

"Isn't that how they describe all the small towns in those slasher flicks?" he asked grimly.

The irony wasn't lost on me. "I guess it is."

He stood outside and watched me unlock the front door, waiting until I rebolted it from the inside before he walked home, just like Nick would have.

Once I was in the sanctuary of my room, I suddenly had an urge to talk to Karen again. I'd been pretty good about not having any contact with the people back home while I was there. I'd only caved in and called her that one time. I figured no matter what happened, by the time the phone records mattered, I would be back in Buffalo and there would be no more cover left to blow.

I didn't bother texting. Karen answered her cell on the first ring. She sounded like she had a mouth full of food.

"Hello?"

"It's me."

"Oh my God, are you okay? You sound terrible. Are you still there? Can we talk?"

"I just wanted to hear a familiar voice. I had a bad night."

"You called because you're lonely?" she asked. I pictured her lying on the couch in her pajamas. "Don't be. You're not missing much up here. How's the case coming?"

"I've got a new theory. Of course, I'm discounting the possibility that some psycho randomly picked that house and kidnapped those girls."

"What did Bill's profile say? Who does he say you're looking for?"

I thought for a moment. "He hasn't given it to me. He didn't want to prejudice me, send me on a false trail. But I think I'm on to something. You know, secrets, like you said."

"If you think you're on to something now, wouldn't it help?"

"You're probably right." I rolled over onto my stomach, propping myself up on my elbows. "But I don't want to talk about that. I just need to hear something normal, some news from home."

"Well, I do have some news for you, but how normal it is I can't say. Guess who I ran into this weekend on Chippewa Street?"

Chippewa Street was Buffalo's downtown party bar area. It could've literally been anyone. "I don't know, who?"

"Aiden. He was all freaked out when I saw him. He practically chased me down in the bar. He said he wants to talk to you."

Aiden Tischler was my FBI agent ex-boyfriend. He'd also been my backup during the Roberts case. That was how we met. During the Roberts detail I lived in an FBI safe house. He was one of the agents assigned to me. We spent every minute together, night and day, except when I was in school. Everything was going fine, until the incident when Roberts attacked me and I almost got slaughtered. It was his legs I saw coming across the lawn and his gun going off. When I woke up in the hospital emergency room, he was there sobbing, while they frantically tried to stitch me up and remove the glass lodged in my knees and arms and hands. He said that they shouldn't have called for clearance to break cover, that they should have just gone into the basement to get me. His guilt at not being able to protect me had killed our relationship. I guess my nightmares were nothing compared to his, because last I'd heard he was in drug rehab and had been asked to resign from the Bureau. I hadn't seen him in months. He'd shown up at my apartment late one night asking for money. I had given him twenty bucks and told him not to ever come back.

He hadn't.

"I hope you told him I was out of town."

"I did. Then I said I was meeting a friend. I didn't want to get into a full-blown conversation with him. He told me to tell you he was all right, doing better."

"How did he look?"

"Like a train wreck. He had this scraggly beard and he's lost about twenty-five pounds. He smelled like he'd been drinking for three days straight."

"There but for the grace of God . . ."

"Bullshit. He got used too, I get that. But he had problems before he got assigned to you and the Bureau ignored them. As long as he was producing, as long as the numbers were there, they didn't care. Maybe, if Bill had been a better supervisor, Aiden would have gotten the help he needed. Instead, he let Aiden play supercop, and he self-destructed."

"Go easy on Bill. I'm still playing supercop."

"True," she agreed. "And you're still getting used. But at least it's on your terms."

We hung up a couple of minutes later. Talking to her had actually made me feel worse and not better. Bill was a user. He'd suck me dry and send me home.

After what had happened to Sarah Rose, I made a decision. It was time to make a move. It was time to throw any shred of morality and ethics I had left out the window.

It was time for me to get to the bottom of what Kayla knew, all of her secrets, once and for all.

## Friday, April 7th

I texted Kayla bright and early the next morning. I asked her what was on our social calendar for the evening. She told me Jim Jordan was having a party at his dad's house. Since we had no other plans, we decided to make an appearance. I had to take Mrs. Parker's car to get her some eggs from the store and passed by Sarah Rose's house. The front window was boarded up and the house looked empty and still. I tried to put it out of my mind. I had done what I thought was the right thing at the time. There was no use in second-guessing myself.

That afternoon the FBI announced that Will Garrette was being extradited to Texas without being charged in the girls' disappearance. They stopped short of saying he was no longer a suspect, but I knew better. Nick called after they were informed of all this to tell me he was staying another night with his mother. Her hysteria had reverted to an almost catatonic state. Her doctor was worried because she wouldn't eat. I told him to take all the time he needed with her.

The chief kept trying to get ahold of me, but I didn't want to talk to him. I was sick of his ego and had tried cooperation long enough. He had scared me the night before with Jake. I was going to get something out of Kayla without his help. And I knew he wouldn't support what I planned to do.

Kayla walked down to the boardinghouse around four thirty. She'd heard about Will Garrette and was upset about the FBI announcement. We sat together in my little room in front of the bay window. Her brown hair fell across her face as she sat in my overstuffed chair. "I feel so weird. I'm glad he wasn't charged, because that means they might still be alive. But now we don't know. It's started all over again." She put her face in her hands. "This is killing me."

I reached over and rubbed her shoulder. "I'm so sorry, Kayla."

She sniffed away some tears. "Thanks." She leaned her head way back, eyes closed. "I just want to go out and get smashed. I mean totally loaded."

Which had been my plan all along.

Jenna called a little while later. She picked up Maddie and they came over. Maddie had stolen a bottle of cheap vodka from her dad's bar. I went downstairs and raided the fridge for iced tea so we had some kind of mixer.

Mrs. Parker was standing at the kitchen counter, putting some stuff together for a pie she was baking. "Are you and your girlfriends all right? Do you want some sandwiches or chips?" she asked, looking up from her mixing bowl. I knew she knew about Sarah Rose, but she hadn't mentioned it at all.

"We're fine," I said, grabbing some plastic tumblers from the cupboard and picking up the pitcher.

"It's such a beautiful day; it's a shame for you girls to be cooped up in the house," she observed. She had a smudge of flour across her nose that I wanted to wipe off for her. But I'm a bad person, so not only did I not wipe it off, I didn't even tell her it was there.

"We're going to a get-together in a barn later."

"How wonderful. You girls have fun," she called after me. I took the iced tea upstairs and began mixing drinks. I made everyone's really weak at first. Even though I didn't drink much myself as a rule, I could mix up a storm. My tolerance being much higher than those girls', I knew I had to be careful. I was really walking the line this time.

We sat around watching YouTube videos and talking. It started off a sad, depressed conversation. Maddie took big gulps of her vodka and iced tea with one hand, vaping with her blinged-out Juul with the other. I inwardly shuddered. I could not get into vaping, but at least my room wasn't going to reek of smoke, like my apartment back home. No wonder Karen was always complaining no quality guys asked her out. *Who'd want to kiss that mouth?* I thought. Might as well make out with an ashtray.

"You know what I think about sometimes?" Maddie was sitting on the floor by the bed, her nose stud replaced for the evening with a thin gold ring.

"What?" Jenna asked absently.

"Dying. Not like really dying, but ways of dying."

"Like driving your car off a cliff?" Kayla asked, looking over.

"No, not like that," Maddie said, sitting up. "Something beautiful. Like jumping out of a plane, but before you do it, taking a pill so that you blacked out just at the instant you would hit the ground. So there you would be, spiraling in space, toward the ground. What a rush."

"Wow," Jenna said in awe. "You are so weird. Stop watching Netflix."

"I don't think so," Kayla disagreed. "I think it's kind of cool. Like a lover's leap. Like in that movie where the girl jumps off a cliff because her true love dies."

"Nobody loves like that anymore," Jenna replied, holding up her phone. "Every guy I swipe on Tinder wants more pictures before they meet me. To see if I'm real enough or hot enough. Then they send me pictures of their junk. It's so disgusting. No one wants to be in a relationship; everyone just wants to hook up."

"Does anyone love anyone?" Maddie said, filling her glass from the pitcher. "Really, I mean every couple I know of, including my parents, are messed up. No one seems happy. They all seem bored, like they settled for something, even if they get along. Maybe it's only in the movies or on television."

"I think the strongest love is unreturned love. You never want what you can have; you always want what you can't. Or what's bad for you," I threw in, joining the conversation.

"Holy crap, that's deep," Maddie giggled. Most of her drink sloshed over the side onto the leg of her jeans.

"I think that's true. Look at Skyler and Joe. He beat her up, cheated on her, did sick things like in the cemetery. But she couldn't stay away from him and he couldn't give her up either." Kayla stretched out over my bed. "I don't get it."

"Did Olivia or Emma have a boyfriend?" I asked. Since we were actually sipping tea, I was hoping to get a couple of the ladies to spill some, and not just on their jeans.

"Olivia dated a lot, but she never really went out with anyone for a long time," Jenna explained. "She was all about school. Like, really focused. Compared to the rest of us."

*No*, I thought, *she was trying to figure out where she fit in. And your normal wasn't her normal. She just hadn't told you yet.*

"Except Billy Kilmer. He was older, one of Nick's friends. They went out for, like, six months straight, and then she dumped him out of the blue. But they stayed friends, still went out now and then when he was back home. He goes to college in

Wisconsin," Kayla told me as she fiddled with her iPhone. She made a duck face into the screen, snapping a selfie.

"I forgot about him," Jenna said, almost to herself. "Anyway, Emma was so shy, she only had a couple of dates. She hooked up now and then, but she never liked anyone that liked her. Except Nick; she had a wicked crush on Nick."

"Everyone has a crush on Nick," Maddie laughed. Wearing her sparkly tank top that matched her highlights, she was like a bright pink disco ball lighting up my bedroom.

"And you got him." Jenna socked me in the leg.

"Ow." I rubbed my shin dramatically. "I think you left a mark."

"So are you going to take him to the Freshman Fling?" Kayla asked. "If you go with him, then I can ask Zach."

"Nick is twenty-one years old. He's not going to want to go."

Kayla dismissed that thought with the wave of her hand. "He'll go. He's really into you. I think he's whipped."

"That's not a compliment," I told her, absolutely complimented.

"Nick Stansfield does not date anyone," Maddie told me. "He went out with one girl, like, four years ago, but she's married now. That's it." Maddie took another big swig from her plastic cup. "And no offense, but I would have thought he would have gone out with some Ivy League type, not a girl from Harris Community College."

"None taken," I replied, totally offended.

"He hooked up with my sister's friend Tammy one night at Bingo's about six months ago," Jenna piped up. "I guess she was all over him, making out with him in the bar and everything. She wanted to get a hotel room, but he wouldn't. He got her number, but he never called her."

"He is definitely the goods." Maddie mixed more vodka into her glass.

"So I guess I'm lucky, huh?" Lick it up, Maddie, I thought. You jealous harpy.

"The man pool is pretty shallow in this town," Kayla said, laughing. "Nick's the only guy around with any kind of a future."

"What about you and Zach?" Jenna asked Kayla.

Flipping her hair back so she could take a sip from her glass, she frowned. "I'm so into Zach, but he thinks I'm too young for him."

"Why do you think that?" I asked. "What did he say when you last talked to him?"

"That I was too young for him." She sighed. "But that hasn't stopped him from texting me ten times a day."

"Maybe he just wants to get a piece," Maddie teased.

"I wish," Kayla replied, and made another drink for herself. The pitcher was getting low. "I think he thinks if we do, Nick will kill him."

"Nick wouldn't do that," I said.

"That's what I keep telling him. But Zach's all into the whole 'bro code' thing. Bros don't screw other bros' relatives. Blah, blah, blah. It's so stupid."

"Wow. I'm so glad most of my relatives are dead," I threw in, making iced tea come out of Jenna's nose as she snorted with laughter. And so it went, on and on, until about eight o'clock. It was then decided I would drive Jenna's mother's car, since I was sober. Kayla was already half in the bag when we left. And she was in a wild mood.

She couldn't wait to get to Jim Jordan's house. Jordan's father owned what used to be a huge dairy farm. His father was one of only two lawyers in town, and they were a very well-off family. "Wait until you see this place," she told me. "It's like something out of a movie."

As soon as we walked in, I was amazed. Music was blasting from the loft above us.

The Jordans had restored the barn on their back lot into a kind of rec hall. It was ripped out of a copy of *Betters Homes and Gardens*. With all the work they'd done to the barn, Jim wouldn't let just anyone up in the loft. There was a pool table up there, full bar, and an electronic dartboard. To get into the loft, they had this kind of platform elevator that worked with pulleys. It was considered a big thing to be one of the chosen few who got to be up on the second floor and not down in the barn. There had to be a hundred people on the ground floor: couples making out in the old horse stalls in the corner, guys crowded around cases of beer set on old wooden pallets, and girls shifting from foot to foot, waiting in line for the lone bathroom.

We fished our cans of beer out of Maddie's black backpack and started to mingle. As I walked through the crowd, I heard someone yelling to us from the loft.

I looked up to see five guys from the hockey team hanging over the railing, waving to us. "Come on up. We'll send the platform down."

I didn't know any of their names, except Tyler's, but the rest of the girls did, so we all got on the lift they sent down while they worked the pulleys.

And up we went.

I could see why Jim didn't want a lot of random people in the loft except the invited few. Besides the slate pool table, which we could see from the bottom, there was a big-screen TV complete with game consoles. Two of the hockey players were fighting their way through a zombie apocalypse with virtual shovels.

There were maybe ten guys and two other girls up there with us. Tyler kept looking at Kayla, but she ignored him completely. "What's up with you and Ty?" I asked as she breezed by him.

"We are so done." She looked back at him over her shoulder. "And I don't even care. He got pissed that I left him to go to Bingo's that night. If I'm going to waste my time on a guy, it's going to be Zach." She shrugged and held up her beer. "This is me, moving on!"

I clinked my beer can to hers. "To moving on!"

The next thing I knew, I was behind the bar making all the nastiest drinks I could think of. It became a game. Someone would call out a drink and see if I knew how to make it. If I did, they had to drink it.

Jim Jordan had pulled out a bartender's guide from behind the bar to make sure I was mixing them right. If I got one wrong, I had to drink it. I never got one wrong.

A heavyset guy wearing a Buffalo Sabres jersey grabbed the book from his hand, paged through it, and called out, "A vodka and orange juice, a Long Island Iced Tea, and a Grasshopper."

"We don't have crème de menthe, or crème de cacao, so no Grasshoppers." I checked the minifridge under the polished wood bar. "I got orange juice, so vodka and orange juice, coming up." I put the jug in front of me. "And no way am I making you a Long Island Iced Tea. You'll puke your guts out."

"Where did you learn to make so many drinks?" Jim asked as I blended the orange juice and vodka in a silver shaker. I poured straight orange juice into red plastic cups under the bar, added some grenadine, handed them out, and kept the real mixed drink for myself. It was an old bartender's trick.

"My parents owned a tavern in Buffalo." It was actually my grandparents. "I used to work there on weekends sometimes." A half-truth, not so bad, coming out of my filthy lying mouth.

"Hey, Tyler! You wanna try some of this?" Jim held his glass up to Tyler at the other end of the bar. He slid it down with a smile, and Tyler chugged the whole nonalcoholic thing.

Bartending duties abandoned, Kayla and I ended up dancing next to the pool table in our socks. Jenna was making out with some guy I'd never seen before in a recliner in front of the big screen.

I was twirling Kayla around, laughing, when someone slipped their arms around my waist.

It was Nick, smiling at me.

"What are you doing here?" I asked in surprise.

"My mom snapped out of it a little, ate something, and sent me home. I knew you'd be here. I wanted to see you." I threw my arms around his neck and kissed him. "Besides," he said, "happy two-week anniversary."

"What?"

"We were at Bingo's together two weeks ago tonight."

I nuzzled my face into his soft, brown-checked flannel shirt and said, "That was a great night."

"So is tonight." He tipped my chin up, kissed me on the mouth, and grabbed my beer out of my hand. I didn't want another one. I wanted to keep my hands on Nick, but I had a job to do.

Kayla was totally smashed. I needed to get her back to my place and alone. I told Nick I was feeling a little drunk and it was getting late, so he finished my beer and we decided to go.

She didn't want to leave, but Nick played the older-cousin card. "I'll drive," he told her, giving a hockey player with eyes on Kayla a look that said *back off.*

"I want to go with Jenna," she protested, looking over Nick's shoulder at the guy who had tried to initiate contact. He was in a holding pattern, like a hovering raptor, waiting for his chance to swoop in on the drunk girl.

"You're sleeping at my house," I reminded her as we searched for her shoes under the pool table. Jenna and Maddie were already waiting for us on the ground floor.

"Third wheel," she sang, holding on to my shoulder, trying to slip her boot on. "I'm officially the third wheel."

"I wish you came with three wheels," I told her as I helped her onto the lift with Nick on her other side.

"Hit me up!" she called to the vulture, who was still eyeing her as we were lowered down.

She came with us to Nick's truck, protesting the whole way that she'd be single forever because we sucked so bad. We poured her into the seat, buckling her in. "You're here for two weeks and hook up. I'm here for life and can't get laid. Except maybe by Tyler."

I smothered a huge laugh as Nick got in the driver's side. "Don't say things like that in front of me," he admonished her, slamming his door shut.

"What? Laid. Laid. Laid. If Shea can get laid, so can I."

"Okay, but can we not talk about it?" He put the truck into gear. "We're still family, you know?"

Jenna pulled up in front of us, and Nick flashed his lights. Nick followed Jenna to make sure they got home okay and then drove to my house. Mrs. Parker was downstairs in her night-dress, making a snack in the kitchen. "I swear he's just helping me get her to my room. He'll leave in a few minutes."

She looked Kayla up and down with a knowing eye. "All right," she said. "But you're calling your aunt and telling her," she told Nick. "And try to keep the noise down; people are trying to sleep." I was wearing out my welcome fast, even at the boardinghouse.

Nick helped me get Kayla into my room, and he called her mom to let her know she was staying with me. We weren't there two minutes when Kayla started getting sick. She didn't want anyone with her, so she shut herself in my bathroom and puked her guts out.

Knowing we only had a few minutes, I practically attacked Nick as soon as the bathroom door closed. I ripped his flannel shirt open, popping off two buttons, sending them scuttling across the floor.

I couldn't keep my hands off his chest, his abs, his thighs. He kept trying to stop me from waking up the rest of the house. "Shhh, shhh," he shushed against my mouth as I pulled his belt through every loop.

While Kayla was vomiting in the bathroom, we were having sex on my bed. Not very romantic, but definitely frantic. I tried to be quiet, but I couldn't help giggling every time Kayla heaved, causing Nick to try to hush me with a kiss, which made it worse, or better, depending on the angle.

We finished up quickly because I was afraid Kayla would walk out. Or her retching would wake up Henry, who'd walk down to see what was going on. Or Mrs. Parker would see the truck still parked outside and come to remind me about male guests.

I propped my head on his arm, pulling the sheet up with my other hand. "I guess there goes your whole nice-guy image once and for all."

He dipped in and lightly kissed me as he pulled his jeans over his dark-blue boxer briefs. "It was worth it."

Gathering up my clothes, I said, "I wish you didn't have to go now."

He tried to button his flannel shirt over his black T-shirt, realized the buttons were gone, and grinned at me. "Yeah. Me either, but I don't want to get on Mrs. Parker's bad side. Anyway, do you want to come to the church with me tomorrow morning? I have to check on the location center and the money from the fund raiser."

"Are you asking me to a house of God after we have sinned?" I kidded, tugging my shirt back over my head. I watched his flawless ass in his faded jeans make its way across the room. His body was ridiculous, clothed or not.

"Of course. I'm going to marry you, kid." He opened the door. "I'll call you in the morning," he whispered, and pulled it shut behind him with barely a click.

Suddenly, my head was crystal clear. Even if he was kidding, this guy had totally stolen my heart in two weeks. Could this wonderful, unbelievable, sweet guy be the person I had been waiting for my whole life?

And if he was, what was I?

I was a dirty, lying spy who'd infiltrated his life to find out what had happened to his sister by any means necessary, right?

Right.

This relationship based on fiction was sure to work out.

*Hrrrkkk! Hwrkkk!*

Kayla continued to hurl into my toilet, so I had a little time to get myself together before we got down to business. After five minutes or so, she finally came out. She was pale and shaky as I helped her to the bed.

"I'm so sick," she moaned. "I feel like I'm going to die." Outside, I heard Nick's truck roaring off.

"Just take it easy." I tucked her in and got the wastepaper basket from the bathroom and placed it beside the bed. Kayla was still smashed, hopelessly drunk, and that was the way I needed her.

"Kayla?" I asked gently, rocking her. "What happened the night Olivia Skyler, and Emma disappeared?"

"What?" she groaned, trying to turn over. "I already told you."

"No, I mean, what else happened? Why were Skyler and Joe fighting? What happened between them that day? Why would someone take them?"

"I don't know," she whined, chin sinking forward into her chest. I shook her a little, trying to keep her focused.

"Kayla, this is important. Think."

She shook her head. "Joe was mad at Skyler because he said her friends were more important to her than him. He's a jerk." She hiccupped. "I screwed Joe before. When I was a senior in high school. Did you know that?"

I did know that. Maddie had told me in the bathroom at school earlier in the week. "No, I didn't."

"It was awful. He's got a really, really small—"

"What else, Kayla?"

"I already told you," she complained, trying to close her eyes.

Shaking her a little harder, I pressed, "No, you didn't. Tell me now."

She tried to sit up a bit, her eyes struggling to focus on me. "Joe was mad because Skyler wanted to take care of Emma."

That was not the answer I'd been expecting. "What was wrong with Emma?"

She shook her head. "I can't tell you."

"You can tell me."

Kayla mashed her lips together like a little girl. "I said I wouldn't tell."

"But you can tell me," I insisted. "I don't know anyone around here, remember?"

Her eyes narrowed. "You can't tell Jenna or Maddie, because they don't know."

I nodded. "Okay. I promise."

Covering her face with her hands, she squeaked out, "Emma was pregnant, at least she thought she was, and Skyler said she would help take care of her."

"She was pregnant?"

She nodded into her hands, still covering her face. "Yeah, and they were going to think of ways to tell Emma's parents because she wanted to keep the baby. Something was wrong, though."

This was it. What I had come and lied and manipulated for. "What was wrong?"

"I don't know. That's all she would say. I would have found out if I had gone to Olivia's that night. We were all going to talk about what she should do. Joe was mad we were leaving, but he didn't know why. He thought Skyler should stay with him."

"Who was the father?" I pushed. "Do you know?"

She lifted her head, snot trailing from her nose, mascara raccooning her eyes. "No, she never said. She was going to tell us the whole story later that night. The only thing she said was that he was older. I didn't even know she wasn't a virgin anymore."

I couldn't believe she knew all that and hadn't told anyone. "Why didn't you tell the police?"

Kayla started to sob. "Because she thought she was pregnant. I figured they really might have gone away, so she could go off and have the baby without anyone knowing. I thought they'd be back and that's why when they caught Will Garrette I was so upset. They were supposed to come home." With that she puked in the wastebasket and then passed out cold.

I had the break. I had the motive. Pulling the bedspread over Kayla with one hand, I snagged my phone off the nightstand with the other. I called Bill.

"It's almost five o'clock in the morning." He sounded groggy, like I'd woken him up out of a deep sleep, which I probably had. Somewhere in the background a dog barked, and he shushed it.

"Emma Lansing was pregnant." With Kayla passed out, I didn't have to worry about blowing my cover. "The girls left that party to figure out what to do about it."

251

Now he sounded wide awake. "How did you find this out?"

"Kayla got drunk and I got it out of her. She won't even remember in the morning. She said she didn't tell the police because she was convinced they ran away so Emma could have the baby without anyone knowing."

"Do you think that's true?"

"I think Kayla thinks it's true." I pushed the puke-filled wastebasket away from me with my foot as I sat on the edge of my bed. "But my guess would be, if they were going there to discuss the situation, maybe the father was going there too."

"Did she say who the father was?"

"Kayla didn't know, only that he was older."

"An older man in Emma's life?" Bill pondered this. "Maybe a married man? Someone with a lot to lose?"

"I think I know who it may be, but I'll hold off on voicing my conclusions until tomorrow. I want a chance to check this out."

He took a second to mull that over. "I'd like a name, but if you're only asking for one day, you got it. This is definitely the break we've been looking for. Great job. You call or text me as soon as you know something. Better yet, maybe I should come down there?"

"Don't start uncorking the bubbly yet. Just give me twenty-four hours."

I hung up with him and started working some things out in my head. What had Emma's mom told me? She was a follower, easily led astray. By someone older. Someone she knew. Someone she trusted enough to open the door to. Someone they'd all leave with. Probably an authority figure in their lives. Someone whose life would be ruined if this ever got out.

Someone like Father O'Halloran.

And what a happy coincidence for me, I was going to see him the next day.

**Saturday, April 8th**

Nick called early that morning. I had gotten maybe three or four hours of sleep. Kayla was still out, breathing thickly and moaning a little as she lay sprawled on my bed. I had to sleep in my overstuffed chair, wrapped in an old blanket I'd found in the closet.

"You awake? Is Kayla all right?"

"I think she'll sleep for a while yet. Are we still going to the church today?"

"Yeah, I called to wake you up. Get ready; I'll be there in a half hour."

"Yes, sir."

"Don't get smart," he laughed into the phone. "See you soon. Good-bye." I clicked end and put my cell on the bedside table.

I went over to the closet and had started grabbing my clothes when I heard Kayla making this horrible choking sound. I turned around to find her hugging the wastebasket to her chest and heaving. "Are you okay?" I asked, coming over and rubbing her back.

"No," she wailed, and kept on vomiting.

There wasn't much I could do for her. "I'll put some clothes on and bring you some toast from the kitchen," I offered. "It'll make you feel better." She nodded and coughed. I got dressed in the bathroom, which was a smelly, disgusting wreck. I could hear Kayla coughing loudly as I tromped down the stairs. The kitchen was empty, for once, and I quickly popped a piece of bread in the toaster and hunted through the fridge for something cold for her to drink.

Kayla was still in that fetal position when I came back with a piece of dry toast and a glass of soda. She ate as much as she could and went back to sleep. I had a feeling she wouldn't be able to keep that toast down long, so I kept the wastebasket next to her.

Nick beeped his horn and I walked down the stairs and out the front door. It dawned on me I had forgotten to call both Bill and the chief. "Nick, can you wait a second? I forgot something." I ran back into the house and called Bill from the hallway phone.

"Bill, what do we know about Father O'Halloran?"

"The priest?"

"I forgot about the whole privileged-communication thing. I was a little drunk last night. It'd be stupid to go over to the church and not tell you. And it would have been stupid of you to let me." But he would have let me go. He would have let me put myself in danger. "I think it could be him. Emma taught Sunday school for him. She was a quiet, shy girl, someone easily taken advantage of."

Priests were covered under special guidelines because confessions were considered privileged communication. Bill would have to run everything by his higher-ups and his legal department.

"This changes everything."

"I won't question him about anything. I'll just go with Nick for his scheduled visit and keep my eyes and ears open."

I could hear him shuffling around. I wondered if he was home or at his office. "Very good. Act like it's just another day. I'll get on this ASAP. As a matter of fact, I'm going to make some phone calls right now and hop in the car. I'll be down there in a couple of hours." More paper shuffling. "I think the good father was one of the people who fell into the 'home watching TV' crowd. I'll have to look it up."

"I don't have time for that. I'll get back to you. If you could, look into a girl who committed suicide five years ago named Carol Losi. She was involved in his church too. It could all be connected."

I hung up on him, something I'd never done before, and decided to call the chief. I was done flying blind.

He must have just gotten into his office, because he sounded annoyed. Or more annoyed with me than usual.

"What now, Shea?"

"I think I have a suspect. I got a huge break last night. Kayla got drunk and told me Emma Lansing was pregnant. She didn't know the father's name, but I'm convinced I know who it is."

There was a long pause, then, "Who is it?" he asked in disbelief.

"Father O'Halloran. She taught Sunday school for him. She wasn't very experienced with men. None of her friends knew she wasn't a virgin." I was so amped up I had to catch my breath. "Why wouldn't she tell her friends? Unless she couldn't. An affair like that would be sworn to secrecy."

There was a long pause on his end, and then he said, "Shea, you're a genius. I can't believe I didn't see the connection. I've been jumping at shadows, like Garrette, and this was right under my nose. What's our next move on this? Did you tell Bill?"

"I told him. But because he's a priest, there may be privileged communication involved. Bill has to talk to his bosses and run it by their legal department. He's coming here later today. Nick is waiting to take me to the priest's office right now. I'm just going to sit back and observe. I'll let you know how it goes."

"Be careful. Don't blow your cover."

Relief flooded through me. He was backing me on this. "I won't."

"Where is Kayla now?"

"In my room, still half-drunk and sick. I'll meet you at the boardinghouse when I'm done."

"Call me if anything changes. I'm going to run our priest friend's record, see if anything pops up. Watch your back. If it is him, he's very, very dangerous."

I wanted to hurry him off the phone. "I get it. I will."

We hung up, and I ran back out to Nick's truck. "Sorry about that," I said, fastening my seat belt. "I had to call my uncle."

"You should just have run across the street." He smiled. "It'd have been just as quick."

He started off down the street, and my head was swimming. I was so tense and excited I thought I was going to explode. I was trying hard to mask it, afraid Nick would notice. I turned my face to look out the window, the whole time mulling scenarios over and over in my mind.

"Last night was great," Nick said, reaching over, grabbing my hand.

"Sorry about your shirt," I told him, trying to sound semi-normal as the town's landscape blew by my window.

"Every time I button a shirt, I'm going to think of you."

I turned my eyes to him, drinking in his high cheekbones and the five-o'clock shadow that scratched my face when he kissed me hello. "You'll be thinking of me a lot, then."

He stared straight ahead at the road. "I already do."

The church parking lot was empty, except for the white church van. It hit me that the van could have been what he used to drive off with the girls. I wanted my gun on me, or any weapon. In my gut, I wanted to hurt this guy for all he had done to the people of this town. I also wanted to protect myself, because criminals can have a weird sixth sense when their number is up.

We walked through the side door into the basement. Off to the left where the offices were located, I could see into the missing girls' information center. It seemed so quiet compared to the last time I had been there. No phones ringing, no people rushing around with tips and search grids waiting to be assigned. Now there were just piles of missing posters and empty coffee cups with brown kraft-colored rings around them sat on the desks, as if everyone had exited in a big hurry. But in actuality they had just been discarded, left behind, as leads had dried up and the volunteers had gone on with their lives.

Out in the yard, we could hear the Saturday religious ed kids playing, trying to enjoy the church's playground on a spring day.

Nick knocked on one of the doors marked *Private*. "Father O'Halloran?" he asked hesitantly, as if he was afraid to interrupt him.

"Come on in," the priest called. Opening the door, we stepped inside. O'Halloran's office was bigger and more elaborate than I'd thought it would be. The walls were covered with framed pictures of him and his parish community, as well as stretched-canvas landscapes, black-and-white close-ups of flowers, and wildlife shots, all nicely grouped and displayed in clusters.

He noticed my curiosity over the pictures and smiled at me from his desk. "Don't look so amazed. I'm an amateur photographer and a ham. I have been for years. Take a seat, kids, before I grab my camera and take a picture of you two. My assistant went to get us coffee."

We sat down on a faux-suede couch along the wall. The whole office had the feel of a parlor rather than a place to conduct business. It was comforting and comfortable. Exactly the type of place to seduce a naïve young girl. On the large coffee table in front of the couch, I noticed a picture of him and Emma taken at a picnic somewhere. It was sandwiched between a letter of thanks from some politician and a picture of a tropical bird taken at a zoo.

"How much money did we raise the other night for the center?" Nick asked anxiously. He was twisting the hem of his jacket fiercely, his knuckles white. It was painful to see how stressful this was for him.

"At twenty dollars a head, three hundred tickets sold total. That makes six thousand dollars minus a few costs associated with the party. That'll keep us going for a little while longer, but I really thought we'd make more. I want to organize another search party, now that the snow is melted, just to be sure we didn't miss anything. I want to try to contact some magazines and some investigative shows. Maybe if we can keep getting their pictures shown, someone will recognize one of the girls."

"Sounds good, Father. I don't want people to forget about my sister."

"Not as long as I can help it," Father O'Halloran told him. There was a tap on the office door, and his secretary pushed it open with her hip. Silver haired, with about twenty jangling bangles on her wrist, she expertly balanced a large tray with three coffee mugs and an old-fashioned ceramic cow creamer on it.

"Here you go, Father." She set it down on his desk with a clank. She handed us each a steaming coffee mug, and when she offered us cream or sugar, we both politely declined. "I've got to go help out with the kids. It's time for pickup."

"Thank you, Katherine. I think you're all set for the day. We'll see you in the morning," he said, pouring the cream into his coffee. She gave us a wide smile as she exited. The exact knowing smile Mrs. Parker gave me whenever she asked about Nick.

The priest was in no hurry to continue with business. His morning masses said and the religious ed kids gone, I suspected it was his time to kick back and we were encroaching on it.

There was a thick Saturday newspaper folded on the tray. He picked it up, unfolded it, and shook it out a little, just like my dad still did.

"I hope you'll excuse me, but I always like to see what's in the *Buffalo News* headlines first thing. I get the Rochester *Democrat and Chronicle* as well. I can only get the weekend editions out here, so these are a real treat for me. I have to read them online the rest of the week. I know it's old-fashioned to still get the paper . . ." His voice trailed off.

He looked up at me, startled.

"What?"

"You're here about me, aren't you?" he asked, the paper rattling in his hands. "Do you think it's me?"

I was so stunned I couldn't speak.

"Father?" Nick asked. He looked from him to me for an answer.

Father O'Halloran threw the copy of the *Buffalo News* down on the floor in front of us. On the front page were two huge full-color pictures. One was of Terry Roberts in orange prison overalls, her short blonde hair spiked up, thick black-framed glasses on, standing demurely with her court-appointed lawyer. The other was the picture from my official police ID of me in uniform, with the headline above: *Judge Jeremy Casey Unseals Gag Order. Teresa "Terry" Roberts Competent to Stand Trial in School Girl Murders.* Then in smaller letters: *Buffalo police officer Shea O'Connor to be awarded commendation for heroism for undercover work in serial killer case.* Another headline blazed, *What*

*Makes Women Kill?* There was some sort of article underneath, but I was too dumbfounded to look at it. I was smiling out of the newspaper in my police hat for all the world to see.

And I realized my cover could not have been blown at a worse time.

Nick stared at it, not comprehending, and then he looked at me. "You're a cop?" he asked, face turning red.

"Do you think I kidnapped those girls?" the priest demanded.

I didn't know what to do. I started sputtering, "Kayla Johnson told me Emma Lansing was pregnant. The only thing she knew about the father was that he was an older man. Do you know anything about that?"

"Father, did you—" Nick jumped up from the couch, face contorted with rage. He dropped his coffee mug to the floor, the black liquid sinking onto the gray carpet. He started toward the priest, but Father O'Halloran pulled a revolver from his desk.

"Sit down, Nick," he told him calmly. Nick was breathing so hard he was almost panting. I grabbed his arm and pulled him back down on the couch.

"Who else knows about what Kayla told you? Tell me who you told," he demanded. "The chief?"

"Yes. Him and a special agent with the FBI in Buffalo," I lied. "The chief knew I was on my way over here. I called him right before I left. He was on his way to talk to Kayla himself, so why don't we put the gun down. This time there's no alibi. Let's talk about this." I had to stall for time.

"We have to go. Kayla is in trouble," the priest said, getting up. He was still training his gun on us. Walking over to Nick, he seized him by the shirt pointing the gun at his chest. Nick swung his arm, ripping away from him.

"Nick! Don't!" I yelled as he tried to lunge at O'Halloran.

"Don't," the priest repeated, stopping him in his tracks by pointing the gun at me.

Nick stood red-faced, enraged and uncertain, frozen in place by the gun pointed at my head. Without a word the priest took ahold of Nick's shirt again, never losing aim at my face. There was a small supply closet in the back of the room. Father O'Halloran pushed Nick into it. He stood numbly for a second, staring at me until the priest closed and locked the door with an old-fashioned key he produced from his pocket.

Then Nick went wild, pounding on the door and yelling out to us.

"That should give us a minute or two before he breaks the lock." The priest turned to me. "It's for his own protection. He's too emotional to be any good, and his mother couldn't take the loss of her only child now." With that, he handed me the gun. "Follow me. We have to go get Kayla before it's too late."

I stared down at the gun in my hand, not understanding what was going on. Grabbing me by the shoulders, he shook hard. "It wasn't me! Do you understand? We have to go now. Kayla is in trouble."

With Nick still pounding on the closet door, I followed him out to the back of the church lot, where the white van was parked. As we walked, I tried to puzzle out what was going on. He got in the passenger's side and motioned for me to get in the driver's side. After I got in, he pressed the van's keys into my hand.

"I'm only going to say this once, so listen carefully. Emma came to me the afternoon she disappeared. She told me she was pregnant. She said the chief was the father and she was going to tell him right after she left me."

"Why didn't you tell the police?"

"I couldn't," he hissed at me. "She came to me in confidence."

"In the confessional?"

"No. She wanted advice, not forgiveness." He looked out the window at the trees, just starting to bud into life. Shaking his head, he turned back to me. "She said she was leaving town with Skylar Santana, to go have the baby in secret. She wanted to tell Chief Bishop and Skyler said no, but I think Emma told him anyway."

"And you're just coming forward now?" I couldn't believe it. He'd sat on this information for months while the parents and families searched and agonized.

"There were no bodies. I suspected. I thought he must have done something to them. But I had no proof, just my word against his. And what if the girls turned up? I thought if we searched long enough, we could find the girls and the baby if they were out there somewhere. She had talked about private adoptions and how prospective parents would pay for an apartment until the baby was born. Skyler had told her about that. Apparently, she'd had a scare last year and looked into it."

"So you kept the information center going and organized searches?"

He nodded. "And if he'd done something to them, I thought if we could just locate the bodies, there would be evidence, something linking him to their disappearance. But I cannot let anything happen to you or Kayla. This has to stop now."

"Why the gun?"

"Protection. I didn't trust him not to figure out she might have told me something. I should have done things differently, but I'm not going to let him hurt another girl."

I threw the van into gear and floored it. "The chief won't know you told me any of this. He thinks I suspect you, so I need you to call the state police and wait for them. I'll get Kayla out of my house. Tell them to call Bill Walters, from the FBI, if you can remember. He needs to know right now what's going on."

I pulled over around the corner from my house at a little small engine repair shop. I parked the van and we both got out. I tucked the gun into the waistband of my jeans along the small of my back. "You call the state police and tell the dispatcher 'Off-duty officer needs assistance' and wait for them here. Do not dial 911. That'll patch you through to our police department and he'll know. I'll try to get her out."

He nodded and ducked inside to use the phone while I ran through the yards to my house. I came up my walk in a jog and looked up at my window. There seemed to be someone moving around. I hoped it was just Kayla. I'd been gone over twenty minutes by then. Maybe the chief hadn't wandered over yet. Opening the front door, I slipped in as quietly as I could, kicking my shoes off into the corner.

I could hear Marlene fiddling around in the kitchen. Marlene must have heard me come in. "Back already?" she said, coming into the hall. I nodded and padded up the stairs. If she thought I was acting odd, she didn't say anything and just went back to whatever she was doing.

I was fully expecting to find Kayla puking in my sink when I got to my room. Faint gagging noises were coming from my room as I made my way down the hall.

I opened my door to find the chief straddling Kayla on my bed. He was sitting on her chest, arms pulled over her head with his left hand and the other over her mouth. She was choking on her own vomit.

I ran at him, into him, ramming him as hard as I could from behind. He wasn't expecting it, so I succeeded in knocking him off the bed. Kayla lurched forward and sprayed the wall with vomit, choking and sobbing. "Are you all right?" I asked in a panic, trying to grab her. She was still gagging, not breathing right.

I felt a sharp pain in my head, like a firecracker had exploded inside it, and I hit the ground. I lay there dazed, trying to focus my eyes. When the blur cleared, I could see the chief standing in front of me with his service weapon in my face. "You should have stayed away. They were going to have to send you back today anyway. Blew your cover. Blew it. I saw the paper on my iPad right before I came over here."

"Please," I begged, trying to sit up. "I can help you."

He shook his head. "Of course, you ruined Kayla's little accident—choking on her own vomit. I was going to strangle her, but when I came in I thought that was so much better. Then everyone would blame you for getting her drunk. It was perfect. Was. But now—"

"You can't kill us both. It's over."

"Accidents happen all the time. If I say there is no crime, then there is no crime."

I stood up with my hands held out toward him, not knowing what to do next. I hadn't expected this. Who the hell would?

He sat down in my easy chair, facing me. "You came here to find the girls, but you found me instead. And Nick. What a frigging joke this whole thing turned out to be."

Kayla's face was milk white, and she looked like she was in shock. There were ugly bruises coming up already on her wrists and arms. Her breathing had become a raspy whisper and she wasn't moving.

"Roy, we can talk about this. I know—"

"Don't give me any of your psychological bullshit. If Kayla goes and you go, no more worries, except for Father O'Halloran, and I got that covered. You know how it is. You can be a number-one suspect, but they have to have evidence to charge you. No bodies, no physical evidence, no jail." He smiled. "Congrats on your award. That picture looked old, though. It doesn't do you justice."

"Where are they?" I asked softly.

"I have a different spot planned for you two." He thought for a second. "But don't worry, those bones are just where they belong." He got up from the chair then and came toward me. Grabbing my face, he pulled it close to his. The barrel of the gun was pressed against my temple, the cold metal gouging into my skin.

"She was just a kid," I ground out between my teeth.

"She was eighteen. She knew exactly what she was doing when we got involved. She knew we had to be careful. And she screwed me over. She threatened my good name, and what's a man in a town like this without that?" he asked as his fingertips dug into my cheeks.

Vaguely, I remembered him making a comment like that when we'd talked about Carol Losi.

"It was good, until then. I was so careful, but not careful enough."

And then he laughed. He pushed me hard by my face and I hit the wall, smacking my head against the dresser. Blood started pouring down the side of my cheek, my neck, soaking into my shirt.

"It was quick," he continued, sinking back down into the chair, like he hadn't just cracked my skull. It was all I could do to focus on him; my head was spinning like a carnival ride. "I did them quick. Except for Skyler; she fought with me, so it was harder on her. More painful."

He was pointing the gun at me, staring at me through the sights like a hunter zeroing in on a twelve-point buck.

"I've always had time to think things through. To do things right." He waved the gun in a circle in front of him. "But now I feel rushed. I need to make a decision, a choice about you and your friend here. Right now."

"Take your time," I offered weakly, picking up a dirty T-shirt from the floor next to me and pressing it against the side of my head. "You can't shoot us here."

"Time is something we don't have, and you know what? It doesn't matter where I shoot you." He straightened his arm, aligning the sights on his Glock, and aimed for my head.

"Honey? What's all that crazy noise?" Marlene came through the door, startling the chief, who jerked his arm up and shot her through the shoulder. She tumbled back, screaming, into the doorway. I scrambled over the top of her, through the door and into the hall. I leaned up against the wall, next to the doorframe, dropping the bloody shirt and yanking the revolver from the back of my jeans.

Marlene was howling from shock and pain, blocking the doorway, clutching at her shoulder. The chief came after me, striding over Marlene and out the door. I stepped up on him as he came through and pressed my gun in his cheek.

"Move and I'll blow your head off," I breathed into the side of his face. "Throw your gun down now."

He tossed his Glock across the hall with a loud clang. My heart was pounding in my chest, making my head throb. He had his hands up on either side of his head, but he was too close.

"Take a step back," I hissed. "Keep your hands up."

"Scared?" he asked.

But he didn't move.

A trickle of blood ran down my forehead, dripping onto my cheek. I dipped my head to try to wipe it off on my shoulder, so I could see without moving the gun aimed at his head. "Shut up."

"You're bleeding. From the head. It'll make you weak, dizzy. Marlene and Kayla are hurt bad."

"Shut up," I repeated, cocking the hammer.

"You won't shoot me. And by the time anyone comes to help you, Kayla and Marlene will be dead. You'll lose consciousness from all the blood you're losing—"

"I said shut up."

"I knew Walters suspected me, and I knew you didn't. I knew it right up until you walked through that door. He set you up, made you a sitting duck. I could have taken you out at any time. And made it look like an accident. They put you with me like a sacrificial lamb. Just so Walters could keep a perfect record. What do you say you give me the gun, and I'll walk out of here and drive off into the sunset and no one will know you weren't smart enough to suspect me?"

*That son of a bitch Walters*, I thought. He knew better than anyone that damage attracts damage.

"I'm going to see you suffer for what you did," I said, trying to keep my focus. My head was getting light, my eyes blurry.

"For the girls?"

"Yes, for the girls."

"Because they're like friends to you now, right? Because you came here to find out what happened?"

"Take a step back," I demanded, trying to put some distance between us.

"You're starting to sound fuzzy. That gun's heavy, isn't it? I can see your hands shaking. Why don't you just let it drop?"

"You know what, Uncle Roy?" I spit a wad of blood out of my mouth, down the front of my shirt.

"What?" He moved a fraction of an inch closer to me.

"I may not have been smart enough to suspect you, but I was smart enough to do one thing."

He came in closer. "And what was that?"

"To call for backup."

His eyes went wide and he looked toward the staircase. At that moment two state troopers came running up the stairs, guns drawn. "Nobody move!" the lead trooper screamed, bearing down on us.

With one swift motion Roy Bishop reached up, wrapped his hand around mine, and pulled the trigger, literally blowing his brains out, spattering the floral wallpaper with gray matter and skull fragments. He fell backward, onto Marlene, with a dull thud.

I crumpled against the wall, dropping the gun.

*　*　*

I must have blacked out, because the next thing I knew I was on my back with someone holding a cloth to my head. I tried to sit up and realized I must be strapped down.

"Don't try to get up," I heard a man say. A moment of panic swept over me as the thought of Terry Roberts filled my mind. I started to struggle against the restraints.

"Easy, easy. You're in an ambulance. You're on your way to the county hospital. You hit your head pretty hard."

My eyes started to focus, and I could make out a face over me, an EMT. "Are Kayla and Marlene okay?"

"The girl might have alcohol poisoning, maybe a broken wrist and some bruised ribs."

"He was sitting on her chest."

The guy was in his early thirties, balding already, sweat beading up on his forehead. *Why the hell is he sweating?* I thought, trying to focus on the words coming out of his mouth. "The woman's shoulder is shattered. We won't be able to determine the extent of their injuries until we get to the hospital."

"The chief?"

"I can't say."

"I guess he's dead then."

"Why don't you take it easy now, okay?" He pulled a thin blanket up to my chest.

I closed my eyes again, and the next thing I knew I was in the emergency room, on a bed. A young doctor was preparing to stitch up my head. Bill Walters was sitting in a vinyl chair next to me.

"How'd you get here so fast?" I asked him once my double vision cleared.

"I started driving down as soon as you called this morning."

Anger bubbled up in me, but I had to keep myself calm. "You set me up, Bill. You knew it was him the whole time, and you had me running around like a fool. You knew that newspaper article was coming out and you didn't warn me. You let my cover get blown. Kayla and Marlene could have been killed."

"I wanted to force Bishop's hand. It was the only way."

I shook my head. "No, it wasn't. It was your way. It's always been your way."

He ignored that. "How are you feeling?" he asked.

I touched the left side of my head. It was bandaged, awaiting the stitches. "How many?" I asked.

"You'll need about twelve to close that gash," the doctor said, threading the needle. "I have to give you this shot to numb you up." He put the clamped, threaded needle down on a surgical tray and picked up a syringe.

I tried to keep talking while he sewed, to keep my mind off it. Bill still hadn't explained himself to me.

"He was going to kill me, Bill. When Marlene walked in, he was about to blow my head off."

"I'm sorry; this is all my fault." And he did sound genuinely sorry, as sorry as a man like Bill can be. "I was already on my way down when Father O'Halloran called for the police."

"When did you suspect Roy?" I could feel the doctor sliding the needle into my skin, but the pain was coming from somewhere deeper.

"Right away."

"That's why you had me at Mrs. Parker's and not living with him." I grabbed at my head as another wave of crushing pain passed over me. The doctor had to stop stitching. I could feel him yanking the thread, tightening it. My stomach rolled. "I'm so stupid. I should have known right there."

I closed my eyes, but Bill kept talking, justifying himself. "It was just a hunch, but he fit my profile. I just needed the motive. I didn't know what any of the girls could have done to set him off. Or if he was just a psychopath, like Roberts. As soon as you said Emma Lansing had been pregnant, I should have pulled you out."

"But you didn't. You let this happen. You let me think I was crazy, having people watching me, parking outside my house, keeping an eye on me and Roy. But not today, huh? Not today, of all days."

"I never expected this would happen."

I closed my eyes. "You didn't expect it, but you hoped for it."

The doctor finished with the stitches and gave me some pills. The red plastic medical waste bucket next to my bed was soaked with bloody bandages. I struggled to sit up, and Bill handed me one of those little bed adjusters. I clicked it until I was upright and looked around. "What time is it?"

"Almost six o'clock now. They didn't want to numb your head until you woke up."

I fingered the bandage covering my stitches. "My head feels like someone dropped a brick on it."

"You remember he killed himself, don't you?"

"I remember everything." So much for sleeping without nightmares.

"Did he tell you where they are?" Bill pressed.

"No, but if you help me out of this bed, I think I have an idea." We argued back and forth for a minute or two, but I insisted. This could not wait a minute longer. Bill called the state police for backup, as well as the FBI agents assigned to the case.

The doctor working on me protested and then berated Bill as he helped me into a wheelchair. "She has a possible concussion. This woman needs to be treated."

"I'll bring her right back," he assured him, wheeling me down the hall toward the exit. He didn't care if he was making my injuries worse. He had business to take care of. For the last time, I agreed with him.

I noticed two state troopers had been posted outside my room. Now they ran to catch up with us to find out what was going on. Bill gave them instructions. They called it in to their superiors, and the next thing I knew I was in Bill's car, following the trooper vehicles out of the lot. I saw news vans parked in front of the main entrance as we passed.

Bill drove slowly so I wouldn't get bounced around. Two trooper cars led our way, lights revolving, but no sirens blaring. I still had my jeans on, but someone had cut my bloody shirt off and replaced it with one of those paper-thin hospital gowns. Thankfully, Bill had draped his jacket over my shoulders. My stitches simultaneously itched, burned, and throbbed. My fingers wandered over the bandage on my head again. The numbing shot the doctor had given me was wearing off, and I was starting to feel the full extent of my injuries.

"Are you sure about this?" Bill asked, as if he actually cared.

"What was the number-one trait, according to your profile, of someone who would commit this kind of crime?"

"Arrogance."

"Exactly. He would be arrogant enough to want to show off his crime, some way." I watched the town roll past my window. "He said, 'Their bones are just where they belong.'"

The state troopers who had been driving in front of us forced open the black iron gate, and we pulled into the cemetery just after seven o'clock. The sun was setting, lighting the sky in pinks and oranges and reds. Our entourage had grown as we drove from the hospital to about twenty cop, Fed, and trooper cars. Officers began spilling out of vehicles, all staring as Bill gently helped me get out of his car. The spring wind whipped around my bare legs as I clutched Bill's jacket around me. My black flats, now splashed with blood and gore, barely stayed on my feet as I tried to get my balance on the uneven ground.

"I can do it," I told him when he wanted to carry me. I had to let him slip an arm around me and lean heavily against him, but I was walking this one on my own.

In the falling light the cemetery looked even more neglected and shabby, despite a few yellow daffodils some mourner had planted at their loved ones' headstone. They looked out of place, too bright and cheerful. Was it ever really spring in a graveyard?

"We went through here at least five times during the original search," one of the troopers walking alongside me commented. He was a barrel-chested guy with a purple Stetson perched perfectly over his crew cut. The kind of guy who looked down on us Buffalo cops as the dirty bottom-of-the-barrel misfits, only good for working in the shit of the city.

"But not with the cadaver dogs," I said, clutching Bill's coat sleeve.

"Of course not. It's a cemetery."

"Did you ever open any of the tombs?" I asked, navigating over a fallen headstone with Bill's help.

"No," the random trooper admitted. "Why would we?"

We came upon the tomb still marked off with crime scene tape. I walked up to the iron gate in front of the door and put my hand on it, feeling the cold seep into my fingers. I could barely find my voice as the eyes of every cop who had followed me into the cemetery stared. "They're in here."

"This is still a sealed crime scene," one of Bill's agents said, fingering the tape across the entrance.

"Open it," Bill told them.

There was a look of uncertainty that passed through the crowd of cops. Everyone remained frozen, trying to decide if Bill had the authority to make that call.

Finally, one of the local county sheriffs stepped up. "I know Emma's dad," he declared. "And I have two daughters." He started to wedge his flashlight into the gap in the gate. Two other officers, from where I couldn't make out, joined in, ripping down the crime scene tape. A yell went up for crowbars, tire irons, anything anyone had in the trunks of their vehicles. I was holding on to Bill's arm for support as they started forcing open the tomb's entrance. I was looking away, but I didn't need to see or hear their reaction. The smell that hit me told me I was right.

Now the calls were going up for a supervisor, for evidence and photography units, to maintain crime scene integrity. "That brilliant bastard," Bill whispered under his breath. "With Skyler gone as a witness, he knew he'd have to keep the scene sealed. No one would have ever found them."

All around me people swirled, whipped into action by the discovery, frenzied to get it done right. The stench overpowered me and I started to vomit. Doubled over, retching, tears streaming down my face, I dropped to my knees. Bill hustled me to the car, but not before I caught a glimpse of a decomposing hand in the entranceway of the tomb. Apologizing, Bill told me he couldn't come with me, he had to supervise the scene. Of course he did.

Bill had a different random trooper drive me back to the hospital. I kept the window open the whole way. The trooper tried to talk to me, but I just held my head in my hands, trying not to throw up again. As we came around the back way, there were nurses at the door and the angry doctor waiting for me. Someone must have called ahead. Hands gripped me under my armpits, lifting me out of the car, Bill's jacket sliding off onto the pavement. The next and last thing I knew I was on a gurney, where they gave me a sedative. I was grateful for it, because I knew that at least for one night, I would not dream.

## Sunday, April 9<sup>th</sup>

That next day was absolute chaos. Every news magazine, tabloid, newspaper, TV show, and prime-time producer was outside the hospital clamoring for my story. I made headlines across the country as some kind of supercop, an undercover lady Sherlock Holmes. The Roberts case had generated a lot of media attention, but my identity had never been disclosed. Now with the revelation of my involvement with both cases, I was dubbed the Nancy Drew Detective.

Bill called a press conference from the hospital to explain the facts. I watched it from my room while eating my Jell-O. They also showed reactions from the people in town. Most expressed disbelief at the chief's involvement and outrage that I had posed as a student in their community college. They showed people I had never even seen before, let alone knew, giving interviews on how they'd suspected all along I was somehow not right. Other people took the time to stop and tell the news media how I was the town slut and had worked my way through every man in the community to get the information that broke the case. Every rumor, lie, half-truth, and prediction got its airtime, and it was mostly at my expense.

I sat up when they showed Nick's family ducking into their house. In all of the chaos the day before, I had forgotten all about him. I wondered who had let him out of the closet.

Nick came out to shoo the reporters away, and one female closest to him asked, "What do you think of Shea O'Connor's participation as an undercover agent to find your sister?"

Nick turned a pale face toward the camera and said, "No comment," in a cold voice and went back into the house. The footage then cut to an earlier taped portion that had Mr. and Mrs. Stansfield outside the hospital. Mr. Stansfield had an arm draped around his wife's shoulders as he spoke into the microphones set up around a podium outside the front doors.

"My family and I are very grateful to the FBI and state police for all they have done to find my daughter. We're especially grateful to Shea O'Connor for her role. She has given us justice and peace, and we support the way she was used in the investigation." His voice broke and they stepped down. I figured their lawyer must have prepared that little speech, but it was relieving, just the same, to hear it. Nick hadn't tried to contact me yet, and I was beginning to wonder if he ever would.

I had armed guards at my door to keep the press and nuts out. I had already started getting death threats from anti-government groups, calling me a spy and a threat to democracy. Twitter was going crazy with the hashtag *#nostudentspies*.

One of my guards popped his head into my room. "Miss O'Connor? Kayla Johnson wants to see you."

My friend Kayla Johnson, whom I'd used and lied to and manipulated to get information from, had come to visit me.

I nodded. "Let her in."

Sitting in a wheelchair, she came rolling in with a brace on her wrist and a hospital gown on. She had bruises around her mouth where Roy Bishop had clamped his hand over it. Kayla's brown hair was pulled back in a tight ponytail, exposing her face and neck. Her eyes were purple and swollen, but that, I think, was from crying. She looked old to me suddenly. Old and tired.

She slowly wheeled herself up to my bed. She didn't say anything at first; she just studied my face intently.

I broke the silence first. "How are you?"

All she could manage was a small harsh whisper. "I feel like crap; what do you think?"

"Maybe you shouldn't be talking," I told her. Mostly because I was afraid of what I knew she was about to say.

"I know I shouldn't, but I have some things I need to say to you, Shea. Shea O'Connor."

The venom in her voice made me flinch. "I'm sorry. I didn't mean for any of this to happen."

"How old are you really? Who are you really?" she rasped.

"I'm twenty-three years old, and I'm a Buffalo police officer. I was planted in your college by the FBI to find out what happened to your friends."

"And now what? You just disappear? What about me? And Maddie and Jenna? I thought we were all friends, or was that part of your act?"

My head was throbbing again. "We're still friends. I wasn't faking that."

"What about Nick? Were you just using him? Were you just using all of us? I can't believe this." Her voice rose, scratchy and harsh. I knew she was going to have a hard time dealing with everything that was about to come out. I should have expected it, tried to comfort her, but I was tired and emotionally drained and too worn out to make excuses for myself. So I went on the defensive.

"Would you rather not know what happened to your friends? That they stayed in that tomb?" It came out sounding harsher than I'd meant it to.

I might as well have slapped her in the face. She sucked in a deep stuttering breath and stared at me. Now I was both a liar and a raging bitch.

"That's not fair," she said softly. And it wasn't. I saw her shudder and I knew what she was picturing in her mind. For a second, I saw it again too. The decomposing hand outstretched on the cold marble floor, the other bodies heaped beside the first. The smell creeping out, heavy and choking as the police forced open the door. I pressed my eyes shut and tried to force the images away.

I tried again. "I'm sorry for what happened to your friends and I'm sorry it had to come to this. I didn't lie about everything. The things we talked about, laughed about? That was me. The real me. Buried underneath the bullshit lies."

Red splotches checkered her face. "It's just so hard. To believe they're gone and you're not you. How do I deal with this?" Tears rolled down her cheeks. "I don't know what's real anymore."

"I'm real." I touched my hand to my chest. "I'm right here."

We both were silent for a while, neither of us knowing what to say to the other. After what seemed like hours, she asked uncertainly, "Do I get to keep you as my friend?"

I exhaled a breath of relief. "Always."

She rolled herself over to my bed, and I hugged her tight.

"Thank you," she whispered in my ear.

I stroked her hair with my IV'ed hand. I couldn't say *you're welcome* or *don't mention it* or any other meaningless platitude. There was so much I wanted to tell her, to say to her, and yet I had no words. So I just held on to her.

"Who do you think will play me in the movie?" she finally croaked out. I laughed and she laughed, and then we both cried until neither of us had a tear left.

I told the troopers guarding my door to tell our nurses she wanted to stay in my room with me. She didn't remember much about what had happened in my bedroom at the boardinghouse, but she'd had a nightmare that night in the hospital and didn't want to be alone.

A nightmare. Imagine that.

## Wednesday, April 12<sup>th</sup>

I got a shaky handwritten note from the Stansfields on Tuesday saying they understood the role I had played and that they were grateful. They also invited me to the funeral service. I had been released from the hospital on Monday and went home to Buffalo. I debated driving back down there. I still hadn't heard from Nick.

I decided to attend because I could not get my mind off all that had happened. It replayed in my head on an endless loop. And the press and constant phone calls and interview requests weren't helping with that. I drove to Kelly's Falls Wednesday morning with Bill. He was going to make one of his agents come with us for protection, as I was receiving death threats, but I told him not to. It seemed official now that almost everyone I met wanted to kill me: teachers, cops, people who watched twenty-four-hour news stations. One talk show host actually called me the most dangerous threat to American civil liberties alive. Then she tweeted my parents' street address in South Buffalo, since Karen's name was on our lease. Nice.

Bill and I missed the funeral mass at the church, so we drove over to the cemetery. Olivia was being buried in nearby Whitesville for obvious reasons. We walked up to the crowd as Father O'Halloran was finishing the blessing. There had to be three hundred mourners gathered around the open grave. Jenna, Kayla, and Maddie were there, right up front, clutching white roses. Kayla was still wearing her wrist brace but had lost her wheelchair. They didn't look at me. I didn't expect them to. It wasn't about me; it was about Olivia.

They began to lower the casket into the ground, and the sobs became a little louder. I could see Nick holding his mother up. He was wearing a dark suit that matched the circles under his eyes. His dad had a hand on his shoulder, as if to steady himself. A three-person house of cards, ready to crumble at any moment.

The girls came forward and dropped their roses one by one on the sinking pink casket, already covered in flowers and stuffed animals. The service was over. Olivia was at rest.

The crowd began to drift apart, back to their cars to head to the funeral breakfast. I noticed people staring at me, whispering as they passed. I took the roses I had brought with me and stepped forward. I dropped them down onto her casket, and I thought how I'd never seen her face, not even in death. I prayed over the roses for a moment, praying for her family, and maybe praying for myself. As I turned to walk away, Mrs. Stansfield caught my arm. She just looked at me for a second and then hugged me to her. "Thank you," she whispered in my ear.

"I'm so sorry," I told her as I pulled away. Her husband was standing next to her, hands stuffed deep in his pockets, just like his son did sometimes. My eyes darted behind her. I was looking for Nick.

"Go and talk to him, please." She directed my gaze toward him. He was leaning against a long black limo waiting on the road, arms crossed against his chest, face turned away from us.

She patted my shoulder gently, as if to send me his way. Taking a deep breath, I navigated the headstones over to him.

"Nick."

He wouldn't look at me. "I don't want to talk to you." His voice was cold and empty.

"Please believe me; the way I feel about you, it's not an act."

His head snapped around, eyes burning into mine. "It was all a lie. All of it. You left me locked in a closet and almost got yourself and Kayla killed—" He cut himself off, like all that didn't matter now. "I just buried my sister. And I guess I'm burying my girlfriend, too." He grabbed the limo door handle and got in, leaving me standing there on the road.

The windows were tinted, so I couldn't see him. I wanted to pound on the glass, demand that he listen to me, but I didn't want to create a scene at his sister's funeral. From on top of a small hill across the cemetery I could see reporters and cameras set up, filming everything. We could give them another good show. Frigging vultures.

I walked back to where Bill was waiting with the car, and we drove back to Buffalo.

On the way home Bill asked me, "So, have you given any thought about coming to the Bureau?"

I was tracing circles on the passenger's side window with my finger and counting cows. It was a game I used to play with my grandfather on road trips. You counted cows on your side of the car, and if you passed a cemetery, you lost them all and had to start over. I had twenty-three cows. "As a matter of fact, I have given the matter some thought. If you would have extended a real offer after the Roberts case, I would have said yes. You dangled that carrot to get me to do this case. 'Poor Shea, so unappreciated.'" I mimicked his voice. "'Here's your chance to do some real good instead of writing tickets.'"

"It was the only way," he protested, glancing at me. "If you'd have known, he would have sensed it. I knew you could handle it. That was my confidence in you."

"If I had been two minutes later, Kayla Johnson would be dead now. The Roberts case wrecked me. Wrecked me." I took a shuddering breath. "And you used it against me. I'm not you; I won't solve cases at any cost. I can't. I'm done with this. As it is, I'll probably never get another good night's sleep again."

"If you change your mind—"

I held up a hand. "I won't. I can forgive a lot of things. I can forgive what you did to me, but not to Kayla. No way."

And that was the end of that.

I couldn't forgive myself for what I'd done to Nick. I should have turned him down when he asked me out that first night. I should never have given him my number. The pain of losing his sister was now being compounded by the betrayal he must be feeling from me. My own feelings toward him were stronger than I'd ever expected them to be. It had been a long time since I'd let someone into my life, and it had been a lie. Now I had to be back in Buffalo and get on with my life and try to forget him, as if that was going to be possible.

I let Bill drop me off in front of my apartment building. There were reporters standing around waiting to get a sound bite. I pushed past them, trying to cover my face. Karen was smoking a cigarette on the couch when I came in.

"So how did it go?"

I fanned the air with my hand as I sat down next to her. "Terrible."

I slipped off my pumps and rubbed my toes. "How long have the reporters been outside, and why are you smoking in the house?"

"Since this morning. Every couple of hours I open up the window and throw those slices of cheese we had left over from our New Year's party on them."

"You've been raining moldy cheese on the news media?"

She shrugged. "Maybe they're hungry."

"And the smoking?"

"One: there are reporters outside. And two: you aren't the boss of me."

"Marcus and Jamal will freak out."

She motioned to the jungle of baskets and flowers stuck on every single available surface in our apartment. "I don't think they'll mind."

I leaned my head back against the couch. "He didn't even want to talk to me."

"What do you expect? Hello. His sister was murdered by someone he trusted with his life, and guess what? The girl he thought was his girlfriend dresses up like a hooker once in a while or a high school student or whatever to catch criminals and everything they had together was an act orchestrated to obtain information from him."

"That's not true."

"It's not?" She cocked a perfectly arched eyebrow at me. "Fill me in on what part? Cause it sounds awfully close to the truth to me. And probably to him, too."

"Are you done making me feel like shit?"

She butted her cigarette out in the antique ashtray shaped like a lily pad she'd found at an Allentown garage sale. "No, but we can take a break if you want."

I excused myself to a hot bath and tried to block everything out. I poured half a bottle of bath bubbles into the tub with me, trying to hide myself in it. Outside the bathroom window I could hear the reporters on the sidewalk making their six o'clock reports to their stations. The buzz coming from them was enough to drive me crazy. I knew I could never explain to Nick what had happened. That everything we'd felt together was real and true.

But it had been a lie at the same time. What had I expected by going to the funeral? That he would forgive me, like Kayla? He hadn't confided in Kayla his deepest fears and heartache, and he definitely hadn't had sex with her. I had no right to ask for his forgiveness. And I sure as hell didn't deserve it. It had been wrong to be with Nick. Period. But I wanted him. Pure and simple. I was selfish, and it had blown up in both our faces.

Sliding down, I let the water wash over me. My stitches itched like crazy, but the doctors assured me they'd dissolve in time. Just melt away. Like Nick's feelings for me. Maybe they already had. I had to pray for him to go on with his life and stop being selfish. I stayed under until I thought my lungs would burst, then popped back to the surface.

I had to let him go.

## Wednesday, May 24th

I stayed in Buffalo, but I couldn't go back to work right away. The media attention I was getting made it impossible, so I was put on paid administrative leave. Even Karen was getting bothered at work by the press, trying to get some scoop into my life. It was the story of the month, and we tried to ride it out until it was over. I was still getting death threats and hate mail, so we had to dump our apartment. Marcus and Jamal had another rental property a few streets away and moved us out in the middle of the night.

I kept in touch with Kayla, which made me feel better about everything, because she didn't blame me for anything that had happened to her, although I blamed myself. She told me Nick refused to talk about me, which I knew had to be true because I must have called and texted him a hundred times. As time went on I missed him more, not less. After about two weeks I stopped calling, hoping he'd wonder why and call me. He didn't.

About three weeks after I had gotten back to Buffalo, I received an actual letter, on paper, from Joe Styles. I'd never gotten a handwritten letter in the mail before, not counting the death threats written in crayon I'd been getting at my old apartment. Joe had sent it to Bill, at his office, and Bill had for-warded it to me. I was surprised to hear from him, since he didn't seem to be the letter-writing type. But that was Joe, someone I never could figure out. It read:

Dear Shea,

Kayla told me you moved and wouldn't give me your new address so I'm sending it to the guy who you worked for. I just wanted to thank you for finding Skyler and for believing it wasn't me. Not a whole lot of people in this town have a high opinion of me and I can't blame them but it's one thing to have them think you robbed some tires. It's another when they think you killed three peo-ple. I don't think I'm going to go back to school again this year either, so I'll probably leave town soon. I wanted to get my GED but maybe that type of thing is not for guys like me.

I heard there's construction jobs in North Carolina, so maybe I'll head down there and check them out. If I don't ever see you again, I just want you to know I'm glad you did what you did. A lot of people around here feel like that, but I know there are some people who say you shouldn't have done it. I say I knew you personally and I'm glad you did. (I knew you were the one who dimed out Will Garrette once I heard who you really were, but that's okay because you were doing your job, I guess.)

I thought you were a really good person, even if you were faking it.

He'd signed it *JOE*, in messy, uneven block letters, and that was the last I ever heard from him.

I had pretty much given up hope of seeing Nick again, even though he was in my thoughts constantly. It didn't help that all I had to do was turn on one of the news channels and eventually they'd show the family photo that hung above their fireplace. Him and Olivia sitting under a tree with their parents standing behind them, all smiling radiantly in matching white shirts and khaki pants. A picture where they looked perfect. The perfect he hated so much.

Nick deactivated his Instagram, Snapchat, and Twitter accounts, so I couldn't follow him.

I stopped looking at the pictures I had of us on my cell phone. It was too painful. So I moped around my new apartment while Karen was at work. I binge-watched movies on Netflix and those talk shows where grown women get on stage and tell how they cheated on their boyfriends with their best friends and then all yell at each other. When they were over, I watched game shows and then reruns of *Supernatural.* At least Sam and Dean always got to slay their demons.

On that particular day in late May, I had a box of chocolates from Park Side Candy in one hand and the remote in the other when the doorbell rang.

I reluctantly got up to answer it, because the show was just getting good and we were out of cheese if it was a reporter. Most of the reporters had learned not to bother us at the new apartment, because Karen had moved up from throwing moldy cheese from the window to spraying them with Cheez Whiz when she opened the door.

The doorbell rang again. "I'm coming," I called, looking for the spray can that was usually on the hallway table. It was gone. I'd just have to wing it.

I opened the door, and there was Nick.

"Hi," he said in an awkward, quiet voice. He was wearing a denim shirt and faded jeans. His dark hair was shorter than when I had last seen it, and he was thinner. He looked older. The toll that his sister's death had taken on him was written all over his face.

"What are you doing here?" I asked in disbelief.

"I got your address from Mr. Walters. I have to talk to you, and I wanted to give you this." He thrust a book toward me.

It was a Harris Community College yearbook. I stared at it for a second, mostly because I couldn't look Nick in the eyes. Then, like it was some radioactive relic from the Manhattan Project, I took it from him and gingerly fingered through it, afraid of what I'd find. There was a collage in the front with some candid shots of the girls and some poems written for them by their classmates. It was a little memorial from their friends.

"Look in the back," he said, "near the end." Skimming to the back of the book, there was my picture. Under the name *Shea Anderson* was the caption *Best Dressed*. I remembered when the picture was taken. I had been coming out of the student union when some of the photography nerds stopped me and Kayla. I was looking at her and laughing when a guy named Hector snapped it. Another one of them had tried in earnest to get me to join the yearbook staff by saying that it counted as a credit hour toward your general education requirements, but I had declined, for obvious reasons. I'd been surprised they even had a yearbook at a school so small and tried to remember if the university I graduated from had one. If they did, I'd never bought a copy. Now here I was, holding a yearbook with a picture of me as a fake student with a fake name in front of my real ex-boyfriend.

I backed up into my apartment, letting him inch his way in, closing the door behind him.

We ended up facing each other in my living room, the tension so thick you could cut it with a chainsaw.

"Thank you. For this." I held it up, then tossed it gently on my couch. The weather had been warm all week, and he already had a smattering of sunburn across his nose, like he'd been helping his mom in the garden. Suddenly, I was self-conscious in my yoga pants and ripped sweat shirt. I was a stranger to this man.

"Is this why you came all the way here? To show me this book?" I couldn't get my hopes up, not again. Not with him. My heart might shatter into a million pieces if this was good-bye forever.

His hands were stuffed down in his pockets, in that habit I was so familiar with. "No. I came to ask you a question."

I folded my arms across my chest to keep my hands from shaking and sat down on my couch. I was so nervous I could barely speak. "Go ahead."

"When you told me how you felt about me wasn't an act, did you mean that? Or was it all just to solve Olivia's murder? Did you feel anything for me?"

"Of course I did." I could hardly get the words out, even though I had rehearsed what I would say a million times, if I got this chance. "I still do. Nick, I didn't pretend to want to be with you. I should have stayed away from you, but I couldn't. I know you don't understand and I don't expect you to. I can only hope you'll forgive me." I was trying to be tough, to keep myself together, not to cry.

"Do you know how I found out how old you are?" Now his anger came bubbling up. "Where you came from? That your parents are alive and your favorite color? I read about it in blogs and I saw it on the television and online. I don't know what to think, or what to do. I was falling in love with you."

I was so paralyzed with the helplessness of the situation. I couldn't turn back time. I didn't want to. The truth was, I wouldn't have given up a second of our time together. I was sick and sad and brokenhearted all at once. I swallowed hard, pulling up as much courage as I could muster. "I've called and texted, over and over. I'd get down on my knees and beg you for forgiveness if I thought you'd accept it. I don't blame you for how you must feel. Either you can forgive me or you can't. But I don't expect you to. It's too much for me to ask."

The weight of the situation came crashing down on me. I felt myself sinking into the couch, my whole body seeming to crumple in on itself. I was tired of being strong. Exhausted from it.

"I'm here because I don't want—" He reached for words he couldn't find as he knelt down in front of me. "I lost someone I love, and I don't want to lose someone else." He tipped my chin up with his finger. "I'll get down on my knees so you don't have to. I needed time to think about things, to try to see things your way. I'm not all the way there yet, but I know what you felt for me was real, because I felt it too."

He folded himself forward, resting his head in my lap, and wrapped his hands around my waist. Hesitantly, like he was a puff of smoke that would dissolve at my touch at any moment, I ran my fingers through his hair, remembering the silky warmth of it. And the smell of him. I drank in the smell of him so near me. This was what I missed. Just being close to him. Just hearing him breathe. Finally, he looked up at me.

"That's very mushy," I told him with a weak smile.

"Yes, it is," he agreed, smiling too. "But can you live with dating a younger man?"

I wrapped my arms around his neck. "I want to find out."

\* \* \*

Nick stayed with me that night and the rest of the weekend. Some things were awkward; some were surprising. There was a lot of talking and crying. We knew it would take us a while to get to know each other all over again. But we were trying, and that's what mattered.

Nick decided to transfer to the University at Buffalo for the fall term to finish out his last semester before grad school. Karen finally snagged her hot doctor, so Nick moved in with me when she moved out. His parents weren't thrilled; holidays and birthdays were awkward affairs, tense and sad. After every dinner Nick floored his truck to get back to Buffalo. His house, that town, had too many ghosts for him now.

I went back to work and tried to get back into the flow of the job. I grabbed a female rookie fresh out of the academy to partner with and tried to start over. I had finally gained the respect of my coworkers, so in that area I was happier than I had been before. I was starting to think maybe my days with the department weren't numbered. John Krause, my old partner, even called me one day out of the blue to tell me congratulations on Terry Roberts getting a life sentence despite her plea deal and on cracking the case in Kelly's Falls. We ended up talking for two hours. Nick and I went out for a drink with him and his new girlfriend at his insistence and agreed at the end of the night to get together more often.

Nick's forgiveness meant a lot to me. Some of my old wounds were finally healing.

The cable movie came out and made everyone look ridiculously devious, corny, or stupid.

The movie had a happy ending, of course, and tied up all the pesky loose ends neat and clean. In real life questions don't always get answered. The FBI had done some checking into Roy Bishop after it was all over and found out that a young, married mother of two who'd happened to be one of his neighbors in Ithaca had disappeared without a trace when he was in high school. She's never been found.

No one will ever know what really happened between the chief and Emma. No one will ever know what snapped in him, made him kill. No one will ever know how many others there might have been, and why, because in the end, he killed himself.

Those things went with him when he wrapped his finger around mine and pulled the trigger. Nick and I have each other to get through the questions and doubts. We're still reintroducing ourselves to each other, in some way, almost every day. Nick has lost a lot of buttons in the process. It isn't always easy, and even though we've moved in together, we're taking it slow and hoping things work out.

Is he my happily ever after? Am I his?

I don't know. I'm not thinking that far ahead.

Yesterday, October second, just when I had thought everything had blown over and I could resume a somewhat normal life, I got a letter from the city, forwarded from Amber Wray's attorney. It was a notice of claim. She's suing me, the FBI, and the Buffalo police for twenty-seven million dollars for violating her civil rights.

God bless America.